Never Steal a Cockatiel

by Edie Claire

Book Nine of the
Leigh Koslow Mystery Series

Dedication

For Liking blurry pictures of random plants, snow, and chocolate.
For guessing what bizarre location I'm off to next.
For Commenting on stuff even when it's boring.
But mainly, just for being there —
Reminding me every minute that readers are real.

This one's for my Facebook buds.
Thank you.

Chapter 1

Leigh refused to open her eyes. She lay in bed, motionless and content. The sound she'd just heard wasn't what she thought it was. Really, it wasn't.

Tap, tap, tap.

She sighed. It was exactly what she thought it was. Someone was rapping gently on her bedroom window, trying to wake her up without disturbing anyone else in the house. As if that were possible. Warren slept like the dead, and both of their kids had inherited the trait. Leigh, on the other hand, had suffered from insomnia even before her husband hit forty and started snoring like a chainsaw.

She opened her eyes and looked at her clock. It was 4:30 AM.

Lovely.

She rose. An ordinary person, she thought to herself, would likely be concerned about either a burglar or an emergency. Leigh Koslow, advertising copywriter, mother of two, and supernatural magnet for mayhem of all descriptions, was concerned about neither.

Tap, tap, tap.

She crossed to her window with a yawn. No burglar would intentionally try to wake her up, and a true emergency would rate use of the doorbell. Taps on her window in the middle of the night, in her unfortunately vast experience, indicated a *family* emergency. And that was something different entirely.

She rolled up the shade expecting to see her cousin waiting outside. Cara lived at the farmhouse next door, attracted a fair amount of mayhem in her own right, and was by far the most frequent tapper on that particular window.

It wasn't Cara. Leigh blinked away the cobwebs and attempted to focus her eyes. It was Mason Dublin, Cara's father.

Leigh stared at him in confusion. Mason was in his mid sixties, with a full head of once-red hair now turned a soft gray and eyes of the same sparkling blue-green as his daughter's. He looked back at her with an embarrassed grin and gestured toward the front of the house.

Leigh rolled the shade back down.

What could he want? She had always liked Mason, despite the fact that neither she nor Cara had met the man until they were in their thirties. His nefarious behavior as a newlywed had led Cara's mother to banish him from their child's life, but after serving his time and proving a sincere interest in his adult daughter's well-being, he had — albeit with great reluctance on the part of his ex-wife — gradually returned to the relatively good graces of the family. Most of the family, anyway.

Leigh crossed to her closet, threw on a robe, and stumbled toward the front door. It was July, it was hot in the house even without a robe, and dog hair stuck to her feet as she walked across the carpet. What could Mason possibly have to say to her that couldn't wait until morning?

She turned on her porch light, unlocked the door, and swung it open. Mason stood before her, blinking. He had a sheepish smile on his face. He also had a cat under one arm and a partially covered birdcage by his side.

"Are you kidding me?" Leigh asked drowsily, wondering if she might still be asleep. That would be nice.

"Sorry, kid," he replied, scratching his head nervously with his free hand. "I hate to do this to you, but I need a favor."

Leigh took a closer look at his cargo. A small, cream and gray tortie nestled in the crook of his arm. It was curled up tight and hiding its head as if trying to make itself invisible. Whatever was in the bird cage, Leigh couldn't see. The three-foot-tall wire box had a towel wrapped around its top half.

"You need money?" Leigh asked hopefully.

Mason frowned at her. "Of course not. When have I ever asked you for money?"

She felt a twinge of guilt. Mason's youthful lust for riches had been his downfall, and he was still a bit sensitive on the topic. "Never," she admitted.

"Look," he began, shifting his feet awkwardly. "I really do hate to ask, but could you possibly take care of these guys for me? For just a couple days... I mean, like... a week?"

Leigh shook her head in confusion. Surely she was only dreaming this. "Mason," she asked, "since when do you even have a cat? Or a bird?"

"I don't. They're not mine. The cat's my next-door neighbor's. At my apartment in Bellevue, I mean. He asked me to take care of her if anything—" His eyes flickered with distress. "I mean, if he went out of town. I don't know where the bird came from, but I couldn't just leave it there, could I? And I've got to get to the airport. My flight leaves at six."

Leigh's forehead wrinkled in confusion. Mason had just said so many things that made no sense, she wasn't sure where to begin. Besides which, he didn't look like himself.

"Listen," he said quickly, shifting the tightly curled ball of fur to his other arm. "I know I'm not making any sense. But the long and short of it is, I promised my buddy Kyle I'd take care of his cat, but I didn't know he was leaving *this* week, and this week I've got to be somewhere else. I would have taken them to Cara's, but Lenna's afraid of birds, and I knew you and Allison would know how to take care of it."

Leigh blinked three times in quick succession, determined to wake herself up. It didn't work.

She let out a sigh. Mason's last statement, at least, did make sense. His granddaughter Lenna was afraid of a great many things. Leigh's own daughter, Allison, wasn't afraid of nearly enough.

"Could you watch them until I get back?" he begged. "Please, Leigh? I can pay for their board, if you like."

"You will not," she protested. "Don't be silly."

"You'll do it, then?" His expression softened, and with a slight cock of his head to the side, he gave her a dashing smile, his bright eyes sparkling mischievously. Her resistance crumbled. It wasn't difficult to see how her Aunt Lydie had once been charmed into single motherhood.

Leigh gritted her teeth, swung the door open wider, and gestured him inside. "I'm sure Allison would love to pet sit," she conceded. "But I still don't get it. Where are you going?"

He hesitated. "Las Vegas. Pawnbrokers' convention."

Leigh quirked an eyebrow. Mason was usually a better liar. He wasn't even trying.

He carried the cage inside and set it down, then extended the cat to Leigh. "Her name's Peep," he said apologetically. "I, um... I forgot to bring her food. Sorry. She did just eat a big meal, though.

Poor thing woke me up, crying so loud next door. Good thing Kyle gave me a spare key. I don't know how long her bowl had been empty…"

His voice trailed off uncertainly. Leigh reached out and tucked the cat under her own arm on autopilot, her brain still mired in confusion. There was definitely more to this story than Mason was telling her. If she was fully awake, she would interrogate him until she figured it out. But all she really wanted right now was to crawl back into bed.

"When will you get back?" she asked, settling for the most obvious question.

"Friday," he said, "Probably. I'll let you know. You have my number."

"Fine," Leigh said with a yawn. "Go catch your plane. To that *convention*."

Mason cracked a knowing grin. They had always understood each other. "Thanks, kid," he said tenderly, leaning in to plant a fatherly kiss on her cheek. "I owe you one."

"Damn straight," Leigh responded.

He turned to let himself out, but swung around again at the door. "Oh, and Leigh—" he said, sounding uncomfortable again. "It's kind of important. Could we keep this arrangement a secret? Where these guys came from, I mean?"

Leigh's vision began to blur. She was so, so tired. Tuning out Warren's snores had always been difficult, but since he'd caught a summer cold, she'd hardly slept a wink. She knew she should be doing more to understand what the hell was going on here, and that if she didn't, she would kick herself later. She rallied her neurons and made the effort. "And why, pray," she asked heavily, "must we do that?"

"Maybe no reason," Mason answered smoothly. "But with a boy like Kyle… Well, you never know. I'd feel better if the critters stayed here incognito."

Leigh had no earthly idea who Kyle was. She tried to care. She failed. "Whatever," she croaked.

Mason grinned at her again. "I meant what I said," he assured as he stepped out. "I owe you one." With a wink, he closed the door behind him.

Leigh locked it and turned around. Finally… to bed!

Hssssstttttt!!!!

She froze. A black ball of bristled cat fur stood perched on the back of the recliner in front of her, its gold eyes filled with fire.

Oh, crap. She had completely forgotten she was holding an alien cat.

Leigh's own ancient Persian, swelled to twice her ordinary miniscule size, aimed her flat little nose at the lump in Leigh's arms and spat. Then, hissing with a venom not seen since the day the corgi pup had arrived, she coiled her wiry body, ready to spring.

"Easy, Mao!" Leigh soothed, clamping down on the now-struggling tortie and backing quickly away toward the stairs. "No worries. Peep here was just leaving!"

Mao Tse continued to growl. Leigh opened the door to the basement and fled down the stairs while the tortie crawled up her face. "Okay, okay!" she acceded, bending over the giant bean bag in the floor to detach the cat from her scalp. The tortie jumped into the center of the bag, burrowed down into its folds and made herself as small as possible. "Sorry," Leigh apologized half-heartedly, feeling her cheek for signs of blood. "I guess I should have seen that coming. But don't worry. You'll be perfectly safe down here. Mao Tse is strictly an above-stairs kind of cat."

Leigh glanced around the cluttered den with a sigh. She didn't keep a litter box here, since Mao never came down. She'd have to rig one up. Like now.

Five minutes later, she slid a box lid covered with a trash bag and some litter into the corner behind the bean bag, then rounded up a clean dog bowl and filled it with water. The cat hadn't moved, but she seemed a little less tightly curled, and Leigh leaned in to try and stroke her. The cat didn't purr, but she didn't shrink away, either. "That's a good Peep," Leigh said with a smile. "You make yourself at home. Breakfast will be served at seven." She yawned again. "*Ish.*"

Now... bed.

Leigh had trudged only halfway up the stairs before an unfamiliar sound met her ears. Something halfway between a squawk and a cluck. What could Mao possibly be—

The bird!

Leigh shot the rest of the way up the steps and across the living room to find the towel off the cage, one of Mao Tse's skinny black paws sticking through the bars, and whitish-yellow wings flapping frantically.

"No, no, no!" Leigh chastised, reaching to pick up the cage just as the Persian coincidentally lost all interest, withdrew her paw, and jumped back up on top of the recliner.

"Not buying it, Mao," Leigh said, rolling her eyes as the cat gave a casual lick to a back leg, the picture of innocence.

Leigh looked into the cage and studied the bird, which was now scooting back and forth along a perch, bobbing and flapping with agitation. It was a cockatiel of the lutino variety, with a white and yellowish body, yellow crest, and bright orange cheek patches. Leigh was no avian expert, but she had watched her veterinarian father treat enough pet birds to assure herself that despite the scare, the bird showed no obvious signs of injury. "Easy, fellow," she attempted to soothe, moving the cage away from the cat. "You'll be all right. I'm sure we can find you some private accommodations somewhere in this madhouse."

She carried the cage toward her son's room and popped open the door. Eleven-year-old Ethan was sleeping soundly, arms and legs sprawled haphazardly on top of his covers. A sable and white corgi, equally unconscious, slept with its muzzle draped across one of the boy's ankles. Leigh shook her head with a smile. A watchdog, Chewie was not.

She closed the door and moved down the hall to her daughter's room. Having not been favored by the corgi's presence this particular night, Allison would no doubt be thrilled to have a surprise guest. Leigh opened the door and peeked in. Ethan's much smaller twin sister was curled up beneath a sheet adorned with running mustangs. Despite the girl's adeptness at playing possum, Leigh knew that Allison was actually asleep. If the child had heard her "Grandpa Mason" arrive, she would have been up and investigating immediately.

Leigh stepped into the room, settled the cage just inside the door, and reset its towel covering. The cockatiel remained antsy, but was at least not squawking. Leigh checked to make sure the bird had water, then closed the door behind her with a yawn. Just a couple more hours of sleep. Then she would figure out what to feed them both. With luck, the bird would wake Allison first and the precocious young animal lover would have a detailed care plan ready to go by the time Leigh dragged her own butt back out of bed.

She looked down the hall to see the imperious Mao Tse standing in the living room doorway glowering at her. *You are no fun at all,* the cat's gold eyes proclaimed.

"Yeah, I know," Leigh cooed, scooping up the geriatric cat and scratching her under the chin. "You wouldn't have eaten it. You only wanted to play with it a while. Sorry to disappoint."

She put the cat down near her bedroom door, then moved to the kitchen to get sticky notes and a pen. After alerting whoever might rise first to the presence of their new guests and the inadvisability of letting either Mao or Chewie into the basement or Allison's room, she at last returned to her pillow and settled down with a cat on her stomach.

Unfortunately, she was now fully awake.

She stared at her bedroom ceiling with frustration. Warren's snores had progressed from chain saw to jackhammer. Even Mao's purr seemed louder than usual. Worse still, she now remembered what day it was. Her mother was having some long-overdue surgery this morning — for bunions. Frances would be off her feet for two solid weeks, during which the other Morton women would be taking shifts to help her around the house. Leigh was first up.

Her eyes closed. She really, really wished this day was just a dream.

What was it that had been so odd about Mason, anyway? What was causing the uneasy feeling that only continued to increase the more alert she became?

Her eyes flew open. She propped herself up on her elbows, tilting an annoyed Mao Tse. "Apartment in Bellevue?" she whispered aloud. "What apartment in Bellevue?"

Leigh's and Cara's families lived in a suburb well north of Pittsburgh, but Bellevue was a small borough just beyond the city's North Side. It was positioned between West View, where Leigh and Cara had grown up and where Leigh's parents and Cara's mother still lived, and Avalon, where Leigh's father's veterinary clinic was located. But for over a decade now, ever since Mason had returned to Pennsylvania and reunited with his daughter, he had lived nearly two hours away at his own family home in Jennerstown, where he supported both himself and his invalid sister by running a pawn shop. Trudy, a recovering alcoholic, had died of cirrhosis a year ago; but Leigh hadn't heard a word about Mason moving to Pittsburgh. Was it supposed to be a secret?

She fell back onto her mattress with a frown. What exactly was Mason playing at? She couldn't fault him for lack of devotion to his daughter and grandchildren — no one could. Even Frances had to concede that his willingness to drive into town on a moment's notice for any and every event of significance in Cara and her children's lives was nothing short of heroic. Furthermore, he had always treated Ethan and Allison as if they were his own grandchildren. The man never forgot a birthday, and his soft spot for baseball had brought him to nearly as many Little League games as Warren or Gil.

But he was definitely hiding something now.

Leigh considered his appearance. He had looked different somehow... more dapper. Mason had always been a handsome fellow, and age had done nothing to diminish his considerable charm. But he had never had any —

Leigh's breath caught. Money.

She knew the pawn shop was doing well, and had done well for years. But the family property in Jennerstown was run-down and in need of repair, and Trudy's care expenses had been high. Mason had always managed for himself, never asking anyone in the family for help. But he had never been what you'd call flush, either.

Yet he had headed for the airport just now in the spiffiest outfit she had ever seen him wear. Business casual in the height of style. Everything Mason sported — including his shoes, if she remembered correctly — looked brand-spanking new and fit him like a glove. And unless he had sold the house in Jennerstown, the new apartment marked a second home.

Leigh sucked in an anxious breath. She wasn't imagining things. The man had money. Where had he gotten it? And where was he flying off to in such a rush this morning?

An uncomfortable ache arose in her middle, just underneath the purring cat. No one, least of all Mason himself, could deny that for the first half of his life he had been somewhat "ethically challenged." Although he didn't have a violent bone in his body, he had served time in a federal penitentiary for counterfeiting, and with his long and unhappy history of get-rich-quick schemes, if he were any less wily he probably would have served more. Prison had had the desired effect, however; he had emerged a changed man who went to great effort to avoid so much as bending the law. Ever since Leigh had known him, he had been — if not the soul of propriety — a model ex-con.

So why did his newfound wealth make her so nervous? Did she not believe him capable of earning it honestly?

That depended. Who was this mysterious Kyle person? She tried to remember exactly what Mason had said. He asked me to take care of her if anything — I mean, if he went out of town.

Mason obviously hadn't expected that "the boy" would go off at this particular time, leaving the cat without warning and without food. But both of them must have known that Kyle's sudden disappearance was a possibility. Otherwise, why give Mason a key?

And where the hell had the cockatiel come from?

The nonsense of it all continued to swirl in Leigh's head, maddeningly and unproductively, until some time later she was roused into full consciousness by a raucous avian squawking, followed closely by the delighted squeal of a young girl and the indignant woofs of a suddenly protective corgi.

"Don't let Chewie in here!" Allison ordered from her room. "He'll scare the bird!"

Ethan's mattress squeaked and the house vibrated as his heels hit the floor. "What bird?"

Warren awakened with a start, running a hand through his bushy head of hair and looking annoyingly refreshed. "What's all the yelling about?" he asked curiously.

The alarm on Leigh's bedside table erupted with piercing beeps.

From the basement below came the muffled sound of a feline howl. Mao Tse's claws sank into Leigh's abdomen.

"Leigh!" Warren exclaimed suddenly, staring at her. "My God, what happened to your face? Did Mao do that to you?"

Leigh shut her eyes and breathed in slowly.

Her day had officially begun.

Chapter 2

"But where did the bird come from?" Allison demanded, staring at her mother across the kitchen table a few minutes later. "Did you put it in my room because Mao freaked out? Who brought it here?"

Leigh took a sip of cola — straight up. Her coffee was still percolating; she couldn't wait that long. Her son and husband both stared at her expectantly. The bird in the bedroom continued to squawk.

"It was an old friend of mine," she answered hesitantly. She would tell Warren the full story later, of course, but for now it seemed best to keep Mason's name out of it. She could hardly ask the kids *not* to mention to their second cousins, Mathias and Lenna, that the animals had come from their grandfather. And if Mason said it was better that nobody knew…

"She agreed to pet sit for someone else, but then she had a family emergency of her own and had to take an early flight this morning."

Warren threw his wife a skeptical look, but said nothing.

A hiss from Mao Tse drew their attention to the basement door. The Persian had planted herself at its base, much to the consternation of the corgi, who whined pathetically as he paced in semicircles a safe distance away.

"Oh," Leigh said dully, fingering the scratch on her cheek, which extended from just below her eye nearly to her chin. It was shallow, but had gotten tender and swollen overnight. "There's a cat, too. In the basement. Her name's Peep, and she seems perfectly sweet. At least when she's not being hissed at and dragged down a staircase."

Allison blinked at her mother with disbelief. Then she sidled carefully around Mao Tse and slipped through the basement door.

"Chill, Chewie," Ethan soothed, scooping up the near-frantic corgi and carrying him toward the back patio. "It's just another cat. Let's go throw the ball."

Leigh breathed out a sigh of relief as Warren collected the first drips of coffee into a cup and handed it to her. "So what's the real story?" he demanded quietly, sitting beside her in the now-empty kitchen.

She drained the half inch of coffee, then shared what she knew, being careful to keep her voice nearly inaudible. Allison's powers of eavesdropping could not be overestimated.

"Did you know Mason had an apartment in town?" she whispered.

Warren shook his head. "The whole thing does sound a bit shady. But Mason's kept his nose clean for ages now. He's given us no reason *not* to trust him." His brown eyes focused on her intently. "Unless, of course, there's something else I don't know."

Leigh shook her head thoughtfully. "No… not this time."

Warren frowned at her just as Allison's squeal echoed up the stairwell. "Mom! Her leg is gone!"

Leigh sprang up and hustled down the stairs, seeing horrifying images of the tortie with a paw stuck somewhere, bleeding to death. It wasn't until she reached the basement and saw Allison calmly cuddling the purring cat in the middle of the giant bean bag that she found she was able to breathe again. "*What* did you say?" she gasped.

"Look," Allison said, holding up the cat to reveal its underside. "She's an amputee!"

Leigh looked. Sure enough, the spot where the cat's left front leg should be showed nothing but a tuft of fur. Now that she thought about it, the cat's mad scramble up her person last night had seemed a bit clumsy. But whatever had happened to the cat, it had obviously happened a long time ago. "Oh," Leigh exhaled with relief. "I see."

"What do you think happened to her?" Allison mused, studying the tortie's teeth. Playing veterinarian always made the girl seem much older than her eleven years, perhaps because in both looks and manner she was a carbon copy of her grandfather Randall. "It probably was an accident, rather than cancer or something. She's only a few years old." She looked up at her mother with a studious gaze. "Your friend didn't tell you?"

Leigh whirled around quickly, hiding her eyes. She had never been a particularly good liar. "No," she answered, starting back up the stairs. "It was a short conversation. She was in a hurry. Why don't you open that new bag of cat food and offer some to Peep? Then we'll figure out what to do with the bird."

Three hours, a trip to the grocery store, and much chopping of fruits and vegetables later, Leigh at last sank back into a recliner with her second cup of coffee. She could only hope that the bird would become less finicky after settling in. Despite the veritable cockatiel smorgasbord she and Allison had prepared, the bird had turned up its beak at everything except a few of the seeds. Furthermore, it had kept up the irritating squawking at random intervals all morning, making Chewie so beside himself with curiosity that he kept accidentally invading Mao Tse's personal space — a lapse which posed a very real risk to his eyeballs.

A knock sounded on the patio door, followed closely by the sound of the door opening. "Leigh?" Cara's voice called. "Can I come in?"

"You may," Leigh called back, grateful not to have to get up again. "I'm in here."

A few seconds later, Leigh's slightly younger cousin dropped onto the couch across from her. The forehead of Cara's pretty, well-preserved face was furrowed. "I got a call from the police this morning," she stated flatly.

Of course you did.

Leigh closed her eyes and inhaled deeply. She knew she had no reason to complain. It had been months since the last time her name had appeared on a police report; clearly, she was due. The fact that whatever Cara was about to tell her would have to be dealt with in concert with Frances Koslow's bunion surgery should — given Leigh's spectacular relationship with bad karma — have been entirely expected.

"Go on," she croaked, her eyes still closed.

"It was the Bellevue police department," Cara continued, lowering her voice. "Where is Allison?"

"In the basement with Lenna."

"Right. Let me know if you hear the door."

"Will do."

"Leigh, would you open your eyes please? That's a nasty scratch you've got on your face, by the way."

"I am aware," Leigh sighed, opening her eyes.

"They were looking for my father," Cara continued, her voice uneasy. "He's not in any trouble or anything, they made sure to tell me that. But something happened at an apartment complex down there this morning, and... Well, they said they wanted to talk to him because he lives in the apartment next door."

Leigh raised a hand to her mouth and started nibbling on a nail.

"The thing is," Cara continued. "I didn't know he *had* an apartment in Bellevue. He never said a thing about it. But the landlord is saying he's been there two weeks." She shot a look at her cousin, and her brow furrowed further. "You're biting your nails. That means you know something. Spill it."

Leigh pulled her hand down. Cara knew her entirely too well to attempt deception. "He tapped on my window at 4:30 this morning to drop off a neighbor's pets he got stuck taking care of," she said succinctly. "He said he had to catch a six o'clock flight to Vegas for a pawnbrokers' convention."

Cara stared at her a moment. Then she began nibbling on her own fingernail. "I didn't realize his convention was this week," she mumbled. "That explains why the police couldn't reach him on his cell phone; he must have been on the plane. But it doesn't explain why he didn't tell me about the apartment."

Leigh felt another jolt of angst. Mason had clearly given his daughter the same itinerary he had given Leigh. Only Cara had believed it.

"That's a pretty strange thing to leave out of a conversation, wouldn't you say?" Cara continued, her blue-green eyes flashing. "I mean, I just talked to him on the phone three days ago!"

"Maybe he wanted to surprise everyone," Leigh suggested lamely, feeling more and more uncomfortable. "Did the police say what happened at the apartment next door?"

Cara looked at her as though the question were irrelevant. "Somebody broke into it, I think. They wanted to know if my dad saw or heard anything, but if his flight left at six there's no way. They said they were looking for people who'd been at the building between six and seven this morning."

The bird squawked.

"The kids told me you were babysitting a cockatiel and a three-legged cat," Cara remarked suspiciously. "They didn't say that their grandfather had brought them."

"He seemed to think it was best if the kids didn't know," Leigh answered carefully. "Although he didn't say why."

Cara's eyes narrowed. "And did he say *which* neighbor they came from?"

Leigh's gaze met her cousin's. But before she could open her mouth to answer, the house landline rang. She threw a glance at her watch and struggled up. "That's probably my dad. Mom's surgery should have been over a while ago."

Leigh moved to the kitchen counter, checked the caller ID, and picked up the phone. "Hey, Dad," she greeted. "Everything go okay?"

Randall Koslow, VMD, cleared his throat. "Your mother's surgery went perfectly. No problems." He drew in a breath as if to say something else, then didn't.

Leigh walked back into the living room. "So… are you ready for me to come over?"

Another pause ensued. "Well, er," Randall began again. "The thing is, we had a bit of an accident on our way back into the house. Your mother's not used to the walker yet, and she lost her balance on the top front step."

Leigh's breath caught. "Is she okay?"

"Yes," Randall said, his voice oddly embarrassed. "Your mother's fine, except for a few bruises. But it looks like… well, I might have broken my ankle."

Oh, no. "What do you mean 'might have?'"

"Well, it's sprained for sure," he answered. "But Jim next door drove me up to urgent care, and they splinted it until I could get to the orthopod. So, for the moment I'm afraid I'm on crutches."

Leigh sank slowly onto the back of the couch.

"I can still work," Randall said quickly. "No reason I can't sit on a stool and see patients. But I'm going to need a little extra help getting to the clinic and back. And your mother… well, I know we'd planned on my taking care of her in the evenings, but—"

"We'll manage," Leigh said quickly, even as her heart dropped into her shoes. She, Cara, and their Aunt Bess would have to alternate staying overnight, as well as handling the daytime shifts. If only her Aunt Lydie, who lived next door to her parents, were not out of town! But despite all their careful planning, Frances's surgeon had rescheduled her procedure at the last minute, right on top of Lydie's much-anticipated historical symposium in Hershey. They had all assured Lydie they could handle the situation without her, at least for the first week. But that was when they thought they only needed to cover the hours Randall was at work.

"It'll be fine, Dad," Leigh insisted, attempting a cheerful tone. "My work is mostly portable, and Cara and Aunt Bess will help out. No worries. Where are you now?"

"Home," he answered. "But I was hoping to get to the clinic as soon as possible. My appointments start in a hour."

Leigh assured her father that she was on her way, hung up the phone, and explained the situation to Cara.

"We'll manage," Cara echoed, forcing a tone of cheer only slightly more convincing than Leigh's. "You go ahead. I'll give Aunt Bess a call and we'll pop over later and hash out the details."

"Mom?" Allison's small voice piped up from just behind Leigh's elbow.

Leigh jumped. She really wished she could train herself not to be surprised every time her daughter crept up on her, considering how frequently it happened. She could only hope the regular exercise was strengthening her ankles.

"I can go to the clinic with Grandpa," Allison suggested. "He'll need somebody to stay in the room and hand him things. I wanted to go today anyway, to ask him about the bird."

Leigh nodded in agreement, but before she could speak, her cell phone rang. She crossed to the kitchen counter, looked at the screen, and swooped it up. "Hey! Cara's been trying to—"

"I know," Mason interrupted. "I just got off the phone with the Bellevue police. Listen, Leigh, don't say anything else out loud, okay? You never know when Allison's listening."

Leigh stifled a snort. He was telling her?

"It's really, really important you don't tell anyone those animals came from Kyle's place. Or even from me," he said earnestly.

"Are you going to tell me what's—"

"I have to shut off the phone again in a second," he said quickly. "We're taking off. I just wanted to warn you that Kyle has… well, some people after him, and I don't want you guys getting dragged into his mess. There's no reason you would, so long as no one but you and me knows where those animals came from."

Leigh looked around to see three faces staring at her curiously. She had to be careful what she said. "Cara and Warren?"

"You mean— Oh, I guess so. But no one else, okay? Maybe I'm being too cautious, but if any of the kids—" He broke off again. Leigh could hear what sounded like a flight attendant over a loudspeaker. "I've got to shut down," he finished. "No worries, okay? Ciao!"

"But what—" Leigh began. She was too late. The line was dead. She put the phone down.

Cara's eyes held hers. "We'll talk later."

Leigh nodded, and her head began to spin. So, the mysterious Kyle had *people after him*. People who had, perchance, broken into his apartment this morning?

An unwelcome chill slid up Leigh's spine.

It was going to be a very long day, indeed.

Chapter 3

"Er, Allison, could you—" Randall Koslow began, gesturing toward the exam room counter. His granddaughter was already on it. She had scooped up the toenail clippers and was holding them out to him as he started to speak. "Thanks, sweetheart," he praised.

Leigh watched with an unsettled feeling as her father sat awkwardly on the clinic stool with his splinted foot sticking straight out beneath him. His stoic face bore no sign of self-pity, but she knew his ankle had to ache, and the lower-than-usual stool would do his back no favors, either. But she knew better than to try and talk him out of seeing his previously scheduled patients. The late start had already backed up his schedule, and the waiting room was full to bursting.

His longest employed and trustiest technician, Jeanine, stood on the other side of the exam table holding a geriatric cockapoo to her chest while extending its front paw for a nail trim.

"There's something I've been meaning to ask you," trilled the dog's owner, a nervous-looking woman in her seventies who fidgeted beside the table, alternately checking the clasp on her purse and rerolling her dog's leash.

"What's that?" Randall asked, clipping the dog's toenails with his usual quiet efficiency.

"I was wondering if there was some sort of tracker I could get for her," the woman inquired, her face reddening as she spoke. "You know, like a microchip, where if she ran away, I could tell where she was?"

Randall looked at the woman curiously, and Leigh found herself doing the same. The dog in question was sixteen years old if she was a day, crippled with arthritis, and nearly blind. Her unused toenails had grown so long they were curled round nearly into circles.

"You think Peaches is planning to make a run for it?" Randall asked without sarcasm.

"Well," the woman replied unsteadily, working the leash furiously in her hands. "You never know. I'd just hate to—" her voice choked a little. "Lose her. Is there such a thing I could get?"

Randall switched to the dog's back feet. "A microchip won't give you a pet's location," he explained in a rote manner. "It just gives identifying information that can be read by someone checking the animal with a scanner."

Leigh's eyebrows perked at his tone. The veterinarian was answering the bizarre question as if it were an issue that came up every day.

"To track a pet's location, you'd need a GPS collar," he continued. "They exist, but they're bulky, and they only work in a limited range."

The woman's face fell. "But anyone could just take off a collar!"

"That's true," Randall confirmed without looking up. "Anything else you're worried about with Peaches, besides those nails?"

"No," the woman said shortly.

"She taking her medication okay?" the veterinarian questioned.

"Fine," she replied, still agitated. "But I need refills."

"No problem," Randall responded. He finished up his examination and the technician led both the dog and its owner back out to the reception area.

Leigh frowned as she watched them leave, and she noticed that Allison was doing the same. Mother and daughter exchanged a knowing look. Randall Koslow's skills of observation might be second to none with regard to the appearance and behavior of his animal patients, but when it came to reading people, the poor man was oblivious.

"Dad," Leigh asked tentatively, "That woman seemed a little uptight. Why do you think she was asking about GPS?"

He shrugged. "I've had a bunch of people asking about that lately. Must be a new ad running somewhere, trying to scare people into thinking every pet needs a tracking collar. It's not a bad idea — it could help with the chronic runaways — but somebody needs to make the devices smaller and improve the battery life first."

The technician returned, this time leading a black lab mix with a limp, and Leigh moved toward the exit. Clearly, her father could manage with his splint; her continued presence in the already crowded exam room was not required. She dispensed a few final instructions for Allison, then slipped out the back way.

Emerging into the clinic's tiny parking lot, she smiled absently at two clients engaged in conversation near their cars. She stepped around them and into the street.

"Has anyone told the police?" a hushed voice hissed.

"I don't know what you'd tell them!" another replied.

Leigh's steps slowed. She fished around in her pocket for an imaginary piece of trash, then changed course and headed toward the dumpster.

"Well, somebody ought to say something!" the first voice demanded, no longer whispering.

"I'd be too scared!" the second insisted. "You don't want to be next, do you?"

Leigh lingered at the dumpster as long as she dared, but as the women moved away toward the clinic's front door, their voices became inaudible. What she did overhear disturbed her, even as she told herself that whatever the police *should* be told didn't necessarily have anything to do with her father's clinic. Avalon was a small borough; many of his clients were already neighbors or friends. For all Leigh knew, the women could have been talking about missing change at a bake sale.

Reminding herself that she had trouble enough at the moment without borrowing more, Leigh hopped into her van and headed back to her parents' house in West View. Another neighbor had offered to be "on call" while Leigh took her father to work, but she knew that her mother would be anxious for her return. One could only impose on one's neighbors so much, Frances would say. Conscription of family was another matter.

Leigh parked on the street outside the two-story brick foursquare house in which she had grown up. The neighborhood had changed little since her girlhood, except for the trees. One of the old maples lining her block had toppled in a storm, and three others had been taken out by the city when their roots buckled the sidewalks. New trees had been planted, but it would be a long time before the street was as shady as she remembered.

She inhaled deeply before opening the front door. Frances had still been in panic mode when Leigh had arrived to fetch her injured father, but by now Frances was likely to have moved into Disaster Response Stage Two: The Action Plan. And as fearsome as Frances's panicked tirades could be, her steeliness in the action stage could be even scarier.

"Leigh, dear, there you are," a determined voice announced before the door had closed. *"Come sit."*

Leigh turned to the living room. Her mother was sitting sideways on her 1970s-era floral-upholstered sofa, which had been carefully pre-covered with protective sheets for the occasion. Frances had both feet straight ahead of her, propped up on plastic-covered pillows and encased in wrappings and bags of ice. She sat bolt upright.

"Um…" Leigh stammered, moving closer. "Are you sure you're comfortable like that?"

"Perfectly," Frances replied, patting the wingback chair next to her. "Sit."

Leigh sat.

"What in heaven's name did you do to your face?" Frances asked accusingly.

"I made a cat scratch me. In retrospect, it was probably a bad idea."

Frances frowned with disapproval, then threw out her chest and folded her hands neatly in her lap. "I have made a decision," she announced.

Leigh tensed. "About what, exactly?"

"About your father's disability, of course. He'll need to reduce his appointment schedule significantly, but he needn't be idle. The current situation will afford the perfect opportunity for him to catch up on that paperwork he is perpetually avoiding, because for the next several weeks *I* will be available to help him!"

Leigh faked a look of enthusiasm. She could not pretend the work didn't need doing. Her father was an excellent clinician, but a notoriously horrible administrator. The clinic's profits had always ebbed and flowed predictably, based not on the local economy but on whether or not competent office help was employed. Randall's last business manager had gotten married and moved to New Brighton six months ago, and Leigh had not seen the top of her father's desk since. The last time she'd peeked in his basement office, she could not even see the floor.

Randall was aware that he needed to address the situation. But his preferred solution was to eventually get around to posting a want ad and then cross his fingers and hope that whoever took the job could at least manage to dig themselves out before deciding to marry, move, have a baby, go back to school, or fake their own death. The idea of transporting a vanful of file boxes, loose paper, unsorted mail, and flash drives full of spreadsheet data home to his living room to be picked through, pored over, dissected, and criticized by his anal-retentive wife — with him being *present*, for God's sake — would make the man's blood freeze.

But there was nothing Leigh could do about it. Debating with Frances was inadvisable when she was in the best of moods. Challenging her primal need to keep busy post-surgery could be downright dangerous. Besides, Leigh thought selfishly, her mother could have come up with a worse idea. Like deciding again that *this* time, Leigh Eleanor Koslow was *going* to learn to sew.

"That sounds great, Mom!" she answered with enthusiasm. "I know Dad can use the help."

Traitor.

"I thought you would agree," Frances said with a smile. "Now go back to the clinic and load up whatever is currently cluttering that surface your father calls a desk. I'd like to get started. No time like the present!"

"You..." Leigh asked uncertainly, "want me to leave you here alone and go back? Right now?"

Frances patted the cell phone at her side. "I'll be perfectly fine for half an hour or so. Virginia said she'd be home all afternoon and not to hesitate to call her if I needed anything. However, before you leave, I should like to use the restroom. If you'll just help me up the stairs, I'll—"

"The stairs?" Leigh interrupted, casting a glance at the relatively narrow staircase that led to the three small bedrooms and full bath on the second floor. Even with Randall helping earlier, Frances hadn't been able to make it up the half-dozen steps to the front porch. "Mom, that's ridiculous," Leigh protested. "You don't need to go upstairs. You can use the half bath down here."

Frances drew herself up indignantly, her lips pursed. "You know perfectly well that the powder room is reserved for guests!"

Leigh sighed. Her mother's feelings about the half bath went deep. The room was not original to the house, but had been added on by the previous owners for the sake of "convenience." To Frances, however, "sheer laziness" was hardly justification for sacrificing both a kitchen broom closet and what must have been a "perfectly lovely" built-in china cabinet in the dining room. The ill-gotten powder room was thus forbidden to family members, kept pristine at all times, and largely forgotten — except for those still-regular occasions when Frances bemoaned her lack of dish storage space.

"Mom," Leigh said reasonably. "These are hardly ordinary circumstances."

"I can make it up the stairs just fine!" Frances insisted.

Leigh received inspiration. "You probably could, but what if *I* were to fall trying to help you? How many sprained ankles can the family handle?"

Frances's lips curled down into a frown. "I see your point."

Leigh smiled in triumph.

"I will use the powder room," Frances announced, reaching for her walker. "But *someone* is going to have to keep it cleaned properly while I am indisposed."

Leigh's smile faded. She helped her mother shuffle the short distance to the hall and back, then she reluctantly returned to the van and headed back to the clinic. Randall would not be pleased to see papers from his office being carted out the door, but with luck, she could conduct her mission covertly and get by with leaving him a note.

Coward!

She had successfully sneaked into the basement office and was in the process of scooping neglected piles of mail off the desktop and into a cardboard box when Allison silently materialized at her side.

"What are you doing, Mom?"

Leigh tried hard not to jump again. "Grandma wants to help Grandpa catch up on his office work."

"Oh," Allison remarked heavily. The child was nothing if not perceptive. "Listen, Mom," she said, her tone turning urgent. "There's something weird going on around here. You know how nervous Mrs. Lippert was about Peaches getting lost? Well, she's not the only one. I've been getting the strangest vibe from people, like everybody's scared of something. Grandpa says it's nothing, but..."

Leigh's curiosity battled with her conscience. Her daughter was undoubtedly right; Leigh had gotten the same feeling when listening to the women talk in the parking lot. It was as if some rumor were circulating — a very troubling rumor. And if whatever it was did involve the animal hospital specifically, Randall needed to know. If Leigh could, she would hang around herself until she got to the bottom of it. But she couldn't. Her mother needed her. Would it be so wrong to let Allison give it a try?

Yes, of course it would. The last thing the overly inquisitive girl needed was encouragement to spy on people. It would be sending the wrong parental message. Never mind that Allison was incredibly good at it. Never mind that, in a matter of hours, the child could almost certainly acquire more information than Leigh could in an entire day. And all without being detected, or most likely even suspected. Randall frequently had youngsters interested in veterinary medicine hanging around to observe — Allison's presence was no more notable than that of a fly on the wall.

Besides, the girl was going to do it anyway. Right?

"Well," Leigh said carefully. "If you do figure it out, be sure to let me know. It could be important to Grandpa."

Allison beamed. "Will do!" She whirled on a heel and jogged toward the basement steps.

Leigh clenched her jaws and finished filling the box. Had she seriously just given permission — however passively — for her daughter to engage in espionage?

She had.

Bad parent!

She let out a defeated sigh and headed back to her mother's house with the boxful of stolen mail.

She was *so* going to hell.

Chapter 4

"Really, Bess," Frances tutted at her older sister with exasperation. "That's far too large. Why, no one will be able to walk in here!"

Bess shot back a sour look and switched on the air pump, which went to work with a loud hum. "A queen-size mattress is what I have and a queen is what you'll use," she said firmly. "There's plenty of space; it's not like you're going to be doing any formal entertaining the next two weeks!"

Frances continued to frown as the giant inflatable bed swelled to fill a quarter of the foursquare house's living room. The women had piled half the furniture along the wall of the dining room, leaving only the couch, one wingback chair, and the coffee table. If they had left any more, there would be no aisle to walk through.

"This arrangement should be very functional for you, Aunt Frances," Cara said tactfully. "Everything you'll need is right along this path, and all your fragile pieces are out of the way."

"Living rooms are for living, not sleeping," Frances opined. "This just isn't proper!"

"And how exactly do you think the three of us are going to haul both your carcasses up and down that staircase every day?" Bess replied with no tact whatsoever. "You want to harness us up like sled dogs so we can pull you on a stretcher?"

Frances's lips pursed to full protrusion. "I'm not saying it isn't necessary," she snapped back. "I'm saying it isn't proper."

Bess's eyes rolled. "Hey, kiddo," she said to Leigh. "Can you pull that corner over a little?"

Leigh adjusted the mattress to leave walking space between it and the wall.

"Well, the schedule is finished at least through Wednesday night," Cara announced, looking down at the yellow legal tablet in her hands. "By then we should know exactly when Mom is coming home."

"Why wouldn't she come back Wednesday?" Frances asked. "That's when the symposium ends."

"She thought she might want to stay an extra day or two, depending on the weather," Cara explained. "But with Uncle

Randall getting hurt, I'm sure she'll come straight home."

"Tell your mother to stay as long as she likes," Bess insisted, checking the mattress for firmness. "Lydie can use the vacation."

"It's hardly a vacation," Frances argued. "It's an educational opportunity."

Bess scoffed. "Every 'symposium' has a bar somewhere."

"Not everyone drinks with strangers like an ill-bred hussy!" Frances retorted sharply.

Bess shrugged. "The fun ones do."

"Ladies!" Cara interjected smoothly. "If there's no more scheduling to be decided, I need to pick up Lenna and get home to the boys. Leigh, don't worry about dinner. I'll make something for the Pack — just send them to the farm."

Leigh smiled. Bess had brought over a casserole and would be staying the night tonight, so Leigh was officially off-duty as soon as Randall was escorted home. But Warren was hosting a symposium of his own at the University of Pittsburgh this week — some sort of training session on financial management for non-profits — and wouldn't be home till late every evening. That meant she was responsible for all the cooking in the Harmon household, which meant she'd given the issue no thought whatsoever until the middle of the afternoon. "Thanks, Cuz," she said genuinely.

"There!" Bess announced, turning off the pump. "It's perfect. I'll have it made up in a jiffy. Leigh, go fetch your father. We're done here."

Leigh did not need to be excused twice. What sort of evening her father would have being subjected to the sisters' constant bickering, she shuddered to think. Then again, his ability to tune out uninteresting human interaction was highly developed.

She arrived at the clinic for the third time that day to find her father still working, his schedule having been further slowed by his inability to switch between exam rooms filled with already prepped patients. The mood of the clients still waiting in the lobby was tense as Jeanine pulled Leigh to the side of the reception desk. "I'm working on the rescheduling," she confided. "He's off surgery and evenings, but he insisted on seeing appointments between eleven and five, at least. You think that will be okay? Your mother's called down here twice already, and she keeps telling me the exact opposite of what he says—"

Leigh felt a stab of pity for the senior technician who, despite being an irritating know-it-all who routinely bullied the rest of the staff, lived in abject fear of Frances Koslow.

"That sounds perfect," Leigh interrupted. "It's the best my mother could have hoped for, no matter what she says."

"Really?" Jeanine asked with relief, beads of sweat breaking across her upper lip.

"He worked that much after he had his appendix out, didn't he?" Leigh reminded. "It'll be fine." She felt a sudden sensation of hair brushing along the side of her calf and looked down to see a schnauzer trotting merrily toward the back, dragging his leash behind him on the floor. Instinctively, she stepped on the nylon hand loop.

"Axel!" a woman screamed, jumping up from her chair. She turned and checked beneath it, then looked frantically around the waiting room. "He's gone! Oh, my God! He's *gone!*"

"No, he isn't," Leigh said quickly, reaching down and giving a tug on the leash. "He's right here." The escapee promptly reversed direction and trotted out around the desk and into view.

The dog's owner threw both hands over her heart and sank down onto her chair. "Oh, my," she said weakly. "How foolish of me. Come here, Axel."

Leigh watched as the dog returned and was promptly swept up into a bear hug. Another client, sitting on the woman's far side, had drawn his own cocker spaniel into his lap and was clasping it protectively, his face unnaturally pale.

What the heck?

Leigh left the waiting room and walked back to check on Allison. The girl was still in the same exam room with her grandfather, looking on as he expressed an unhappy shih tzu's anal glands. Leigh doubled back to the treatment area and parked herself on a stool, and Allison sidled up to her a few seconds later.

"Grandpa says he'll be another half hour or so," the girl reported. "He's sorry he didn't think to call and warn you he was running late."

"No problem," Leigh replied, noting the keen sparkle in her daughter's dark brown eyes. "You found out something, didn't you?"

Allison nodded, casting a wary glance behind her.

Leigh noted the irony.

"We shouldn't talk about it here," the girl continued. "But... could we maybe walk up to Aunt Mo's real quick? While Grandpa's finishing up? Paige will stay in the room with him."

Leigh felt a pang of anxiety. Allison's "Aunt Mo" wasn't a blood relative, but one of Leigh's best friends from college, who was now a detective with the homicide division of the Allegheny County police force. And although it was unlikely that Allison was concerned about a homicide, at least on this particular day, her determination to talk to Maura Polanski indicated worse trouble than a few idle rumors.

"Sure," Leigh said nervously. She let her father know where they were going and told him to call her cell when he was ready to leave. Then she and Allison headed out and began their walk up the steep cobblestone street. The Polanski duplex was only a short distance away, and Leigh resisted the urge to pump Allison for information before they got there. The girl seemed unusually quiet and thoughtful, which only made Leigh more anxious, and by the time they reached Maura's front porch she felt near to exploding.

Luckily, the detective was at home.

"Koslow! Allie!" Maura boomed enthusiastically, swinging open the door. "What brings you by?"

Leigh cracked a grin. It was difficult not to. Although she had never personally feared her loud, large, and looming policewoman friend — at least not that much — Maura had a longstanding reputation for being able to effectively intimidate perpetrators of either gender. To see her now dressed in a tee shirt and shorts, wearing a bright yellow baby carrier covered with green lizards that held her 11-week-old son sticking out from her middle face-forward and drooling, was really just too cute.

"Hey there, little Eddie!" Allison greeted, reaching up to slip a finger into the baby's tiny hand. The infant grasped it and turned his head toward hers with a sloppy grin.

"See there!" Maura said gleefully, looking at Leigh. "I *told* you he smiles at people!"

Leigh leaned toward the baby, holding out her own hand. "How are you doing, little guy?" she cooed.

The baby swung his head slowly toward her. His pretty blue eyes locked on hers, and his grin disappeared.

Allison giggled. "What did you do to him, Mom?"

"Nothing!" Leigh said miserably. The baby continued to stare at her, his tiny face screwed up into a critical scowl. "He's judging me again," she lamented.

Maura chuckled. "Stop being so dramatic, Koslow. I repeat, what brings you guys by?" She stepped back and waved them inside, and all three took seats in the cozy living room. Maura settled into her recliner, crossing her arms underneath little Eddie and giving him an occasional bounce.

"There's something weird going on at the animal clinic," Leigh replied, trying not to sound in the least dramatic. "Allison's picked up on some things and she wants to run them by you."

"Excellent! I'd love to hear it." Maura turned to Leigh. "Nothing against motherhood, but after two months of limited-duty bedrest and three months of family leave, I'm bored out of my mind. Nobody at work will tell me jack about what's going on. Apparently there's a betting pool laying odds on whether I'll actually go back to work next week, and the ones betting against it don't want me in the loop. They're about to lose their shirts." She turned back to Allison. "Proceed."

The girl sat forward. "Well, for the last couple weeks, Grandpa's been getting more and more questions about tracking devices for pets. Everybody seems worried about their pet getting lost, all at the same time. The funny thing is, it's not just the pets you'd think people would worry about running away. Some are really old dogs and super-fat indoor cats — you know, the kind that never go anywhere except to the vet anyway."

"Interesting," Maura remarked. Little Eddie's gaze was also locked on Allison, and Leigh fought a grin as both mother and son's brows furrowed simultaneously.

"Grandpa didn't really think much about it," Allison continued. "But there's definitely something going on. When he does ask people why they want to know, they don't say anything that makes sense. And they won't talk to the staff, either. But the clients are muttering to each other all over the place. They're scared. All day long in the clinic, everywhere I listened, I heard the same kind of thing. 'Have you heard?' 'Someone should say something!' 'Well, who's going to do it? How can you take that risk?' One client said, 'I'm not sure I believe it,' and the other said, 'Well, it happened just a block away from me!' But when the second person asked who, the first person wouldn't answer. Said they didn't know, really. That no one wanted to say."

"I see," Maura said thoughtfully. "So what are you thinking, Allie?"

The girl squared her thin shoulders. "I think there's a rumor going around that pets are disappearing. But no one knows exactly which ones. And they're all scared that if they talk to someone in authority about it, something bad is going to happen. Like maybe *their* pet will disappear next."

Leigh tried to wrap her mind around the thought. "If that is the rumor, there couldn't possibly be any truth to it. Dad hasn't mentioned any pets going missing. And why would anyone want to snatch old poodles and obese housecats?"

She considered the more horrifying possibilities without listing them out loud. She knew that it wasn't unheard of for dog fighters to use cats and small dogs as training bait, and dealers still sold unwanted animals for laboratory research. But there had to be easier ways to obtain animals than to snatch cosseted pets from the North Boros!

Maura put a hand to her chin. "Other than young purebreds, stealing pet animals for resale wouldn't make sense, no," she agreed. "The financial gain, if any, wouldn't justify the risk. Unless…"

The three of them exchanged looks. It was clear they were all thinking the same, seemingly preposterous thing.

"Ransom," Leigh murmured breathlessly. "A well-loved pet could be kidnapped and returned for a price." She turned to Maura. "Have you ever heard of such a thing before?"

The detective's lips twisted. "It happens," she answered. "But I'm not aware of anything local. Or large-scale. It would still be a very risky business."

"But it makes sense!" Allison piped up. "What if a few animals were petnapped — even one or two — and the owners were instructed to pay up and not say anything to the police? If they followed the instructions and did get their animal back okay, they wouldn't want to report it. But still, they probably couldn't resist telling somebody something."

Maura nodded at Leigh. "She's right, you know. It's pretty

typical for kidnappers to threaten the victim's family, not just with hurting whoever they're holding for ransom at the moment, but with doing the same thing again — or worse — if the family squeals after the fact. In this case, the victims might be afraid to talk to the police, or to anyone they perceive to be in authority. But they'd be tempted to warn friends and neighbors to keep their pets close, without admitting that anything had happened to them personally."

"So," Leigh said unhappily, "there could be some truth behind all this."

Maura nodded. "Or none at all."

Baby Eddie burped. He was staring at Leigh again, his gaze critical.

"There's not a soul around here, or associated with the clinic, who doesn't know by now that I'm a cop," Maura continued. "So if they're really afraid, I'm the last person they'd level with."

Leigh had to agree. Maura had grown up in Avalon as the daughter of the borough's longtime and highly revered police chief, the late Edward Polanski. No local who feared being taken for a squealer would want to be seen anywhere near her. "That would explain why no one wants to talk to my dad, either," Leigh mused. "They'd figure he would just call the police, and they'd be right. He would. And any of the staff would tell my dad."

"No one would talk to me, either," Allison lamented. "I've been hanging around the clinic forever, so they all know who I am."

"But if the threat is real," Maura proposed, "people certainly will want the perpetrators caught. We just need to create a way for people to report what they know anonymously."

"Snail mail!" Leigh suggested. "We can post signs at the reception desk, telling people to mail tips to the clinic. No return address needed, no questions asked."

"Good idea," Maura confirmed. "Send whatever you get to me, and if it looks like there's any real basis to it, I'll get the local force to look into it."

"Thanks, Aunt Mo!" Allison said with a smile. "I knew you'd know what to do!"

Maura looked thoughtful again. "I can't guarantee how much of a priority it would be for the Avalon PD. But hey — I've got another week of maternity leave. We'll see what shakes out."

Leigh's phone rang, and she answered it. Her father was ready to go home. Maura rose and walked Leigh and Allison to the door while a pensive Eddie continued staring at Leigh without humor. "Why do I get the feeling that as soon as this child can talk," Leigh mused, "he's going to start telling you all my deepest and darkest secrets?"

Maura shrugged. "Boring. I already know them."

Eddie hiccupped.

"Mom!" Allison chastised with a laugh. "You are so paranoid! He's just a baby." She played with his hand again. "Bye bye, little Eddie!"

The baby gurgled and gave the girl another toothless smile.

"Bye!" Leigh echoed.

The infant turned to stare at her again. His smile disappeared.

Maura chuckled. "You know, Koslow, you do look a bit scary today. What did you do to her supreme evilness this time, buy the wrong brand of shrimp in aspic?"

Leigh put a hand to her cheek. The scratch still smarted.

"Long story," she said dismissively.

She could only hope it wouldn't get much longer.

Chapter 5

Leigh could hear Bess and Frances arguing even before she popped open the front door for her father.

"Lydie doesn't tell you everything!" Bess scoffed.

"Of course she does!" Frances shot back. "We're twins! We've always shared everything. I couldn't expect you to understand."

"Well, then, Miss Know-it-all," Bess insisted. "Who is she seeing?"

Leigh stopped in her tracks, remaining quiet as her father slowly moved forward on his crutches. It sounded like the women were sitting at the kitchen table, just out of sight. Cara had been obsessing for months because she was convinced that her mother was dating someone, but Lydie flat-out refused to discuss it, either with her daughter or, as far as either of them knew, with her sister Bess. They suspected that Frances knew, but getting sensitive information out of either twin had always been difficult.

"She isn't seeing anyone!" Frances insisted.

"Hogswaddle!" Bess argued. "You're just annoyed because she won't tell you who it is, either! Twins share everything, indeed."

"She did so tell me!" Frances shot back indignantly.

Leigh smirked. Her Aunt Bess was good. If only her father didn't make too much noise coming in the door...

"I don't believe you," Bess baited.

Frances humphed with annoyance. "It's only Cole Harbison again," she snapped. "And it's not serious this time, either. Lydie just enjoys his company. There's nothing improper going on, but she doesn't want Cara thinking—"

"Improper?" Bess chortled with laughter. *"Improper?* Lydie's a middle-aged divorcee! She can do whatever she darn well pleases! You want to hear something improper, just listen to—"

Randall cleared his throat loudly.

Leigh threw him an annoyed look, but he merely raised his eyebrows at her, and with Allison standing directly behind him on the porch Leigh could hardly complain about his wrecking her eavesdropping.

"We're home," Randall called out.

The kitchen went silent.

After a moment, Bess popped out. "Well, come on in and have a seat," she told him pleasantly. "I've got dinner all heated up and ready to go."

Randall hobbled past her and on into the kitchen, and Bess shot a mischievous look at Leigh. "You two can go on home," she told Leigh and Allison cheerfully. "Everything here will be just fine. I've proposed a gin rummy tournament tonight, and I intend to clean your father's clock."

From the kitchen, they heard Randall chuckle. "You just keep talking, Bess."

Leigh smiled. Her parents were clearly in good hands. She thanked her aunt, collected her daughter — who gave no sign of having overheard anything, although with Allison that didn't mean much — and drove back home.

They walked from the garage into the basement to find Peep the cat curled up in another tight ball in the center of the bean bag. "Aw... she's so cute!" Allison exclaimed. But when the girl approached, the cat jumped off the bag and scuttled underneath the television stand. "She's pretty shy," Allison admitted. "But she really took to Lenna earlier. You should have seen them."

A loud complaint from another feline issued from the top of the stairs. Leigh headed up to console Mao Tse, but had only taken three steps when her nose wrinkled.

Oh, no.

Allison sniffed, too. "Uh oh. Is that what I think it is?"

Leigh sighed heavily. "Evidence of her imperial majesty's displeasure, you mean?"

Allison giggled, then held her nose. "Oh, that stinks. Where do you think she did it?"

Oh, please, anywhere but the upholstered furniture, Leigh thought miserably, trudging up the rest of the stairs. *Or the beds...*

Half an hour, a roll of paper towels, and many squirts of odor neutralizer later, Leigh dropped into one of the kitchen chairs at her cousin's farmhouse next door. She was more than ready to call her Monday officially at an end. "It's like the cat drank all the water in both her bowls just to stock up for the occasion," she finished complaining to Cara. "You'd think laminate would be okay, wouldn't you? But the puddle by the basement door soaked into the grooves and now the planks are uneven!" She dropped her forehead onto the table. Her voice turned grim. "Your father *so* owes me."

Cara chuckled. "He certainly does. I guess Mao Tse isn't used to smelling another cat around."

"No, she is not," Leigh lamented. She raised her head. "Look, Cara. Is there any way Lenna could keep Peep over here? We can deal with the bird, but Mao's old, and it's not like she's ever been a fan of change. Every time we've moved, we've lost at least one piece of furniture. Allison said Lenna likes Peep, and it would really help me out." She favored her cousin with her best pathetic look. "Gil won't mind. Provided nobody tells him. Right?"

Cara, who was busy setting her kitchen table, rolled her eyes with a smile. "I'm not convinced he even *is* allergic. He said he broke out in hives once when he was ten, but I think he just doesn't like cats. As many times as he's been over at your house, he's never sneezed once. Sure. Lenna can keep the cat in her room. We'll see if he notices."

They heard a shrill feminine shriek, quickly muffled.

Cara stepped over and swung open the doors to the dining room, revealing the expected two eleven-year-old girls.

Allison smiled innocently and removed her hand from over her second cousin's mouth.

"Can I really, Mom?" Lenna squealed immediately, her pretty blue eyes practically teary. "Can I really keep Peep in my room?"

"Yes, you may," Cara answered, even as her tone expressed her displeasure. "But we're about to eat, so you'll have to wait till after dinner to bring her over."

The girls squealed together and whirled away.

"They're only going to get better at it, you know," Leigh lamented.

"Maybe we should learn sign language," Cara quipped, stepping back to the stove.

"Speaking of eavesdropping..." Leigh rose and went to stand close beside her cousin. She lowered her voice to barely audible and relayed the conversation she'd overheard between Bess and Frances.

Cara shook her head at once. "No. I don't believe it. Your mother probably does know who my mother is seeing, but it's not Cole Harbison."

Leigh cocked an eyebrow. She knew her cousin had nothing against the kindly history buff who had enjoyed Lydie's company for much of the last decade. Whether the two were just friends or more than friends had never been entirely clear, and Leigh had gone back and forth on the question more than once, as had Cara. But Lydie always insisted the relationship was platonic, even as Cara assured her mother that she would be fine with them as a couple. Cole was a nice enough man, even if he was significantly older than Lydie. The only weird thing about a romantic relationship between them, if there was one, was why they would bother hiding it in the first place. "How do you know for sure?" Leigh asked.

Cara blew out a breath. "He's engaged. To another woman from his church. I heard about it through a mutual friend, and Mom confirmed it. She said she's happy for him."

"Oh," Leigh remarked. "Well, I guess that settles it. It's just that…" Her brow furrowed.

"What?" Cara asked.

"It's just that I didn't think my mother was lying. Usually I can tell. Or at least I can tell that she's covering something up. When she said it was Cole Harbison, I believed her. And I thought Bess did, too."

The women exchanged a look.

"*Your* mother wouldn't lie to *my* mother, would she?" Leigh asked incredulously.

Cara's eyes widened. "You know… I don't know."

They stared at each other a moment. The Morton twins had been figuratively joined at the hip their entire lives. They had always lived in West View, first in the same house, then in copycat foursquare houses side by side. One always seemed to know everything the other one knew. There was never any visible discord. Bess and Frances might bicker, but Lydie had always been the peacemaker. Her tolerance for Frances's nonsense seemed boundless. The idea that she would withhold any significant information from her twin seemed preposterous.

Cara shook her head. "No. Your mother must be a better liar than you think. And why not? The whole family had both of us convinced of a total lie about my father for decades!"

"Good point," Leigh conceded.

Cara frowned. "Speaking of my father, I still don't understand why he didn't tell me about the apartment in Bellevue. I tried to call him this afternoon, but he wouldn't pick up. He did send me an email late this morning, but..." Her voice drifted off.

"What?" Leigh asked after a moment's silence.

"I think he's avoiding me," Cara said unhappily. "I mean, why shouldn't he answer his phone? Or at least text to say he's busy? He may be in Vegas, but it's supposed to be a professional conference. You really think all those pawnbrokers are paying such rapt attention to the workshops that they're not even texting?"

Leigh mulled over the thought uncomfortably. She had no idea what Mason was doing, but she was sure he wasn't at any pawnbrokers' convention. And he knew that she knew. Why would he keep his own daughter in the dark and not Leigh?

Her teeth gnashed. One thing she had learned over the years about the enigmatic Mason Dublin, besides the fact that he was light years smarter than he liked to pretend, was that he didn't do anything without a reason. He loved his daughter and grandkids more than anything in the world, and if he was fudging on his whereabouts this week, he must believe that Cara was better off not knowing. Still — the fact that he didn't care if Leigh knew was perplexing. He had no reason to believe that she would keep his confidence if she thought Cara's wellbeing was at stake. So what was the man playing at?

"He's had that apartment in Bellevue for two weeks now," Cara continued. "I did a little digging and found out he's put the house in Jennerstown up for rent. He must be planning on living in Pittsburgh indefinitely. He's got a full-time manager at the pawn shop now, so he can certainly do that. But why wouldn't he tell us?" Her eyes flashed with hurt. "He's never been secretive like this before. Not with me, anyway."

"I don't know, Cara," Leigh soothed. "But there must be a reason. You know he'd never intentionally hurt you. He's spent the last decade twisting himself into a pretzel trying to be the father you always wanted."

Cara smiled sadly. "I know that. You're right, there must be a reason. As much as it ticks me off that he's hiding things from me, I suppose I should assume his motives are good."

"Absolutely," Leigh encouraged. *Until proven otherwise*, she refrained from adding.

"Mom!" Mathias's newly deeper voice rasped as he and Ethan burst into the kitchen. "Grandpa Randall wants to pay me to do some work at the clinic this week. Can I?"

"Me too, Mom!" Ethan said excitedly. "Can I? He wants us to start tomorrow."

"Doing what?" Leigh and Cara asked simultaneously — and somewhat skeptically. The boys were both good workers, but their rambunctious presence within the tight confines of the animal clinic had been problematic in the past.

"Helping Jared move stuff," Mathias answered, referring to the clinic's longtime janitor and kennel cleaner. "He can't lift anything heavy since he hurt his back, and Grandpa hired somebody to help him but they haven't been showing up and now they quit. Jared's flipping out because he's overdue with some cleaning rotation thing he's always done and he's afraid of getting mice. We're supposed to move all the food bags and the freezer and stuff so he can get behind them to clean."

"It'll only take a couple of days," Ethan added. "But with Grandpa on crutches he may need us to help with other stuff, too, like moving the big dogs after surgery. He says the clinic is short on strong arms."

The boys beamed, and Cara and Leigh exchanged a guarded look. As proud as they were of their bright and amiable sons, they knew that Randall must have reached a point of desperation to invite the two back into the clinic after the havoc they had wreaked in their elementary days. The chain link on one of the larger runs in the basement was still bowed and bent from where they used to lock each other inside and race to see who could escape faster.

"Please, Mom?" Ethan cajoled. "He wouldn't have asked us if he didn't think we could handle it."

Leigh considered. With Jared and her father both out of commission, there really wasn't anyone at the clinic to do the heavy lifting. The current staff was both all female and unusually weak in the athletic department. But Mathias was almost fourteen, and Ethan, while more than two years younger, was nearly as brawny as his cousin.

Cara's eyes signaled her approval.

"All right," Leigh agreed. "But you have to promise to mind Jared. You know he'll tell me if you give him any trouble."

Both boys' eyes rolled. "We won't, Mom," Ethan replied.

"Is dinner ready?" Mathias asked hopefully, eyeing the already-set table.

"Five minutes," Cara replied.

The boys promptly disappeared again.

Cara excused herself to go to the bathroom, and Leigh had not been alone in the kitchen for thirty seconds before the landline rang. She saw her aunt's name on the caller ID and picked up immediately.

"Aunt Lydie!" she said happily. "It's Leigh. Cara will be back in a minute. How's Pennsylvania history? Any breaking news?"

Lydie chuckled. "You'd be surprised. Listen, don't bother Cara. I just got off the phone with your mother and Bess; I'm so sorry about your father's accident."

"We all are," Leigh agreed.

"I'll call in a couple days to let you know exactly when I'll get back," Lydie continued. "I just wanted to let Cara know not to worry if I don't answer her right away. Half of this place is below ground level, and the reception is terrible. But she can leave me messages and I'll check in periodically."

"Will do."

"Thanks, dear. Bye-bye, now!"

"Wait, I—" Leigh broke off. Her aunt had hung up already. Leigh set the phone down, puzzled. Lydie had never been the chatty type, but she wasn't one to rush off, either. Leigh was about to brave asking whether Lydie knew anything about her ex-husband's recent move to Pittsburgh, but she needed a little more time to work up to it.

Talking to Lydie about Mason wasn't easy. Although the exes had always been civil with one another and had managed to stay in communication while Cara was growing up, their relationship since his return had been rocky. Although they tried to fake being comfortable around each other at family functions, even now, four decades after the divorce, the tension between them was palpable. As loving and mild-mannered as Lydie was, the humiliation she had endured at her young husband's hands had clearly exceeded her capacity to forgive and forget, because the deeper Mason weaved his way back into the family, the more his presence seemed to irritate her.

Lydie would hardly be pleased to know that he was now living in Pittsburgh. In fact, Leigh thought suddenly, dread of her reaction could very well be the reason Mason had kept the move a secret in the first place.

In retrospect, Leigh was glad she hadn't broached the topic. There had never been a surer way to wipe the smile off her aunt's face than to mention the name Mason Dublin, and just now Lydie had seemed to be in an unusually good mood. In fact, though her words had been both sympathetic and businesslike, her tone had been downright chipper. At times, practically breathless.

Leigh's brow furrowed. Her aunt didn't get away much. And she really did enjoy studying history.

But come on.

Cara returned to the kitchen, and Leigh delivered the message.

"How did she sound?" Cara asked offhandedly, putting on mitts to take her homemade pizzas out of the oven.

"Like she was having a good time," Leigh said carefully.

But not by herself.

Chapter 6

"I feel awful, Mom," Allison said the next morning, her voice close to tears. "I did everything Grandpa said!"

"I know you did, honey," Leigh said sympathetically. She studied the cockatiel with chagrin. Overnight, it had plucked a dime-sized patch of feathers off the center of its chest, leaving a naked circle of bumpy pink skin showing.

"He didn't have any signs of feather picking before," Allison bemoaned. "He looked perfect!"

"It's probably a stress reaction," Leigh suggested. "But we'll take him down and have your Grandpa check him out, just to be sure."

Allison tried to get the bird to hop onto her finger, but it merely fidgeted on its perch and sidled away from her. She frowned. "I think he misses his owner. We should get in touch with them and let them know. Maybe they'd want to come get him."

Leigh's stomach soured. *If only.* She could ask Mason to try and contact the mysterious Kyle, but if she remembered their predawn conversation correctly, Kyle wasn't the bird's real owner either. Still, it was worth a try. The cockatiel wasn't eating right, it looked unhappy, and without some intervention it would almost certainly keep picking at itself.

"Poor thing," Allison said miserably.

"Mom!" Ethan called from the living room. "There was a shooting in Ben Avon last night!"

A *shooting?* Ben Avon was directly adjacent to Avalon.

Leigh hurried out of Allison's room to the television. Ethan was rewinding the DVR. "I just caught the end of it," he explained. "Here's where it starts."

He punched a button on the remote, and the local news segment began.

"We're here in the normally peaceful neighborhood of Ben Avon," a reporter said, standing on the edge of a small park Leigh recognized, "where residents were shocked just after midnight to be awakened by the sound of a gunshot."

The camera panned around to show the front of a small stone

cottage barely visible behind a curtain of dense bushes and trailing vines. "Police say that a Ben Avon resident was sitting on her back porch when she spied a man running and then heard him attempt to enter the fence surrounding her property. The woman claims she fired a warning shot into the ground with a shotgun in order to frighten away the intruder. Ohio Township police received multiple calls from concerned citizens who heard the noise. Shortly afterwards, a thirty-two-year-old man who also resides in Ben Avon called police from his home to report a shot being fired at very close range while he was jogging. The man said he frequently runs in the area and prefers to exercise at night because of the cooler weather. He claims he was jogging between houses as a shortcut to the nearby country club when he accidentally ran into some sort of fence. He then heard a shot fired and believed he was being targeted."

The camera cut to a picture of a short, stocky woman standing in her front doorway while the reporter stuck a microphone in her face. Her dyed-auburn hair was cut short in an androgynous pixie cut, and her pinched and weathered face was tight with displeasure.

"Oh, no," Leigh murmured.

"Skippy!" Allison exclaimed.

"An intruder came onto my property without my permission and I scared him away," the woman said unapologetically, her gray eyes blazing. "It's my right to protect my property, and I'll do it again if I have to. Nobody messes with my birds. *Nobody*. You got that?"

She pointed a crooked finger at the camera, then withdrew inside and shut the door.

The camera switched to another shot of the reporter at the park. "Police say that according to local ordinances, it's illegal to discharge any firearm within the borough, although an exception is made in the case of protecting persons or property. The jogger, who was apparently wearing running gear and a reflective jacket, was unavailable for comment."

"Like, can't you get arrested for shooting at somebody like that?" Ethan asked.

"Whether any crime was committed here is still under investigation," the reporter continued. "In the meantime, night runners beware. Back to you, Dave!"

Ethan stopped the playback. Leigh and Allison remained immobile, staring at the screen. "Well, Mom?" the boy repeated. He turned to his sister. "Who's Skippy?"

Leigh tore her gaze away from the television and shook her head with disbelief. "A client of your grandfather's," she answered.

"Is *that* the crazy bird lady?" Ethan asked.

"She's not crazy!" Allison argued. "She does parrot rescue, and Grandpa says she takes good care of her birds. She's just a little... well, weird. You know."

"Eccentric," Leigh supplied mechanically, her mind reeling. Never mind that Skippy was indeed known as "that crazy bird lady" to pretty much the entire North Boros. She lived with dozens of birds in a small house no one else ever went into or came out of. Her backyard was completely screened in like an aviary, and the local children had worn a path to it from the park so that they could sneak a peek at the colorful parrots. Skippy permitted the gawkers, but woe be unto any child who yelled at the birds, much less poked a stick or threw a pebble! It wasn't the least surprising that a jogger following that path might run into her fencing in the dark.

Despite Skippy's antisocial tendencies, the birds she brought to the clinic were always in good health, at least physically. Psychologically, all the larger, more intelligent pet birds showed problems sooner or later, which is why Skippy, along with the rest of Randall's "bird people," had gotten out of the breeding business over a decade ago. Now, they all focused on taking in troubled parrots no one else wanted — a population which, unfortunately, was only continuing to grow.

"She sounded nuts to me," Ethan said dismissively. "When are we going, Mom?"

Leigh was distracted. Skippy had been a client of Randall's forever — even back when Leigh herself had worked in the clinic as a teenager. The woman had looked exactly the same then as she did now. Ageless. *Nobody messes with my birds,* Skippy had threatened. Was she fired up over the same rumors as everyone else? Had she been so scared that she was sitting on her porch with her gun on her lap, just waiting for someone to try something?

Knowing Skippy, it would be entirely in character. Not that she was your stereotypical paranoid conspiracy theorist. She was, in fact, entirely apolitical, concerned with virtually nothing that didn't directly relate to birds. But if you threatened Skippy's babies, you had best be prepared to defend yourself.

A bulletproof vest was recommended.

"Mom?" Ethan repeated. "When are you taking us to the clinic?"

Leigh tried to focus. "We'll leave around ten," she answered, feeling suddenly bleary. Having been dragged out of bed by Allison's cries of distress, she only now realized that her husband had left for work already. Given that she had gone to bed alone last night, she wondered briefly whether he'd come home at all. But she remembered hearing the chain saw rev up around eleven, and as tired as she currently felt, she doubted she had slept deeply the rest of the night, either.

After several cups of coffee and a lame attempt at accomplishing something on the pile of work she'd brought home from her advertising agency, Leigh bundled her two kids and one disturbed cockatiel into the van, collected Mathias from the farmhouse next door, and drove to the clinic.

She was pulling the van up to the curb across from the clinic's back door when Allison groaned from the back seat.

"Whoa!" Mathias exclaimed from the opposite back seat. "Who is *that?*"

Leigh looked over her shoulder to see a young teenaged girl floating across the parking lot toward the staff entrance. She was petite and generously curvy, with long, loosely curled blond hair that bounced around her shoulders like a model in a shampoo commercial. Leigh shot a glance at Mathias and resisted the urge to laugh out loud at his widened, admiring eyes. She wondered if somewhere in his adolescent mind a pop song was crooning and animated birds were flying around the girl's head.

"Kirsten," Allison answered without enthusiasm. "She's been hanging out observing. She wants to be a vet."

Leigh could hardly miss the derogatory tone in her daughter's voice. "You don't sound too happy about that," she commented. Allison was used to other young veterinary wannabes hanging out at the clinic, particularly during the summer. What was so objectionable about this one?

Allison sighed dramatically. "It's just that she's such a suck-up! Like she thinks that because Grandpa owns the clinic, I can get her into vet school or something. It's annoying."

"She wouldn't annoy me," Mathias joked, still staring.

Allison rolled her eyes at him. "She's fifteen. And she has a boyfriend already. An *older* boyfriend."

Mathias deflated a bit and slouched in his seat. But his gaze continued to follow the girl as she disappeared into the building.

Leigh fought a grin. Mathias, who had only just begun to notice girls, showed signs of inheriting not only his father's ridiculous good looks, but also Gil's tendency toward smug overconfidence. Suspecting they had not heard the last of the bewitching Kirsten, she cast a glance at her own son and was relieved to find him watching his cousin with equal parts amusement and puzzlement.

Thank goodness, she breathed. Having one precocious twin was more than enough.

They all piled out of the van, and as the kids went in through the clinic's back door, Leigh carried the covered birdcage down the steps to the basement entrance. Bringing the cockatiel into the clinic would stress it more, she knew, but it was important that her father make sure it didn't have any kind of physical problem. She stashed the bird away in a relatively quiet corner of her father's office, noticing as she did so that a good deal more of his accumulated paperwork had disappeared from the desk and floor. Then she jogged up the steps into the main part of the clinic to make sure the boys had connected with Jared. She was not surprised to find the three already on their way down to the basement. She *was* surprised to find Randall already parked on his stool in an exam room.

"Dad!" she exclaimed. "You're not supposed to be here yet! I was just leaving to pick you up at the house."

Randall threw her a beleaguered expression. "I, uh... had some things I needed to attend to," he mumbled. "Bess took pity on me."

Leigh exhaled slowly. "That bad, huh?" She envisioned Bess trying to make breakfast while Frances yelled helpful tips from the living room about the proper way to prevent fried eggs from sticking to her cookware. Then she imagined what Bess might do with those eggs...

Randall cleared his throat, but said nothing.

"I see," Leigh declared.

"I have an emergency coming in," Randall said. "And besides, Bess wanted to take more paperwork back home to keep your mother occupied."

I'll bet she did.

Leigh started to explain to him about the cockatiel, but before she could get a sentence out the door to the reception room burst open.

"I'll find him!" a scratchy female voice announced as none other than "that crazy bird lady" invited herself in and lifted a pet carrier onto the tabletop.

"If it's broken," Skippy raged, staring at Randall with her cool gray eyes, "I'll sue every damn one of them!"

"Let's take a look first," Randall said calmly, opening the carrier door. Morgan, one of the newer veterinary assistants on staff, slipped behind Leigh and moved into position to help hold the bird.

"Come on out, lambkins," Skippy crooned, her affected baby-voice striking a sharp contrast to the masculine figure she made in her long-sleeve plaid work shirt and shapeless jeans. "Mama won't let anybody hurt you!"

Leigh watched in silence as a bedraggled and partially featherless African grey stepped tentatively out of the carrier and onto the tabletop, holding one of its wings in an awkward position.

"I've only had her a few months," Skippy explained, seemingly to Leigh, as Morgan gently took hold of the bird for Randall to examine. "She hardly had a feather below the neck when I got her! But she's been doing really well for me in the house, nearly got her flight feathers grown back. Then those damned police came storming in and she went totally bonkers, trying to fly and running into everything!" Skippy turned her attention back to Randall. "She seemed okay right after it happened, but now she's holding her wing all funny-like!"

"You were on the news this morning!" Morgan gushed as she held the bird. "Did you see?"

Leigh cringed. Morgan, a slight and pretty dark-haired girl in her early twenties, was sweet-natured, good with the animals, and amenable to instruction. But when it came to client sensibilities, she had the tact of a preschooler.

"I was?" Skippy barked.

Morgan nodded emphatically, missing Randall's warning glare. "They said you shot at an intruder!" Her eyes glinted with admiration. "But it turned out to be just a jogger," she finished with disappointment.

"I didn't aim at the idiot," Skippy snapped. "Like I told the police, it was just a warning shot. And it worked, too. You'd better believe if he'd tried to snatch one of my birds—" She gestured a trigger pull. "That'd be the end of that!"

Morgan's attractive dark eyes widened. "Have you ever shot anybody before?"

Randall cleared his throat. "Morgan," he said sternly. "I'll need you to—"

"Well, I'll tell you, young lady," Skippy answered, ignoring him. "There was this one time, back in Vietnam—"

"I don't think the wing is broken," Randall proclaimed, pulling Skippy's attention back to the parrot. "But I'd like to take an x-ray, just to make sure." He looked past Leigh. "Allison, would you go get Jeanine for us, please?"

Leigh didn't bother looking behind her. Of course Allison was there.

Vietnam?

"Skippy," Leigh said on impulse, trying to keep her voice casual. "Why were you worried that the jogger might be after your birds? Have you had people try to break in before?"

The woman — *was* she a woman? — shot a shrewd look back. "You can never be too careful," she said grimly.

Jeanine appeared, and she, Morgan, and Allison took the parrot back to the treatment room, leaving Leigh and her father alone with Skippy. No sooner had the others left than Skippy leaned across the table close to Randall's ear. "Nobody else'll tell you," she said in a hoarse whisper. "But I will. There's a pet snatcher on the loose. Dogs and cats both stolen. Who says they wouldn't take a bird? I don't trust nobody. And you ought to keep your own eyes open around here too, Doc. You ask me, somebody's doing this methodical like."

Leigh sucked in a breath. She could tell from her father's long-suffering expression that he gave no credence to the woman's claim. "Doing what exactly?" Leigh asked.

Skippy studied her. As an extension of Randall whom Skippy had known four pant sizes ago, Leigh evidently passed muster for trustworthiness.

"Picking their victims," she answered, "for *ransom.*"

"That seems a bit—" Randall began skeptically.

Leigh jumped in. "What kind of money are we talking about?"

"Thousands," Skippy rasped.

"Shouldn't someone tell the police?" Leigh suggested.

Skippy shrugged. "Only the people whose pets got snatched know enough to bother, and they're all too scared to snitch. So far I hear the critters have all come back all right. But who knows when that'll change? Somebody's got to get this guy!" Her voice turned steely. "And me and my shotgun'd be only too happy to give it a whirl!"

"Has the grey been eating all right?" Randall asked, his tone slightly bored.

Skippy's attention was easily diverted back to her bird. "Better and better all the time!" she answered proudly. "I know how to feed a parrot right. You take my quinoa and navy bean porridge. I could market that stuff. Now, Olan says his birds don't like navy beans; he's all into mixing everything up with yams and yogurt and sweet stuff. But I say…"

Leigh tuned out. Skippy and Olan, another client whose collection of rescue parrots numbered in the double digits, had been feuding over various points of bird care — with no small amount of acrimony — for as long as anyone could remember. The staff liked to joke about what would happen if the two met unexpectedly in the waiting room and someone called out, "Should you clip a pet bird's wings? Discuss!"

The consensus was that neither would emerge alive.

Leigh looked at her watch. She couldn't delay any longer; it was time for her Tuesday shift of Frances-watching to begin. Bess was probably already sitting in her car in the street with the engine running. Leigh had meant to ask Randall's permission to post the signs soliciting anonymous information about the pet snatchings, but it was just as well that Allison did the honors. If Randall thought it was pointless, he would be more likely to humor his granddaughter.

Leigh quietly excused herself from the exam room, apprised Allison of the situation, and exited through the back door. As soon as she was back in the van and out of earshot of any curious bystanders, she picked up her phone and called Mason.

His line went straight to voicemail.

Leigh frowned. "Mason," she said sternly, recording a message. "I need to talk to you. The bird isn't doing well, and we need to contact its owner. Can you get in touch with this Kyle guy, or at least give me his number? It's important."

She hung up, still frowning. The man had a lot of nerve, turning his phone off.

Two women walked past the van on the sidewalk, one of them chattering so loudly Leigh could understand every word even with her windows rolled up.

"So then I said, 'Well, can you make it Thursday?' And she said 'No, only Tuesday.' But she'd just told me she could only make Thursday! That's why I asked her 'Can you make it Thursday?' and she said, 'No, only Tuesday!'"

Leigh looked up to see the clinic's newest receptionist, Amy, heading in to start her shift with another of the veterinary assistants, Paige. The slightly heavy, freckled Amy was a nice enough girl and good with the computer, but Leigh had to wonder at Randall's wisdom in hiring a receptionist who seemed genetically incapable of saying anything only once.

"Hi, Leigh!" Amy said with a wave as the two women cut in front of the van to cross the street to the clinic. "That's Leigh," she informed her companion. "I said 'hi' to her."

Paige, a frizzy-headed blonde in her early thirties who had been employed through at least four different receptionists now, glanced up at Leigh with a beleaguered expression. *Kill me now,* her eyes seemed to be messaging as she offered a wave of her own.

Leigh waved back and then started up the van to head to West View. According to Bess, Frances had found a smudge on the mirror in the half bath last night and responded by setting up a roster of housecleaning duties for all three of the women to carry out. Frances had also determined that Dr. Koslow "needed his books examined," and that Leigh's primary job today would be to "dust all these filthy papers." Leigh's first round of duty was supposed to have started ten minutes ago. It wouldn't end until Cara arrived tomorrow morning.

Kill me now, indeed.

Chapter 7

"Koslow," Maura's voice boomed from Leigh's cell phone. "Are you at home?"

"No," Leigh answered, staring at the pile of file folders on the table before her with despair. Bess must have scooped them up from the clinic's basement floor, because their every surface was encrusted with animal hair, dust bunnies, and a gritty veneer of crumbled kibble. Naturally, Frances refused to even look at the papers until they were cleaned, and a card table — "not the *kitchen* table, for pity's sake!" — was designated as the triage area. Leigh wondered whose bright idea it had been to tell Jared not to touch any of her father's paperwork. Didn't they know the diligent yet mentally challenged kennel cleaner took every instruction literally?

"I'm at my parents' house," Leigh answered.

"Oh, right. Do you think it would be okay if Eddie and I dropped by?"

Deliverance! "How soon can you get here?"

Twenty minutes later the doorbell rang, and Leigh leapt up from her chair. "Maura's here!" she announced to her mother as she headed for the door. Frances, who was planted on the couch poring over another pile of papers spread out on a tray table, dipped her chin to peer at Leigh over the top of her reading glasses.

"How is the file cleaning going?" she asked with suspicion.

"Stupendously," Leigh replied, hastening to open the door.

Maura Polanski looked down at her with a smile; Eddie Polanski looked up at her with a scowl.

Leigh swung open the door. "Come in," she invited, gesturing the twosome into the living room.

Frances sat up immediately and pushed her work table to the side. "Maura, dear!" she greeted with enthusiasm. "Oh, bring that little darling over here!"

"Hello, Ms. Koslow," Maura said cheerfully. She walked over to the couch and stood next to Frances, leaning down to give her and Eddie a better look at each other. Frances reached out a hand and held his, and the infant gurgled with delight.

"Oh, give me a break!" Leigh mumbled.

"All babies like me," Frances said smugly, making a silly face. Eddie practically contorted himself with amusement, and Maura laughed out loud.

Leigh bit back a groan. "Did you need to talk to me about something?" she prompted, wondering if the policewoman had heard about Skippy and tied the incident to the petnapping rumors.

"That I do," Maura said vaguely, throwing Leigh a meaningful look. Whatever she had to say, she preferred to say it in private.

Frances's hawk eyes missed nothing. "Why don't you take Maura up to your room, Leigh?" she suggested sweetly. "Little Eddie and I can get better acquainted."

"You don't have to do that, Ms. Koslow," Maura remarked.

"Nonsense," Frances argued. "It would be a delightful diversion. You just leave this little cherub with me and toddle along. I'll give a yell if we need anything."

Maura thanked Frances for the offer and lifted the infant out of the belly pack.

"Come here, Peanut," Frances cooed, taking him deftly into her arms. She looked up at Leigh and Maura, then shooed them both away toward the stairs. "Off you go. We'll be fine!"

Leigh led the only slightly reluctant new mother up the stairs. The small room that had once been Leigh's own was now outfitted with bunk beds for the grandchildren, so Leigh steered her guest into the sewing room instead, where they settled on a desk chair and a stool. "What's up?" Leigh asked nervously, wondering why Maura hadn't wanted to talk in front of Frances. The petnapping rumors were certainly disturbing, but the Koslow Animal Clinic wasn't directly involved. Was it?

Maura let out a breath. "Do you know where Mason Dublin is?"

Leigh's heart skipped a beat. This wasn't the line of questioning she expected.

It did not bode well.

"I talked to him yesterday," she answered, considering her words. Lying to Maura was pointless, but she was loath to get Mason in trouble, accidentally or otherwise. "He told me he was flying out to a pawnbrokers' convention in Las Vegas."

Maura's face bore no expression. "That's what he said?"

"Yes," Leigh answered honestly, her anxiety rapidly increasing.

"What's this about?"

Maura watched her closely. "Do you know where he is, Koslow?"

Leigh swallowed with discomfort. "No. I don't."

Maura seemed disappointed.

"I repeat, what's this about?" Leigh pressed.

"Hopefully nothing," Maura answered, the muscles in her lower jaw working as they often did when she was thinking. "Look, you know I have nothing against Mason. I never have, even if he's not so crazy about me. I'm not on the job right now and I'm not doing this in any official capacity, but I'd like to speak with him."

Leigh tensed. "You want his number?"

"I have his number. He isn't picking up. I was hoping you could convince him to call me."

Leigh studied her friend's earnest face. The situation was awkward, to say the least. Leigh was under no obligation to pass along any information about Mason, or any other family member. She did believe that Maura's motives were good. But good for whom? "You'll have to give me a little more to go on," she requested.

Maura straightened. "Okay. A buddy of mine called this morning; said he wanted to catch me up on a few things before I came in next week. Clearly, he's betting on the 'Polanski will come back' side."

"Clearly," Leigh agreed, smiling a little.

"So he was trying to whet my appetite," Maura continued. "He gave me the rundown on a couple of cases, and Mason's name came up. Mason's not suspected of anything, but he might know something important. The Bellevue police have already talked to him; nothing I'm telling you is a secret. It's just that he picked a really bad time to leave town. Whether the timing is a coincidence or not, it looks suspicious. They can't order him to come back, not at this point. But I'd like to explain to him that he needs to tread carefully."

Leigh breathed out slowly. "Does this have anything to do with the break-in at the apartment next to his? Cara told me they called her about that."

Maura nodded. Her face took on a pained expression. "The occupant of that apartment has been MIA for a couple days now, which is a problem, because he's wanted for questioning by the state police. Mason may have nothing to do with this guy's disappearance, but they did know each other, which makes the whole business pretty damned messy. And potentially dangerous. Can you convince him to call me?"

"I don't know," Leigh replied. Although Mason had gotten used to Maura's presence at family functions, his cop-avoidance instincts were still firmly ingrained. "I'll try." A heaviness arose in her middle that she knew she would not easily be rid of. Mason was definitely acting weird. Mason suddenly had money. If after all this time on the straight and narrow the man had fallen back onto the wrong side of the law, it would break his daughter's heart. And Leigh's.

Maura rose.

"Wait," Leigh said, getting up herself. Did the police think that Mason had helped Kyle escape the law somehow? If so, they were wrong. She was certain that Mason hadn't known Kyle would leave when he did. Mason had clearly been put out about the timing of his cat-care duties and hadn't expected the bird at all. But she couldn't explain that to Maura without breaking her promise to Mason to keep quiet about the pets.

What a mess.

She decided not to elaborate, at least not now. It would be better if she could convince Mason to talk to Maura himself.

The policewoman stood looking at Leigh expectantly. *Oh, right.* Leigh had been about to say something. She said something else instead. "Have you heard anything about the petnapping rumors? Skippy Titus certainly seems to believe them."

Maura grimaced. "A lot of people do. The locals PDs are aware of what's being said. But no one's filed a complaint, so they've got nothing to go on."

Leigh exhaled. "I see."

With her mind full of thoughts, none of them pleasant, she accompanied Maura to collect the baby and then walked the policewoman back out to her car. No sooner were the mother and son down the street and out of sight than Leigh pulled out her phone and tried again to reach Mason.

Her call went straight to voice mail. Leigh left a second message, then walked back into the house with a sinking heart.

What the hell was the man up to? When he'd said Kyle had "people after him," Leigh hadn't thought he meant the law. She'd been thinking more along the lines of creditors. But why would Mason even bring up the ruse about a pawnbrokers' convention? Could he be running from the law himself?

Leigh stubbornly dismissed the notion. When he'd awoken her before dawn, he hadn't seemed like a man who was sweating over a pursuit by the police or anyone else. He had seemed like a man who was anxious to go somewhere, but was being frustrated by an unexpected nuisance: a.k.a., a neighbor's pets. Once Leigh had said she would take care of the animals, Mason had acted downright chipper.

So where *was* he going?

She returned to her parents' living room to find her mother staring at her with arms crossed and reading glasses removed. "Now," Frances said crisply. "You can tell me what that was all about. What kind of trouble are you in this time?"

"I'm not in any trouble!" Leigh protested, knowing it was pointless. Never mind that she really wasn't in any trouble. This time. She had given the same answer too many times before when it was... perhaps slightly less applicable.

"Oh, patoot!" Frances retorted.

Leigh sighed. Where was the kindly granny who'd been making goofy faces at little Eddie just minutes ago? "I'm *not* in any trouble, Mom," she repeated. Then inspiration struck. "It's just that there's something pet-related going on in Avalon and Ben Avon." She explained about the petnapping rumors and Skippy's overzealous defense of her parrots. "But Maura says the police can't really do anything until an actual crime victim comes to them," she finished.

"I see," Frances said thoughtfully. With one brisk motion, she replaced her reading glasses. "Well, we've got work to do. Well begun is half done. Spit spot!"

Leigh's teeth gritted. She rued the day her mother had ever watched *Mary Poppins*.

After what seemed like a hundred hours — but was actually more like six — Leigh was thrilled to hear the sound of car doors slamming out front. Cara was scheduled to deliver Randall back to the house, and she would have the entire Pack in tow. If Leigh was lucky, Cara would also bring along some sort of food for Leigh to microwave for her parents' dinner.

"So, how did it go?" Leigh asked as she held open the door for her father to hobble inside. It took him a while. "It was frustrating," Randall said tiredly. "But I'll make it."

"We took a bit of a spill on the steps outside the clinic," Cara lamented, walking close beside him with both hands out. "I'm not very good at this, I'm afraid."

"Nonsense," Randall insisted. "I just lost track of my feet."

They moved on through the door, and Leigh looked behind them. Lenna and the boys were waiting in the van, but Allison was standing on the porch holding the cockatiel's cage. "Why do you have that? Aren't we taking the bird back to our house?" Leigh asked, confused. The plan was for Allison and Ethan, along with the corgi, to spend tonight at Cara and Gil's, since Leigh would be in West View and no one knew how late Warren might get home.

"Grandpa wants to watch him here," the girl answered, walking inside.

Leigh closed the door and turned to see Cara helping Randall onto the edge of the inflatable bed. "You should lay down and prop those feet up," Cara suggested, fetching pillows.

Frances's eyes fell on the bird cage. "Ack!" she erupted, her finger wagging in Allison's direction. "You leave that thing right there on the tile, young lady."

Randall sighed. "I thought it would be best if I kept the bird here," he said to Leigh. "I don't believe there's anything physically wrong with it, but having a strange cat and dog around could certainly be a stressor. A little more human activity, on the other hand, could be helpful."

"Excuse me?" Frances protested, glaring at her husband. "Have I been consulted on this matter?"

"We've had birds before," Randall reminded. "It'll only be for the rest of the week."

"The birds we've had before," Frances said slowly, enunciating each word, "have scattered seed husks, feathers, and that deplorable dust throughout the entirety of our home. Which is why we no longer have any."

Leigh looked anxiously from one parent to the other. She remembered well the insane schedule of vacuuming and dusting her mother had insisted on whenever they'd had finches or budgies in the house. When Leigh was very small, there had even been an Amazon that Frances herself had been fond of, despite its nasty tendency to bite anyone or anything that came near its perch. The bird had sealed its place in Frances's heart by learning to screech "clean that up!" every time anyone dropped anything.

"It'll only be for a few days," Randall repeated calmly.

Frances continued to glare at her husband even as her hand reached for her clipboard. "I'll adapt the cleaning schedule," she said dryly.

Leigh and Cara exchanged a look of dread.

"I'm trying to reach the owner to come pick him up," Leigh assured them all. "Hopefully it won't take long."

Frances's glare remained skeptical. She scribbled furiously on her clipboard.

"I told Grandpa I'd come feed the bird and clean his cage," Allison offered.

"That's lovely of you, dear," Frances said, still scribbling. "He'll have to go in the dining room. But the furniture must all be covered first. With plastic sheeting. 10 mil, I think…"

When at last France stopped writing and looked up, it was only to hand out such onerous work assignments that Cara did not actually manage to leave with the Pack for a full half hour, and by the time Frances was satisfied that her dining room was protected to Haz Mat standards, Leigh and Randall were both starving.

Sadly, Cara had not brought any food.

"There's a fresh whole chicken in the refrigerator," Frances insisted. "And potatoes in the basement pantry. If you applied yourself, you could have a proper meal ready in an hour and a half."

Leigh ordered pizza.

Chapter 8

None of the Koslows seemed in the mood for conversation, much less a card game, and the evening dragged. Randall's covert wincing convinced Leigh that he had bruised himself significantly in today's "bit of a spill," and after a solid hour of listening to his wife explain what was wrong with the clinic's filing system, he seemed exhausted. Leigh was happy to get both her parents to bed early, and after sending her own hardworking husband a "what do you look like again?" text, she crawled into the lower bunk of her childhood bedroom certain that she would sleep like a rock.

She was wrong.

After tossing and turning forever, she had been asleep for what felt like only minutes before the ringing of her cell phone woke her up again. She looked at the caller ID and scowled. The area code was unfamiliar. It was only spam. She rejected the call and looked at the time. It was 1:00 AM.

She turned over and closed her eyes again. A minute later they flew back open.

Someone downstairs had coughed. It was a man's cough, but it didn't sound like her father's. She had heard Randall cough through many bouts of cold and flu, and this sound was different. It had the distinctive hacking sound of a smoker's cough.

Leigh swung her feet off the bunk and stood up. Randall had not smoked since he was a teenager. But what if his cough sounded odd because he had fractured a rib or bruised a lung?

She made her way down the stairs and into the living room. It was dark, and she stumbled twice over the rearranged furniture, stubbing a bare toe. But eventually her eyes adjusted enough to see that both her parents were asleep. She stood a moment, watching the rise and fall of the sheet over her father's chest. He didn't cough again. His breathing seemed normal.

Puzzled, but relieved, she started to make her way back to bed. She had just put her throbbing right toe on the first step when she heard the noise.

It was a rasping, sawing noise. As if someone were cutting

through metal, like a screen. And it was coming from the kitchen.

Leigh reached for a cell phone she didn't have. She was barefoot in a sleepshirt. Her phone was upstairs beside the bunk beds. The house's landline was in the kitchen, where both her parents' cellphones were recharging.

She made a quick assessment. If the intruder was a petty thief, he would probably run away as soon as she flipped on the lights or made noise. *But* if she made her presence known now and he was some psycho serial killer, she'd never make it to the kitchen phones. And if she ran upstairs to get her own cell, she'd be leaving her sleeping parents at his mercy.

She drew in a breath and crept stealthily toward the kitchen doorway. The landline was on the wall just inside. She would take a quick look around, make sure she wasn't imagining things, then call 911. As soon as she dialed the number, she would flip the lights on. Most likely, he would run away then. But even if he attacked her with a meat cleaver and she never got a word out, the landline would give the police their location.

She listened as she crept, but the floorboards creaking under her feet nearly obscured the rasping noise.

Leigh's pulse pounded. Had her mother left the windows unlocked? Frances often left the windows open in the summer, rather than "waste money blowing around unnecessarily cool air." But her parents always made sure to shut and lock the windows at bedtime, at least those on the first floor.

A pang of guilt shot through her. Well, *they* weren't even walking at the moment, were they? It was her job to make sure all the windows were locked. They had been closed when she arrived, so she had assumed... but she shouldn't have.

This was all her fault!

With her heart in her throat, she inched her head around the kitchen doorway just far enough to peer in.

Through the window, she could see a pale hand with a knife working to pull down a large flap of screen wire.

Leigh fought to control her breathing and stay silent. She withdrew her head, reached her arm around the corner, felt for the phone cradle, and then lifted the headset. Her hands were shaking as she quickly punched in the numbers. The dial tone had become audible as soon as she picked up the phone... had the intruder heard it?

A sort of a popping sound, followed by a creak, sounded from the kitchen. The window was sliding open.

Leigh's call connected. She could hear it ringing at the other end.

THUMP.

Her heart raced. Something had definitely happened. She heard a scuffling noise. The intruder was coming through!

She knew she should stay out of sight. But she couldn't help herself. She poked her head back around the doorframe.

"Leigh Eleanor Koslow!" Frances hissed from the living room. "Whatever are you doing wandering around down here in the middle of the night?" A dim light shone from behind Leigh as Frances turned on the table lamp in the living room.

Leigh stared into the kitchen. Through the hole in the screen protruded the upper torso of a man — a boy? — wearing a dark gray hoodie with the hood pulled up. He was bent over the window ledge at the waist, awkwardly paused midway through the act of vaulting himself inside. Leigh saw him for only a second, and his face was concealed by the hood. But she was able to discern two things. He was a wiry caucasian with narrow shoulders, and Leigh and her mother had just scared the crap out of him.

He mumbled a four-letter word, braced his hands on the sill, and backed himself out again. Leigh heard another thump as he hit the ground, followed by the predictable pounding of retreating footfalls.

"Nine-one-one," a voice on the phone said calmly. "What is your emergency?"

"Whatever is going on in there?" Frances shouted.

The footsteps were heading toward the street. Leigh dropped the phone, raced around to the front door, turned the bolt, and swung it open.

"Leigh!" Frances persisted.

Leigh stepped out on the porch and looked down the street. She could see the man running. He was wearing jeans and dark shoes… beyond that she couldn't tell much.

She closed and relocked the door, then rushed back to the kitchen and picked up the ancient phone, which was attached to the wall base by a spiral cord. "A man tried to break into my parents' house," Leigh told the dispatcher. She gave the address and a quick description. "He just ran away down the street. Toward Perry Highway."

"Leigh Eleanor!" Frances shrieked. "You come in here and tell us what's happening this instant!"

"Leigh?" her father called blearily. "Is something wrong?"

"Don't you dare get up!" Frances screeched at him.

The cockatiel squawked and fluttered in his cage.

Leigh stretched the phone cord as far as she could move toward the living room. "It's okay," she attempted to soothe. The couple were sitting bolt upright on the inflatable bed, Frances pale with panic and Randall red-faced with frustration, his one good leg swung over on the floor and ready to go. "Somebody tried to break in, but he's gone now," she explained. "Just a minute."

Leigh turned her attention to the dispatcher's questions and moved into the kitchen. The burglar had clearly known what he was doing; the hole in the screen that he had cut so expertly was plenty big enough to admit his entire body. Without interruption, he could probably have slipped inside with a minimum of noise. If her parents had been asleep upstairs as they normally were, they wouldn't have heard a thing. Leigh probably wouldn't have either, if the man hadn't coughed first.

What would have happened if he had surprised her parents in the middle of the living room?

Leigh shuddered. She answered the rest of the dispatcher's questions and hung up to await a visit from the Ross Township police. Her heart was still pounding. Her palms were sweaty and she felt a little light in the head.

How the heck did Maura do this all the time?

And what the devil had the man wanted? If he was after jewelry, he should have broken in during the day, when he could rifle through the bedrooms unmolested. If he was after valuable electronics, he was a moron. One look through the window at her parents' Paleozoic box television should have nipped that idea in the bud. He must have been after cash — most likely a desperate search for drug money. But why target this house at all, with her Aunt Lydie's house sitting empty right next door?

A stab of fear shot through her chest. Had he broken into Lydie's house, too?

She started to turn toward the front door again, but stopped herself. The police could check that out. There was nothing she could do about it now, anyway.

Leigh heard a clunking noise and turned to see her father standing in the kitchen doorway leaning on one crutch. He spied the ruined window screen and exhaled. "It's hard to find that size anymore," he said tiredly.

"Oh, for heaven's sakes, Randall!" Frances shrieked from the living room. "We could have been murdered in our beds!"

"Not much profit in that," he murmured, turning himself around. Leigh followed him out of the kitchen and back to the bed, not at all sure he wouldn't fall again.

"Leigh Eleanor," Frances ordered, her panic now giving way to action. "Go upstairs and put on something decent immediately. You can't talk to the policemen wearing that!"

Leigh looked down at her worn sleep shirt. It had Winnie the Pooh on the front and had been a Christmas gift from the twins when they were four years old. She really, seriously needed to catch up on the laundry.

"And fetch my blue pantsuit," Frances added earnestly. "With a pair of knee-high hose. And oh, heavens! I'll need my hair spray!"

"No, you don't, Mom," Leigh mumbled as she headed up the stairs. No sooner had she returned with her own bathrobe on and two more thrown over her arm than she saw the flashing lights of a police car outside. She handed the robes to her parents and headed for the door.

"I can't talk to the police *in bed!*" Frances protested, frantically shrugging her thick corduroy robe over her shoulders. "It isn't proper! What will they think? Randall, tell them we don't normally sleep down here!"

Leigh's father put on his own robe. He made no response.

Leigh opened the door. She looked out to see a single Ross Township policeman striding up her walk. A short, bearded man who appeared to be somewhere in his thirties, he stopped short on her porch steps and studied her. "Are you Leigh Koslow?" he asked, sounding oddly wary.

"Yes," she replied, feeling suddenly wary herself.

"Don't I know you from somewhere?" he asked.

Crap. "You know Detective Maura Polanski?"

"Yeah, sure." His eyes widened. "Oh, right. You're *that* Leigh

Koslow."

Leigh sighed. The policeman didn't look familiar, but that hardly mattered. Her reputation preceded her. She was never quite sure what that reputation was, since she made a point of never doing anything criminal. The fact that criminal things regularly happened in her vicinity was a metaphysical phenomenon beyond her control.

"Officer Sims. We've met before," he declared. "After the... uh... incident at the theater last spring. But I doubt you'd remember me."

"Sorry," Leigh replied lightly, holding the door open. "Please come inside."

Officer Sims was soon joined by three of his colleagues, lighting up the Koslow stretch of Ridgewood Avenue like the Fourth of July. The police searched through the house and yard, took statements from her and her parents, and checked out Lydie's house next door. They found no damage other than the Koslows' cut window screen, and no conveniently left-behind clues either. No one else had seen the fleeing intruder, and Leigh declined an offer to look at mug shots. The light had been too dim and the hood too concealing for her to notice any identifying features. In fact, after being questioned on the specifics of what she remembered, she couldn't even swear that the intruder was male. She had seen caucasian hands and a skinny torso. But the voice uttering the single four-letter-word wasn't particularly low in pitch and the running figure had been too far away to judge build or height.

Some star witness I am, she thought to herself with disgust.

Having little to go on, the policemen wrapped up the investigation quickly, and the Koslows settled uneasily back to bed. Leigh double-checked the windows and locked them all, chagrined to know that the kitchen window had in fact been closed, but unlocked, when the intruder arrived.

You're a crackerjack babysitter too, she chastised herself.

"There's no way he's coming back tonight," Leigh assured her parents, turning the living room lights off. The porch and backdoor lights, per Frances, she left on.

"If it's drug money he's after," Randall said philosophically, lying back on his pillow, "He'll be trying someplace else before morning. They'll catch up with him."

"Such nonsense," Frances tutted. "These young people today! Were we the last generation to display any morality whatsoever?"

Leigh headed for the stairs without comment. As a child, she had fully believed that drugs, alcohol, and fornication did not exist until the seventies. She was disabused of the notion only when eavesdropping revealed that, long before the moon landing, a youthful Aunt Bess had dabbled in the trifecta.

Leigh climbed the stairs and fell into bed exhausted. Theoretically, she could still catch a couple hours' sleep before daylight. Realistically, she knew it wouldn't happen. She was way too wound up.

Were her parents really the victims of a random break-in? They had lived in the same house for over forty years, and with the exception of the brand new lawn mower someone had lifted from their yard in the eighties, they'd never been stolen from. Why now? She supposed there was always a first time. But still…

There it is again!

Leigh's body stiffened as she heard the same bizarre, hacking cough echoing up from below. It couldn't be the intruder again! It just couldn't. Was the man insane?

She found no comfort in that question.

She sprang out of bed and hurried across the hall to look out the window above the kitchen. The alley between the houses was clearly illuminated. But there was no one below. She ran to the other upstairs windows and looked down from every angle. She saw no one.

This is ridiculous, she told herself. It must be her father coughing. She made her way quietly down the steps to check on the couple. Frances had taken a sedative and appeared to be deeply asleep. Randall also appeared to be sleeping, although as Leigh watched, he shifted position restlessly. She knew that no emotional concern short of imminent death would disturb Randall if he chose to ignore it. But if he had bruised his ribs, he could be physically uncomfortable. Maybe turning over in his sleep earlier had given him a pang, and the unusual cough was a reflex.

Leigh blew out a breath and reversed her steps. There was nothing to worry about. All would be well. She paused at the top of the stairs, then stepped into the other two bedrooms and flipped on the lights. If the intruder did come back, it wouldn't hurt to make him think they were up and watching.

But they wouldn't be. She was too damn tired.

She fell back into the bottom bunk and closed her eyes, only to see a looping mental image of a gray-hooded figure invading the Koslow kitchen. What could he possibly hope to gain? What would have happened if the phone call and the cough hadn't awakened her?

She opened her eyes again and stared at the underside of the top bunk. Ethan had stuck blue chewing gum onto the backside of one of the wooden supports. It had probably been there for years. Once Frances knew about it, it would be gone within seconds.

Another sound.

Leigh's muscles tensed as she listened. What was it? A scratching, flapping noise.

She relaxed again. It was only the bird. She should be glad he hadn't started his morning squawking yet. That spectacle was sure to be popular.

Leigh lay on the bunk another few minutes, straining to listen for the slightest sound, pretending she had a chance in hell of actually falling asleep again. Then she grabbed her pillow and blanket, trudged back down the stairs, and curled up on the uncomfortable couch next to her parents.

Her eyes closed. If a psychopathic serial killer did show up before morning, at least they'd go down together.

Chapter 9

Night turned into morning with no additional sleep and little change to Leigh's frazzled emotional state. Her parents seemed better rested, despite having been awakened at first light by the squawking cockatiel. The bird's display of energy had actually pleased Randall, who believed its feather picking to be stress-related and figured the new environment must be agreeable. Frances was less pleased, insisting that Leigh begin her Wednesday morning by wiping imaginary feather dust off the plastic sheeting.

They spoke little as Leigh served an uninspiring breakfast of microwaved bacon and granola. Over coffee, her parents turned to the morning paper while Leigh perused her phone. None of her email was interesting, but she did notice that her late-night spammer had left a voicemail. Expecting a robo-message in need of deleting, she absently pressed the speaker button while spooning cereal into her mouth.

"Hey, Leigh. It's Mason. Sorry not to get back to you sooner, but I'm not checking my phone too often. It's expensive. Listen, I can't get in touch with Kyle. His phone's out of service and that's the only number I have for him."

Frances's paper lowered. Her dark eyes narrowed at Leigh from behind her glasses.

Crap.

Leigh considered stopping the recording, but knew it would only make the exchange seem more suspicious.

"Don't worry about the bird," Mason continued. "When I get back I promise I'll take both of them off your hands, no matter what's going on with Kyle. Just do the best you can until then, if you don't mind. Sorry if it's a pain. You're the best, kid. See you in a few days!"

The message ended.

Randall lowered his own newspaper. He removed his reading glasses and looked at Leigh. "You got the bird from Mason?"

Leigh nodded. There was hardly any point in denying it. "He was supposed to be taking care of them for a friend, but there was some confusion about the timing, and Mason had to leave town himself."

Frances harrumphed. "I'll just bet he did. Running from the law again, no doubt. I wouldn't trust that man to watch a potato."

Randall turned to his wife with a frown. "It's been *forty years*, Frances. Mason has changed."

"Poppycock!" Frances replied, snapping her newspaper back into place. "We should have nothing to do with him."

Leigh and Randall exchanged a look and a sigh. Mason had expended considerable effort when he first returned to town to earn his way into Frances's good graces. But that battle wasn't merely uphill, it was straight vertical. Frances had never liked Mason. From the day he showed up on the Morton family's front porch — a handsome, fresh-faced, smooth-talking youth peddling expensive steak knives — she had declared him a fraud and a menace. Her attitude had not improved when Lydie fell head over heels in love with him, nor when the couple eloped. The chaos that unfolded over the next few years proved to be one of Frances's greatest "I told you so" triumphs, and it was clear that she intended to savor that glory indefinitely.

Leigh said nothing. She was surprised that her father had bothered. Frances would never accept Mason as a member of the family. Never mind that the younger generations already did. Frances's confidence in her own judgment was unshakable: She would be proven right in the end. Again.

Leigh suffered a moment of indecision. Should she tell her parents specifically not to mention the source of the pets to anyone else? Surely doing so would only make the arrangement sound shady. Despite her derisive comment just now, Frances didn't appear to be overly troubled by the matter. But it would take little encouragement to make her suspect the worst.

Leigh decided to let it go. She could explain to her father later.

Her parents became absorbed in their newspapers again, and Leigh stared down at her phone. Why had Mason's name not shown up on her caller ID? If it had, she would have taken the call last night, and she would have been able to explain to him about Maura's request. But the messages Leigh left hadn't been specific. She had only asked him to call her. She could leave him another voicemail. But what had he meant about it being expensive?

She studied the number on his message. Then she opened her web browser and searched on the area code.

Miami-Dade County, Florida.

What the hell was Mason doing in Miami? And why was he not using his own phone to call her? He must still have his cell with him, or he wouldn't have gotten her message.

"Hello!" Cara's cheerful voice called from outside the front door. "We're here!"

Leigh rose. Ordinarily she would call for her cousin to come in, but this morning she had left the door deadbolted. She admitted Cara and the Pack, all of whom looked happy to be there except Lenna. Cara's daughter's face was sullen, her large blue eyes practically teary.

"Something wrong?" Leigh asked her "niece" as the girl filed by, last in line through the door.

Lenna dipped her chin. "I miss my Peeper-Do," she mumbled, her eyes beginning to water.

Cara circled back around and gave her daughter a hug around the shoulders. "She's become quite attached to that cat," she explained. "She wasn't happy to be leaving for most of the day, but I didn't want her all alone at the farm."

"Don't worry about Peep," Leigh assured Lenna. "As much as cats sleep, she probably dropped off the moment you left and won't wake up until you're home again."

Lenna's perfect rosebud lips smiled a little. She scooted off inside.

"So," Cara asked Leigh. "How did everything go last night?"

Leigh closed the door and deadbolted it. "Peachy," she replied.

Cara eyed her suspiciously.

"Ask my mother after we're gone," Leigh suggested in a whisper. "The Pack doesn't need to hear it." On a whim, she looked over her shoulder. Sure enough, there was Allison. Standing quiet as a ghost.

"How's the cockatiel, Mom?" the girl asked innocently.

"Better, I think," Leigh answered. "He ate all his egg this morning and some of the veggies, too. And he's been moving around a lot more."

Allison smiled and headed off towards the cage.

"Cara," Leigh asked in a whisper. "Does your father have any friends in Miami?"

Cara's brow furrowed. "Miami? Not that I know of. But he doesn't talk much about his acquaintances from the past, for obvious reasons. Why?"

"Just wondering," Leigh said vaguely.

After assuring Cara that they would talk more when they had some privacy, Leigh collected the boys, Allison, and her father and loaded them into the van to go back to the clinic. Her mind was reeling. To everyone else in the car, today was a new day. But to her, the last twenty-four hours had been a continuous blur. Irritating, unresolved questions buzzed around in her brain like gnats, but she couldn't concentrate well enough to address them. She needed to drop off her charges, go home, and get some sleep. Maybe then she could make some sense of the nonsense.

When they arrived at the clinic, the boys went straight to the basement for their next assignment from Jared, while Allison stuck with Leigh and helped walk Randall through the staff entrance. No sooner had they settled the veterinarian on his stool than a gorgeous mane of honey-colored hair appeared in the doorway.

"Good morning, Dr. Koslow!" the teenaged wannabe vet, Kirsten, said cheerfully. "Good morning, Leigh! Good morning, Allison!"

Leigh and her father greeted the girl back. Allison mumbled something under her breath and left the room. Through the doorway, Leigh could see Mathias strutting toward them, fluffing his strawberry blond hair with a comb. Allison rolled her eyes as she passed him and mumbled something else, but Mathias seemed aware of nothing but Kirsten.

"I hope your foot is feeling better today," Kirsten inquired politely of the veterinarian.

"I'll survive, I think," Randall responded. Given the frequency of his poorly hidden winces, Leigh was pretty sure the man actually had broken his ankle, but he was still waiting to see the orthopod to confirm it.

"If you need me to get anything for you, I'll be happy to," Kirsten effused. "Everything I do here helps me learn!"

Leigh proffered a fake smile. Allison was right. Kirsten was a suck-up.

"Grandpa Randall?" Mathias said importantly, shouldering his way into the room in unnecessarily close proximity to Kirsten. "Jared says we should move the freezer away from the wall, but we'll have to unplug it for about half an hour. Is that all right with you?"

Randall looked up at him with an odd expression. "Just keep the lid closed. Jared knows what he's doing."

Leigh stifled a chuckle. No one any less socially oblivious than her father could possibly be puzzled by Mathias's sudden interest in the sanctity of the freezer contents. Kirsten certainly was not.

The girl turned toward Mathias, who was more than a year younger than her but at least three inches taller, with a radiant, yet simpering smile. "That freezer must be so heavy!"

Mathias puffed out his chest.

Leigh resisted the urge to roll her own eyes.

The connecting door to the reception room opened and Morgan poked her head in. "Dr. Koslow? Olan Martin is here. Are you ready for him?"

"Yep," Randall replied, swiveling on his stool and opening a drawer. Mathias directed one last brazen smile at Kirsten, then retreated from the room. Morgan carried in a kennel bearing a large cockatoo and placed it on the exam table. Behind the veterinary assistant walked a short, heavyset man with a wire travel cage containing a pair of yellow-naped Amazons. Allison reappeared and elbowed Kirsten out of the way to take her usual place at Randall's side.

Olan set the cage gently on the floor in the corner. "Hello, Dr. Koslow," he said in a nervous manner. Olan was always nervous. His gaze passed over the younger girls without interest, but stopped on Leigh with a spark of recognition. "Well, hello, Leigh," he said in his pleasant, yet nasally voice. "Haven't seen you in a while! I thought your daughter here had taken over your spot."

Leigh nodded a return greeting. "Hello, Olan. And yes, she has. I'm pretty much useless now."

Like Skippy, Olan had been one of the clinic's most active bird clients for decades. He was an unusual figure of a man, being barely five feet tall and pudgy, with a slightly oversized head, large luminous blue eyes, and a thick crop of forever-mussed hair that had once been blond but was now snow white. He was a soft-spoken man and generally meek, but Leigh knew from personal experience that if Olan feared for his birds, Jekyll could turn into Hyde in a heartbeat.

Olan turned his attention back to the vet. "I couldn't let Zeus go another day without getting those wings clipped!" he bemoaned, wringing his hands. "Last night he made it all the way up to the stovetop! I tell you I nearly had a heart attack! I was cooking pasta, you know. *Anything* could have happened to him!"

"Are all three just here for wing clips?" Randall asked patiently. "Anything else you're concerned about?"

"Patsy needs her beak trimmed again," Olan said quickly. "She just doesn't chew on things like Potsy does. Everyone else just needs their wings done." He opened the kennel door and coaxed out the magnificent cockatoo, which immediately assumed an aggressive posture towards Randall.

"No, no, baby boy!" Olan crooned, taking quick hold of the bird before its beak could reach the vet's knuckles where they rested on the tabletop. Morgan swooped in from behind and placed her own hands around the bird's neck and feet, securing it as Olan himself let go. Leigh looked on, impressed. All of the techs knew how to hold birds if they had to, but few took to the task as effortlessly as Morgan, who had been a volunteer at the National Aviary. Her skill with birds was fortunate, as it was probably the only thing keeping her employed.

"So, I've been meaning to ask," she chirped to Olan as Randall stretched out one of the cockatoo's giant white wings. "Are you straight or gay?"

Randall emitted a loud sound somewhere between a throat clearing and a strangled choke. "Morgan!" he said sternly.

"What?" she asked lightly, blinking her pretty dark eyes.

Allison and Kirsten suppressed giggles.

Olan chuckled himself, albeit awkwardly, then turned to Leigh. "I know that *some people* in this town don't approve of wing clipping," he began, changing the subject. "But *my* first priority is the safety of my birds. It's fine to say that birds need to fly, but what good does that do them if they fly right outside and die of starvation or cold?" His voice gained strength as he launched into the familiar argument. "I know a Quaker that broke its neck flying into a window, and it had lived in that same apartment for years! And don't even get me started about the toilets. The one time someone leaves the lid up will be the one time disaster strikes!"

Leigh nodded patiently. Olan had preached the same sermon with every wing clip since the nineties, when his beloved blue and gold macaw, Ollie, had escaped through a flimsy patio door, never to be seen again.

"I just don't know what I'd do if I lost one of these guys," Olan continued. He pulled a handkerchief from a back pocket and mopped his brow, then lowered his voice to a whisper. "I saw the sign out front asking for anonymous tips. That's a good idea. I do hope *somebody* cooperates with the police! We're all scared to death, you know. Even Skippy!"

Randall continued his work. "Yes, that seems apparent."

"I don't think my birds are in any danger," Olan declared, the tremor in his voice belying his words. "I never leave them outside, you know. Except Zeus here. He gets to be in the patio cage in nice weather. But it's bolted down tight, and no one could snatch him out of it without losing a finger, that's for sure!"

Leigh did not doubt it. In the next instant the cockatoo struggled against Morgan's hold and uttered a shriek that made Leigh's eardrums vibrate.

"You're okay," Morgan and Olan crooned simultaneously.

"He *would* take a finger off, you know," Olan said affectionately, rubbing his own finger along the back of the bird's head. "You be good, and when we get home I'll give you a juicy piece of fresh mango. Eh, boy?" Olan grinned at the girls. "He loves fresh mango. He'll sing the Macarena for it."

Olan's smile faded suddenly, and his face reddened. "I would die if I lost Zeus, Doc," he said soberly. "I mean it. I would just *die*. You have to help the police find this fiend!"

Randall met his eye. "I'll do what I can."

Morgan smiled sweetly at Olan. "So if you died, who'd get your birds?"

Chapter 10

Leigh walked out the front door of the clinic and turned towards her van, savoring dreams of home and bed. But before her feet hit the sidewalk, she noticed a dog limping up the street. The medium-sized, spotted black and white mutt was unaccompanied by a human and wore no collar. A green nylon leash was loosely lassoed around the dog's neck, while the hand loop dragged along the pavement. Puzzled, Leigh turned and approached the dog, expecting to see its owner sprinting along somewhere behind it. But although she could see all the way down to the Ohio River Boulevard, there were no pedestrians in sight.

"Where'd you come from, fella?" she asked. The dog wagged its tail and ducked its head submissively, and she squatted down to pet it. Very gingerly, it lifted a front foot, and Leigh was disturbed to see a smear of blood on its toes. The poor thing had worn its nails to the quick, and one was still actively bleeding. The pads of the paw were rubbed raw. Leigh didn't need to lift the dog's other paws to know that they were likely in the same condition. She had seen such paws many times before — whenever a house pet suddenly found itself running for miles on hard pavement.

"Well, you came to the right place, didn't you?" she praised. "What a smart boy! Follow me." She picked up the lead and led the dog the last few feet into the clinic. "I have a drop-in," she announced. "A runaway with some seriously sore paws. Anybody recognize him?"

Amy was sitting behind the reception desk, and Paige was standing beside it writing something on a chart. The only client in the waiting room was Mrs. Gregg, a staple of the environment who brought in her giant Maine coon cat, Rocky, on a near-daily basis. Randall insisted there was never anything wrong with the cat, and the general consensus of the staff was that the middle-aged widow was simply lonely and liked hanging out at the clinic. This explanation was buttressed by the fact that she routinely waved any number of other clients ahead of her while she waited, and often showed up without either an appointment or the cat.

"Aww," Amy's freckled face cooed. "What a cutie!"

"Do you know who he belongs to?" Leigh asked.

Amy shook her head. "No, but he's a cutie, isn't he?"

"I know that dog," Paige said speculatively, tapping her pen on her chart as she stared at him. "He was here not too long ago." Today the tall and lanky veterinary assistant was wearing turquoise nail polish with pale pink lipstick, a typical fashion choice. She topped it off with dangly red earrings that were already tangled up in her frizzy blond curls. Leigh had suspected Phyllis Diller aspirations until she mentioned the name and the thirty-something Paige had no idea who she was talking about.

"Isn't he Mrs. Ledbetter's dog?" Paige asked, directing the question at Mrs. Gregg, who lived nearby and seemed to know everyone in Avalon. "Lucky?"

The dog perked its ears and turned its head toward Paige.

"Ginny Ledbetter?" Mrs. Gregg said. "Yes, I think you're right."

"Let me double check with the doc," Paige suggested, taking the end of the leash from Leigh. She led the dog around the corner into the exam rooms.

"Ginny adores that dog," Mrs. Gregg said in a frightened whisper. "I can't imagine she'd let him get away from her. What could have happened?" She cuddled her Maine coon closer. "What if somebody tried to snatch him, too? What is this world coming to?"

"To hell in a handbasket," Amy answered cheerfully. "That's what my grandmother always used to say. To hell in a handbasket! Of course, Grandma said lots of other things, too. She had a million sayings. Like: 'Stupid is as stupid does.' She said that even before *Forrest Gump* came out!"

Leigh's mind wandered, as it inevitably did whenever Amy opened her mouth. Mrs. Gregg, on the other hand, seemed fascinated to hear about every saying Amy's grandmother had ever uttered, both the first and second times Amy told her about it.

Leigh was relieved when Paige reappeared with the black and white mutt in tow. The dog wagged its tail happily. "I put some styptic on the nail that was bleeding," Paige reported. "But those paws are going to be sore for a while. Doc wanted to know if you could walk him home before you go, Leigh. Mrs. Ledbetter is just up the street — he said to tell you she's two houses down before your friend Maura's."

Leigh sighed a little as the vision of her soft bed at home withdrew further into the future. "I'll just pop him in the van and drive him up," she agreed, taking the lead.

"No!" Paige said quickly, startling her. "You can't pick him up. He's a total sweetheart most of the time, but he *hates* being held tight or having his belly touched. You pick him up without a muzzle and he'll take your face off."

Leigh looked down at the angelic appearing canine, who was straining on the lead toward the exit. He doggie-smiled up at her, wagging his tail eagerly and whimpering in anticipation. "Oo-kay," she said skeptically, heading for the door. "Think you can make it just a little farther, boy?" she asked.

The dog practically sprang up and down.

It was Lucky who did the leading as Leigh found herself pulled up the cobblestone street. Randall needn't have bothered giving Leigh directions, as the dog knew exactly where it belonged. The mutt trotted nearly to Maura's house before turning up the sidewalk of a similar duplex, then bounding up onto the porch. It scratched at the door with both front feet — sore as they were — and gave an impatient woof.

The door burst open within seconds. An elderly woman gave out a strangled cry, then fell to her knees to envelop the squirming, whimpering dog. "Lucky!" she cried. "Oh, you came back!"

Only some time later, after the dog made clear that the reunion was over by skirting past Ginny and on inside the house, did the woman bother to look up at her other visitor. "Who are you?" she asked, her voice wary.

"I'm Dr. Koslow's daughter, Leigh," she explained. "I found Lucky outside the clinic and they told me he lived here."

Ginny's eyes, which were already puffy from crying, began to water. She faltered a bit as she stood.

"Maybe you should sit down," Leigh suggested.

Ginny nodded and gestured for Leigh to come inside. They settled on a worn couch with Lucky curled up between them. The dog was excited and restless, dropping his head in and out of his owner's lap and whimpering periodically.

"I was afraid I'd never see him again," Ginny said tightly.

Leigh was assaulted by a sudden sick feeling. This was no simple runaway. "Did someone take him?" she asked gently.

Ginny nodded. One large tear dripped off the side of her nose and fell into her lap. "This morning. I put him out at first light, like I always do. He does his business in the yard and then naps on the porch till breakfast. But when I went to let him in, he wasn't there. And I found this." Her hand trembled as she reached out to her cluttered coffee table and picked up a folded piece of plain white paper. "Read it."

Leigh unfolded the note. It was written in pencil, in a nearly illegible scrawl of print letters.

> If u want dog back alive you put $300 cash in yellow bucket in woods behind Avalon park batting cage sunset TONITE with THIS NOTE. Tell anyone - dog dies. Tell cops - dog dies slowly painfully! Now or ever or I'll come get him again!

In the bottom corner of the note was a scribbled signature — in the form of a drawing. It was a skull with a knife handle sticking out of one eye socket.

Leigh felt even sicker. She folded the note back up again. She put out a hand and stroked the dog's furry neck. "I wonder how he got away."

Ginny shook her head. "I don't know how they got him in the first place. Unless they lured him with food. He'd follow anyone for bacon, that's for sure. But they couldn't pick him up! He'd take their face off!"

Leigh withdrew her hand. If there was a story behind that claim, she didn't want to hear it. "It doesn't matter now," she said firmly. "Lucky's home and he's safe. And thanks to his escape and your saving this note, the police may finally be able to catch this devil!"

Ginny's composure wilted. Her hands clutched at her dog. "The note says not to."

"Well, of course it does," Leigh argued. "Because the petnapper knows that if the police get involved, he's going to get caught. But it's the only way to stop him."

Ginny thought a minute, then slowly nodded her head. "He's got to be stopped. I can't let anyone else go through this." Her gaze drifted to her coffee table, and Leigh's eyes followed.

Sitting amidst the clutter, in a neat stack with a rubber band, was a thick pile of twenty-dollar bills.

"I would have paid it," Ginny whispered hoarsely. "I would have paid anything."

"I know," Leigh commiserated, imagining her own Chewie or Mao Tse in the clutches of skull-and-knife. Would she contact the police, or would she be too afraid of what would happen to her pets? She wasn't sure. All she knew was that after she caught up with said villain, the homicide squad would be looking for her.

"I'll take him to my sister's house for a while," Ginny announced, straightening with determination. "She lives all the way over in West Mifflin, and she has a Jack Russell and a nice fenced yard. We'll just visit a while. Until they catch this monster." She raised her red-rimmed eyes to Leigh's. "They will catch him, won't they?"

Leigh smiled. "With this note and your help? Absolutely." She rose. "With your permission, I'll walk this piece of paper straight over to Detective Polanski and let her know what's happened. She'll take it from there. Just keep Lucky safe inside until you hear from her. Okay?"

Ginny nodded and bent over again to bury her face in the ruff of her dog's neck. "Don't you worry about that," she said tearfully. "He's never leaving my sight again!"

Leigh left the happy couple to each other's company and hastened down the street to Maura's house. Remembering the baby, she rapped gently rather than ringing the bell. The detective answered the door almost immediately.

"Koslow?" Maura greeted uneasily, studying her. "I know that look. Is this going to upset me?"

"Most likely," Leigh answered. "Can I come in?"

Maura swung open the door. "Keep your voice down," she ordered. "Eddie just went to sleep, and he had us up half the night. What's going on?"

They settled into chairs. Maura looked as exhausted as Leigh felt. The county detective was obviously unaware of the Koslow family's overnight adventures with the Ross Township police, which was not surprising. Bellevue and Avalon had their own small police forces, but on either side of those two municipalities, West View was policed by Ross Township and Ben Avon by Ohio Township. Maura's county department covered the whole area, but only for homicides and other higher-level crimes. The smattering of break-ins and pet thefts Leigh had the misfortune to be associated with were split over four PDs that might or might not be talking to each other. Looking at the bags under Maura's eyes, Leigh decided it was just as well the new mother didn't know about the Koslow's unwelcome visitor. One crisis at a time.

"I just found Ginny Ledbetter's dog wandering up the street by the clinic with its paws all torn up," Leigh explained. "I took him home, and Ginny told me he disappeared early this morning. After which, she found this." She extended the paper.

"Lucky?" Maura asked with surprise, leaning forward.

Leigh nodded.

"Just set it down there," Maura instructed, nodding at her coffee table.

Oh, right. Fingerprints. Shoot!

Leigh did as instructed, and Maura read the note. Then she swore. "I can't believe anyone would have the gall to snatch a dog just two doors down from me! Who do they think lives here, a couple of nannies? Of all the—" She uttered a few more choice words, then rose and picked up her phone. "Who else knows that the dog came back?"

"People at the clinic," Leigh answered. "I took him inside first."

"Call your dad," Maura ordered. "Have him tell everyone who saw the dog that they need to keep quiet about it, at least for twenty-four hours. If we're lucky, our dognapper won't realize that Mr. Lucky found his own way home."

Of course, Leigh thought with a smile. It wouldn't matter to the petnapper if he had the dog, all that mattered was that Ginny thought he did. Unless he knew for a fact that Lucky had made it home, he would still check for his money tonight, wouldn't he?

"I'll call Ginny," Maura announced. "We don't want her spreading the word either, and she'll have to keep the dog out of sight. The Avalon PD will take it from here."

Leigh completed her assigned phone call and waited for Maura to finish hers. When the detective hung up, her face was flushed and shiny.

"I still can't believe it. The nerve of those—" Maura cast a glance toward the nursery, then cut herself off. "Sorry. I've got to start watching my mouth now, don't I? Crap, that's going to be hard."

Leigh started to chuckle, but Maura's face had turned grim.

The detective dropped back into her chair. "There's something I need to ask you, Koslow."

The look in her eyes made Leigh's pulse race. "Tell me this isn't about Mason," she begged.

"Sorry," Maura returned. "Have you heard from him?"

Leigh explained about the missed call and the voice mail. "But I left him another message this morning," she finished.

Maura looked thoughtful. "A Miami area code, you say? Can I see the number?"

Leigh hesitated. She hated being wedged in between Mason Dublin and the law. She knew Maura wasn't out to get the man, but she also knew that if push came to shove, Maura wouldn't protect him, either. For that matter, should Leigh? And why was she so worried in the first place? Did she really believe that Mason would risk everything now?

She didn't think so. But was she sure?

Her jaws clenched. She pulled out her phone, looked up the number, and read it out. Maura punched the numbers into her own phone, punched in something else, then waited. After a moment, her brow creased.

"Well?" Leigh asked anxiously.

Maura put her phone away again. "I'm going to keep trying to contact him," she announced, avoiding the question. "What I need to know is — are you aware of his doing any gambling lately?"

"Gambling?" Leigh repeated, taken aback. She thought of Mason's spiffy outfit, covert new apartment, and mysterious flight to Miami. "Not that I've heard," she answered honestly.

Maura exhaled. She flashed a look at Leigh that was pure sympathy. "The man really needs to start returning his calls. Soon."

Leigh gulped. Being yelled at, threatened, or ordered around by one Maura Polanski was all in a day's friendship. But when the detective started looking sympathetic?

That was when you worried.

Chapter 11

Leigh intended to pull down her shades and crawl straight into bed. But her bedroom was Mao Tse's sanctuary, off-limits to Chewie. And the bored corgi was so pathetically happy to see a human that he dogged her every step, twice now hovering so close that her heel clipped his chin. Leigh looked down at him with a sigh. The dog's mournful brown eyes could make a sociopath feel guilty. "All right!" she conceded. "Fine. I'll nap on the couch."

She collapsed and kicked her shoes off, and the corgi settled contently beside her. "I know you miss Ethan," she said with a yawn, scratching the dog's giant ears. "He'd take you with him if he could, but we both know how much you *love* the clinic."

Chewie's eyes held hers. *Feed me.*

"Don't give me that," Leigh admonished, rolling over. "You've had three treats since breakfast. Just take a snooze with me." She closed her eyes.

Three minutes later, her cell phone rang. She flung a hand out and groped around on the floor where she had left it, then pulled it in front of her tired eyes.

It was from the area code in Miami. She sat up quickly and tapped to answer. "Mason? Where the hell are you?"

She heard nothing for a moment. "Somewhere I'd rather be doing things other than answering the phone," he remarked dryly. "But apparently I'm a popular guy. I've got another message from you, two from Maura Polanski, and one from the Pennsylvania State Police. What gives? Should I be worried, here?"

Leigh let out the breath she'd been holding. He didn't sound like he felt guilty. "Have you called Maura yet?"

"No," he answered. "I only just got all these. Checking my phone every frickin' hour wasn't part of my getaway plan."

Leigh knew he was joking, but under the circumstances, his word choice was poor. "You need to talk to the police, Mason," she insisted.

"Nothing I'd rather do than shoot the breeze with a copper, as you well know," he said sarcastically. "But I'm not talking to anybody until you give me a heads up about whatever it is that's going on there. And make it fast, because this call is costing me an arm and a leg."

Leigh made a mental note not to let him off the phone until he answered an equal number of her own questions. "It has something to do with your neighbor Kyle. He's disappeared, and the state police are looking for him. Maura says they don't think you're involved necessarily, but that your leaving town when you did looks suspicious. They want to ask you something about Kyle, obviously."

Mason was quiet a moment. Leigh jumped back in. "Now *you* tell *me* why you're in Miami. And why I'm not supposed to tell anyone where these animals came from."

"I'm not in Miami," he said absently.

"Caller ID says you are," Leigh retorted.

"Oh," he replied. "I guess that makes sense. Did Maura say why the state police want to question Kyle?"

"Mason!" Leigh said sharply. "I told you everything I know. Now answer my questions!"

He sighed. "Kyle was afraid he might have to leave town on short notice. He's a professional poker player, but he's had a string of bad luck, and he's in deep with a couple of loan sharks. Last I heard he had a game up in Erie Saturday night — hoped his luck would change. I don't know what happened, but I'm guessing it didn't go well and now somebody's threatening him. All I meant about the pets is — well, some of those guys will use anything to get to a man. Kyle's crazy about that cat, so it's just as well that nobody knows you've got it. You get what I'm saying?"

"I get it," Leigh said heavily.

"I'll call Maura," he promised. "And the state trooper, whoever he is. Sorry to get you involved in all this, kid. But you really don't need to worry about it. Kyle will come back when he's ready. And the first thing he'll do is look me up, wondering where the hell his cat is."

"What about the bird?" Leigh demanded.

"I told you, I don't know jack about the bird. I've got to go. I'm spending a fortune, here."

"Why is this costing you so much?" Leigh pleaded, fearing he would hang up at any second. "And why did Maura ask me if you'd taken up gambling?"

There was another pause. "I'll call her right now. Take care, kid."

"Mason!" she protested. But he had already hung up.

Leigh tossed her phone down on the couch. How could the man be so damned charming and yet so infuriating at the same time? Actually, at the moment he was just infuriating. Why wouldn't he tell her where he was and what he was doing? Didn't she deserve that much for taking care of his blasted friend's cat and his blasted friend's blasted friend's bird?

She wondered, suddenly, if the bird's mysterious owner were as frantic to locate Kyle as the police were. Unless Kyle had explained the whole situation when he took in the cockatiel, that person would have no way of knowing that Mason had intervened.

Fabulous.

Should she let the Bellevue police know that she had Kyle's pets? If the cockatiel's owner came back to claim him, he or she would find Kyle's apartment empty. If they couldn't contact Kyle by phone either, what would they think? Would they hear about the break-in? Might they worry that their bird had been the victim of the pet snatcher, too?

Her tired mind reeled. Aside from Lucky in Avalon, she didn't know where the petnapper's other victims had come from. But the clinic saw clients from all the neighboring boroughs, and everyone seemed to have heard the rumors. It was possible that the poor bird's owner had already called the Bellevue police, trying to find him. But the police wouldn't have any idea what had happened to the bird. Unless Mason happened to volunteer that information during their chat on Monday.

Leigh scoffed. *As if.*

She dropped her head back down on the couch. Now she was stuck. She knew it was the right thing to do to let the police know she had Kyle's pets. But there was no way that doing so wouldn't draw her — and now her entire household — even deeper into Mason Dublin's mess.

Darn the man!

And he had the nerve to whine to her about his calls being expensive! Where the hell was he roaming, anyway?

I'm not in Miami.

Leigh sat up again. She looked at the number he'd just called from and copied it into her browser. She didn't think a reverse search was likely to turn up a private listing. However...

"Aha!" she crowed, swinging her feet onto the floor and startling the sleeping corgi. She *had* gotten a hit on the number. It was listed on a website where people complained about calls from telemarketers. But this number didn't come from a sales outfit. It came from a relay center for cell phone calls bouncing off a satellite... over the ocean.

"A cruise ship!" Leigh said out loud, her face reddening. "I'm stuck here in Pittsburgh cleaning cat urine off my laminate, and he's gambling on a *cruise ship?!*"

She stewed. Why on earth could the man not just tell her that? And why had he lied to Cara about where he was going?

She stewed some more. Then, very slowly, her ire diminished. Mason knew she hadn't believed he was in Las Vegas. He also had to know she could check the number, if she had half a brain. And all of that was before he even knew the police wanted to question him. She had to wonder if, at some level, he *wanted* her to know where he was.

Was this just another gambling junket, or was he with a woman? Someone he wasn't quite ready to tell Cara about? Or rather, the kind of woman no father would ever want to tell his daughter about?

It was possible. He had certainly seemed chipper for a man headed to the airport at four thirty on a Monday morning.

Leigh sighed. She had no desire to plumb the depths of Mason's personal life. Having a nefarious paramour was better than running from the law.

She slipped her shoes back on. The nap wasn't happening. She might as well power through until sunset. She would wait another hour, then call Maura. By then the detective would have talked to Mason herself. If the Bellevue police needed to know about the bird, Maura could relay the message. Kyle's animals were in danger — theoretically — from loan sharks. Not the police.

She stood and stretched. Chewie rose and looked at her hopefully.

Feed me?

Leigh's cell phone rang again. It was Cara.

"Hi, Leigh," her cousin greeted. "You're not still around West

View by any chance, are you?"

"I'm home now. Why?"

"Dang. I should have called sooner. Never mind."

Leigh yawned again. Ten to one odds she would soon be fetching her car keys. "Just tell me what you need," she said tiredly. "There's no way I'm getting any work done this afternoon anyway."

"I was wondering, if you were going to be home the rest of the day, if you might take Lenna back with you and drop her off at the farm. She's driving me crazy fretting over that cat, and she's being a complete ninny about the bird. She's afraid to go anywhere near it — she's just been sitting in the kitchen looking teary and sighing every other second."

"I'll come get her," Leigh said, pulling on her shoes. "I need to talk to you anyway. Outside, maybe."

"Gotcha," Cara replied. "I'll keep an eye out."

Twenty minutes later, Leigh pulled the van up to the curb outside her parents' house. Cara popped immediately out the front door and came to meet her. Leigh rolled down the windows and invited her cousin to have a seat. It was a gorgeous, cool day — unusually cool for Pittsburgh in July.

"Well, hey there, Chewie," Cara greeted as she closed the van door behind her. The corgi made no response. As soon as the van stopped moving, he had hastened to the back to lick any available crumbs out of the seat wells. Cara turned to Leigh. "You've heard from my dad, haven't you?"

Leigh nodded. "I still don't know what's going on with his neighbor Kyle, but apparently Maura does, and she wants to talk to him about it. He said he's going to call her."

Cara's eyes widened. "What does Maura have to do with the break-in at Kyle's? She works homicide!"

Leigh considered a moment, feeling like an idiot. She tended to assume that Maura could and did hear about all sorts of crimes... but why would her co-worker "catch her up" on a case that *wasn't* a homicide?

Holy crap.

"I don't know," Leigh answered weakly. "But I'm going to call her later and find out, I promise you."

Cara's mouth twisted. "Don't you think it's a little strange? The break-in next door to Mason, then the break-in here last night? When was the last time *anyone* you know had a break-in?"

Leigh didn't answer. The various problems affecting her various family members were complicated enough without her trying to artificially connect them all. What could a professional gambler running from loan sharks possibly have in common with her parents, other than a weak link to Mason Dublin? The Mason Dublin who was currently thousands of miles away sipping a mai tai and enjoying the ocean breeze? "Does your father gamble?" she asked instead.

"Gamble?" Cara repeated. "Maybe. He said something not too long ago about how he had been getting really good at Texas Hold'em, which didn't surprise me. He's whip-smart with numbers and you know he could lie his way out of anything. Why do you ask?"

Leigh's eyes caught hers. "He just told me that Kyle is a professional poker player."

Cara blinked back at her a moment. "Dad *has* had more money to spend lately," she mused.

Leigh nodded.

Cara's face flickered briefly with panic, but then just as quickly she drew in a breath and smiled. "Well, gambling on poker isn't illegal," she declared. "There's no reason to assume... anything."

"Of course not," Leigh agreed hastily. She decided to change the subject. There was no point in distressing Cara with any more idle speculation — they would find out what Mason was up to soon enough. "How's everything with my mother?"

"I just finished dusting the plastic sheeting in the dining room."

"I did that already!" Leigh protested.

Cara cracked a grin. "Yes, but not *properly*. And I've vacuumed all the carpet downstairs and dusted all the furniture that's not already covered."

"She'll see dust again by nightfall."

"I'm sure," Cara replied. "But by then, Aunt Bess will be on duty."

The women exchanged a smirk. "When is your mother coming back?" Leigh asked.

Cara's smirk turned into a frown.

"What's wrong?" Leigh asked, alarmed. "Isn't the symposium

supposed to end today?"

Cara nodded, then exhaled with a huff. "It ran Friday night to Wednesday, officially. But she was thinking of staying through this weekend, too. A bunch of her friends from the historical society were planning a sort of post-conference vacation. I get that. But when I told her about your parents both being off their feet, I was sure she'd head straight home after the last session. You know how much she likes to make herself useful, even indispensable, and this time she really *is* needed. None of us would have to stay overnight if she was at home next door, just a phone call — or even a shout — away. But a couple minutes ago I got a text saying not to expect her until Friday or Saturday."

"Really?" Leigh asked with dread. Bess was staying overnight again tonight, but with no Lydie by Thursday, they would have to restart the rotation all over again.

"The text was a bit cryptic, but it sounds like her roommate Cynthia has family near there and really wanted to visit with them before heading home. I guess Mom doesn't want to make her find another ride back, since they drove up together."

"I see." Leigh looked over Cara's shoulder. "Lenna's coming."

Cara's voice dropped. "It's just strange, Leigh. I don't want to think she's lying to me. I really don't. But God knows she's done it before — all in the name of 'protecting' me. And I could absolutely *swear* she's seeing someone romantically, and that she was looking forward to the conference so much because it meant they could spend more time together. But the only name she ever mentions—"

Cara's eyes met Leigh's with a startled expression. Neither woman said a word, but they knew they were both thinking the same, ridiculously impossible, yet somehow tantalizingly plausible thing.

Cynthia?

Lenna skipped up to the van. Leigh hit the button to slide open the side door. "Lenna," she called out, "Before we go, could you grab Chewie's leash and take him out on the grass?"

"Sure, Aunt Leigh," Lenna agreed, reaching in and taking hold of the trailing leash. "Come on, Chewie boy!" She helped the short-legged dog down from the van and led him away into the center of the yard.

Cara lowered her voice to a whisper. "No. She was married! And she's dated —" She broke off and bit a nail. "Hell, she's hardly dated anybody. Not seriously, anyway. Is it possible?"

Leigh shrugged thoughtfully.

"But why would she hide it from me?" Cara asked, her tone showing her hurt.

Leigh shook her head. "Cara, your mom wouldn't worry about you or me, or our husbands, and certainly not about the Pack. If she's hiding something, it's because she's worried about —"

"Aunt Frances," Cara breathed.

Leigh nodded. "Uh huh."

Lenna bounced back to the van and lifted Chewie inside. "Aunt Leigh, Grandma Frances said to tell you that she needs empty banker's boxes. And Mom, she said she's pretty sure that the bird dust is spreading up the stairs and that somebody needs to 'address the situation.'"

Cara and Leigh exchanged a look.

Godspeed, Leigh smiled.

Chapter 12

"I was beginning to think I only imagined being married," Leigh joked, enjoying her husband's embrace. She hadn't laid eyes on the man since he'd left for work Monday morning, but he'd surprised her by coming home in time for supper.

"Sorry," Warren lamented. "The first two dinners were included in the seminar, so I couldn't bail on them. And I need to be there for the evening sessions, even though I'm not leading them. But Wednesday evening was free time for everybody, so here I am."

"How's it going? Your cold seems better, at least," Leigh inquired. She was proud of the work he'd been doing for nonprofits ever since getting out of the political game. Being President of the United States might have been his youthful aim, and he'd been well on his way after having being elected Chair of the County Council in his early thirties. But the lure of politics had faded after the twins were born. Despite Warren's genius with both finances and schmoozing, he was at heart a family man.

"It's all going very well," he answered proudly. "The participants are certainly enthusiastic. And how about you? Are your parents managing all right? I see that Mason returned early."

Leigh stepped back. "Mason? What do you mean?"

Warren blinked at her. "Well... the bird and the other cat are gone."

Leigh exhaled with relief. She'd had enough surprises already today. "No, Mason's still away. The cat is staying at the farm in Lenna's room and my dad is taking care of the cockatiel at their house."

The front door burst open to admit Ethan, whose face lit up immediately at the sight of his father. "Dad! You're home! Can you make dinner tonight? Please?"

Leigh chuckled. She had long since gotten over being offended by remarks about her lack of cooking skills. What was her pride compared to being able to eat decent food? "Yes, Dad," she said jokingly, releasing Warren. "Will you?"

"Only if this one helps me," Warren negotiated, throwing his arm around his son and steering the boy toward the kitchen. No sooner were the two of them out of sight than Allison skipped through the front door. "Look, Mom!" she said excitedly. "We got two letters in the mail today at the clinic that I'm pretty sure are tips! Grandpa said not to open them yet, though. He wants you to check with Aunt Mo first."

Leigh stared at the two envelopes in her daughter's hands with misgiving. Having the clinic serve as a de facto crime stoppers unit had seemed like a good idea at the time. But for reasons she wasn't entirely sure of, her uneasiness about having the kids involved was growing. "Just leave them on the table," she instructed. "I'll call your Aunt Mo in a bit."

She had already tried to call Maura, twice, but the policewoman hadn't answered — only texted that she was busy and they would talk later on.

Allison put the letters on the table. "The bird is *so* much better!" she gushed cheerfully. "He's eating a lot more, and today he started to chirp and even whistle a bit! And he hasn't picked at himself anymore, even without a collar. Can I run over to the farm and see Peep?"

Cara, who had been standing patiently by the doorway, flashed Leigh an unmistakable I-need-to-talk-to-you look.

"Sure," Leigh replied to Allison. "I'll call when it's time for dinner."

Allison banged out the back door and headed for the farmhouse at a jog. Ethan and Warren's voices drifted in from the kitchen, along with the clanging of pots and pans. Leigh turned to her cousin with foreboding. "What is it?"

"Aunt Bess just brought your father back from the orthopedist," Cara answered. "His ankle *is* broken. He's doesn't need surgery, but it's in a cast, and he's not supposed to put any weight on it. He's also supposed to keep it elevated most of the time."

"Oh, no," Leigh murmured. "Can he work at all?"

"He insists he's going to," Cara reported. "But your mother has other ideas."

"Oh, no," Leigh repeated.

"That's what I thought," Cara agreed.

They shared an unspoken moment of sympathy for Bess.

"There's something else, too," Cara said, dropping her voice.

Leigh steadied herself. Having both of her parents with at least one foot non-weight-bearing for at least another week was bad enough. What else could have happened in half an afternoon?

"I heard something," Cara declared, her expression anxious. "I was in the kitchen, and your mom was in the powder room. All the downstairs windows were open because she wanted a breeze, and I didn't think anything about that. It was broad daylight, after all! But I think somebody might have been skulking around outside the house, because I heard a man's cough. Twice."

Leigh froze. "What kind of cough?"

"Like a smoker's cough," Cara answered. "You know, hacking. I ran through the house and looked out every window, but whoever it was had either taken off or was hiding somewhere I couldn't see. I convinced myself it must have come from the sidewalk or a neighbor's window, but then I heard it again, when I was upstairs. I didn't see anything the second time either, but it just sounded so close!" Cara's forehead creased with distress. "I closed and locked all the windows and I told Bess about it when she got there, but I didn't want to worry your parents. They have enough on their minds right now and, well, maybe I was just overreacting."

"I doubt it," Leigh said weakly. "I thought I heard the same thing. Last night. Both before and after I saw the guy at the window."

The women stared at one another.

Cara sucked in a determined breath. "I'll call Bess and tell her that if she or your parents hear *anything*, they should call the police right away. They should leave all the lights on after dark, and I'll talk to Gil about hiring a security guard to send over there."

Leigh nodded.

Cara turned and walked back out, and Leigh picked up her phone. This time, Maura actually answered.

"Hey, Koslow," the detective's deep voice boomed. "Sorry to put you off, but I've been on the horn a lot this afternoon and Eddie's been a real crank. There hasn't been any more trouble at your end, has there?"

"I'm not sure," Leigh answered. She took a deep breath, then launched into a long explanation of the break-in at her parents' house last night and how Cara had heard similar, mysterious coughs again this afternoon.

"That is disturbing," Maura agreed. "How about I give the Ross Township police a call? They can put a cruiser on it. If anybody's casing the place, seeing those flashing lights sweep by at random intervals should be discouraging."

"That would be fabulous," Leigh said, relieved. "Thanks." She sank down on her couch and exhaled. Mao Tse hopped onto her lap.

"Look, Koslow," Maura continued. "I talked to Mason. He says you've got Kyle Claymore's pets."

"Is that a problem?" Leigh asked anxiously.

"I hope not." The policewoman's tone was anything but comforting.

"Will you tell me what's going on, please?" Leigh begged. "Mason told me Kyle split because loan sharks were after him, but that so long as no one knew I had the pets, there shouldn't be a problem."

Maura blew out a breath. "Mr. Claymore's problems are bigger than loan sharks, I'm afraid."

Leigh's heart pounded. "Such as?"

The policewoman hesitated. "Kyle was last seen up in Erie Saturday night at a high-stakes poker game. Not the legal kind. Shots were fired; a man was killed. Kyle hasn't been seen since."

"I see," Leigh mumbled. The cat on her stomach was purring loudly, but Leigh's whole body felt cold.

"Monday morning, before dawn, Mason took off as well," Maura continued. "Then just a few hours later, Kyle's apartment was broken into. Mason and Kyle were known to be associated; they played poker in some of the same circles. You see the problem?"

"But Mason wasn't in Erie Saturday night. Was he?" Leigh squeaked.

"No, he wasn't. Thank God," Maura replied sincerely. "And we have no reason to believe he's done any illegal gambling himself. Although he does seem to be on quite a tear with the casino variety."

Leigh's eyebrows perked. "Really?"

"Really." Maura exhaled again. "Listen, Koslow. I don't think Mason was aware of the shooting up in Erie until I talked to him, and I don't think he knows where Kyle is now. But that's pure instinct talking, and I happen to like the guy. An unbiased investigator is going to find Mason's story harder to swallow. He *looks* like he's in this up to his neck. And with him skipping town and stashing those animals at your place—"

"I don't have them anymore," Leigh admitted. "Not technically. Not here at the house."

"Where are they?" Maura demanded.

Leigh explained. "But it shouldn't matter. I mean, no one knows where they are, either way. Do you think I should let the Bellevue police know about the cockatiel? Mason says he has no idea who Kyle was keeping it for."

Maura was quiet for a moment. "Koslow, how long has the bird been at your dad's house?"

"Since yesterday. Why?"

More quiet. The cat purred. Ethan and Warren laughed about something in the kitchen.

"I do sometimes get crazy ideas that don't pan out to anything," Maura said. "But you do realize that these two break-ins have something in common? Something that was present at both locations — or was *supposed* to be present — when each occurred?"

Leigh jerked upright. Mao Tse sank in her claws and howled with disapproval.

"The cockatiel?" Leigh sputtered. "But that's impossible. No one knew it was there!" Her brain reeled. *Was* it possible?

No, it was not. "Look, Maura," she reasoned. "No one could know that I had Kyle's pets unless they saw Mason leaving with them Monday morning and followed him out here. In which case, why break into Kyle's apartment? Why not break into *this* house? The animals were here alone all afternoon Monday and most of the evening as well!"

"A valid point," Maura agreed. "It does seem far-fetched. But keep thinking about it. There may be some angle we're missing." In the background, Leigh could hear a newborn howl. "Master Eddie requests my presence in the nursery immediately," Maura quipped. "I'll make those calls as soon as I can. Let me know if you or Allison come up with anything."

"But—" The policewoman rang off. Leigh dropped her phone to her side with frustration. She hadn't even gotten around to mentioning the two envelopes on her table that might or might not be from anonymous tipsters.

The evening crawled by slowly. Leigh enjoyed her taco dinner; it was nice to have all four members of the Harmon family gathered together at mealtime, an increasing rarity in the hustle and bustle of midsummer. And Allison had only sulked a little bit when informed she could *not* open the letters unless they were so instructed. But Leigh's mind was uneasy. Her conversation with Maura kept swirling in her head, the various pieces of upsetting information refusing to settle into a comfortable pattern.

It *couldn't* all be about the bird. How could it?

Surely Mason was an innocent bystander in whatever trouble Kyle was in. Mason had seemed sincere, and he would never knowingly involve Leigh and her family in anything truly dangerous. Would he?

Leigh suddenly had doubts. And she hated that she was having them.

The sun set. Leigh's mind drifted to Avalon park and the yellow bucket that would be placed behind the batting cage in hopes of receiving Ginny Ledbetter's thick stack of twenty-dollar bills. With any luck at all, the Avalon police would be catching the petnapper with his hand in that bucket any second now. And then all this mess would be over.

Well, part of the mess, anyway.

Leigh resisted her constant urge to call Maura, vowing to try only once an hour until she got through. So far her efforts had taken her straight to voice mail, meaning that the detective was on the phone. Which, in itself, was less than comforting.

Leigh had sent the kids off for their showers and was cuddled on the couch with her husband and a crossword puzzle when a siren tone announced that she had received a text.

"It's Maura," she said unnecessarily, picking up her phone.

"There's more going on than you've told me, isn't there?" Warren asked suspiciously. "You've been horribly jumpy tonight. What is it?"

Leigh didn't answer immediately. She was opening the text.

> Stakeout was a bust — not even a yellow bucket showed.
> Think back — any ideas who could have tipped off our perp,
> let me know.

Leigh's hopes fizzled. A tip off? How was that possible? Unless the petnapper had good reason to believe that Ginny Ledbetter had squealed to the police, or knew for sure that the dog got home, why not at least set the bucket out? Had the cops doing the stakeout been so inept that he saw them lying in wait?

Or... Leigh chilled at the horribly unpleasant thought. Had the petnapper been tipped off by someone who saw Lucky at the clinic? By someone *at* the clinic?

"Leigh," Warren said heavily, reading the text over her shoulder. "Talk to me."

"Sorry," she apologized. "I don't even know where to begin."

"Does Mason have something to do with this 'stakeout' operation?"

Leigh's jaws clenched. "I certainly hope not."

She tried to picture the scene when she had brought Lucky into the clinic yesterday afternoon. Mrs. Gregg was the only other client in the waiting room, but there were others in the back. And Paige had walked the dog back for Randall to see... pretty much anybody in the clinic at the time could have spotted Lucky. Or heard about it later. There was definitely a lag before she had reached her father to ask him to make a plea for secrecy — and how had he done that, exactly? Couldn't a client have seen the dog and left before getting the message? But why would an uninterested party blab about seeing Lucky in the first place? And what were the odds against some innocent party blabbing about it to the actual perpetrator by sheer coincidence?

It was one coincidence too many.

"I need to go back to West View," Leigh mumbled, rising.

"Now?" Warren protested.

Leigh nodded. She dialed Maura's number again. "I have to get the bird," she mumbled. Maura's line went straight to voice mail. "Call me!" Leigh begged onto the recording. Then she hung up.

She started towards the door, and Warren followed her. "Why do you have to get the bird?"

Leigh grabbed her keys. "Because somebody knows it's there."

"Who knows it's there?" Allison inquired from the doorway to the hall. Standing barefoot with wet hair in a short Bambi nightgown, th
the sharp glint
"Someone v

Chapter 13

Leigh parked the van in the street outside her parents' house a record sixteen minutes later. She jogged up to the door and tested the knob. It was locked. That was good. She rapped on the door. "Aunt Bess! It's me!"

A few seconds later Bess appeared, looking rosy cheeked and delighted to see her. "Well, hey, kiddo," she said, swinging the door open wide and then shutting it behind Leigh. "What's up?" Bess was wearing a floor-length crimson silk kimono with a bright yellow dragon on the front, which for her was a relatively sedate choice of nightwear.

Leigh walked into the living room to find both her parents already settled in bed. Randall sat on top of the covers of the inflatable mattress with his newly casted food propped up on pillows. He was holding a book, but his complexion was on the gray side and his face was lined with discomfort — no doubt because he was refusing to take his pain medication again. Frances sat next to him under the covers with a bathrobe on, her hair in foam curlers and her dark eyes accusing. "Leigh Eleanor," she snapped. "You drove all the way down here wearing *that?*"

Leigh looked down. At some point she had traded her capris for a pair of fuzzy sleep pants adorned with giant Simpsons characters. Oh well.

"Dad, I need to talk to you," she said breathlessly.

Randall set down his book. "Yes?"

Leigh cast an uncomfortable look at Frances and Bess, both of whom blinked back at her with no trace of shame. Bess threw out her chest and Frances crossed her arms stubbornly over her midsection. Leigh sighed. The women weren't going anywhere, and Randall couldn't. They might as well all know the story.

Where to start?

"I need to know what happened after I brought the dog, Lucky, into the clinic this afternoon," she began. "I told you we thought that he had escaped from the petnapper. Well, somehow the petnapper found out that he was back. And..." Leigh paused a moment. Her father was not going to like this. He would, in fact, resist the idea strenuously. "And Maura and I have reason to believe he found out that information from someone who saw Lucky at the clinic."

The wrinkles in Randall's already furrowed brow deepened. "I asked the staff not to say anything," he replied. "But anyone could have seen you walking Lucky up the street to Mrs. Ledbetter's house."

Leigh sucked in a breath. "That's true. But we have other reasons to think that someone at the clinic may be involved."

"Nonsense," Randall said immediately. "There were clients about, too. Any number of people could have mentioned seeing the dog."

Leigh noticed that Bess swayed a bit as she sat perched on the arm of the couch. In one hand she held a small glass containing an amber liquid. Periodically, she swished it.

Periodically, Frances turned and scowled at her.

So *that* was how Bess got through the evening!

"Dad," Leigh tried again. "I know this sounds crazy, but there's a chance — just a chance — that the reason someone broke in the house last night was to get the cockatiel."

Frances scoffed. "Oh, for heaven's sake! I told the police last night, I'm sure they were after my cookware. They did come in the kitchen, and everyone in the neighborhood knows how important an even heating temperature is to—"

"Oh, stifle yourself, Francie!" Bess cut in. "Nobody wants your precious pots and pans!" She looked at Leigh. "Although I can't imagine why anyone would want the likes of that bird, either. No sooner did the sun set than the little devil started screaming like a banshee!"

"I told you," Randall said calmly. "The vocalization is a good sign. It means he's getting more comfortable with the environment."

"Well, he can get comfortable with another one," Frances protested. She turned to Bess. "That reminds me, when I was in the powder room I checked the slats on the air vent. And there *has too* been a significant amount of dust accumulation since—"

"Dad!" Leigh interrupted desperately. "I'm serious, here. Maybe it's not the cockatiel that the burglar wanted and maybe it wasn't anybody at the clinic who tipped off the petnapper about Lucky.

But if the burglar *was* after the cockatiel, how else could he have known it was here? *I* didn't even know you were going to take the bird home yesterday! But practically anyone at the clinic could have found that out."

Randall frowned. "Or anyone could have seen Allison carry the cage out to Cara's van. Or from the van into this house."

Leigh sighed. It would take a whole lot more evidence than one flimsy hunch to convince her father that anyone or any part of his veterinary clinic was involved in such a drama. Randall Koslow, VMD didn't believe in drama.

"It can't hurt for me to move the bird someplace else, just in case," Leigh insisted. "I was thinking maybe Skippy would take him in. She doesn't have any animals other than birds, he'd be well cared for, and no one in their right mind would break into her place after she practically shot that jogger the other night. What do you think?"

Randall considered. "Well, I suppose. But I still think you should leave the bird here. He's been doing really well, and the change to another environment could set him back again."

Leigh stood her ground. "The bird's temporary psychological state is not my first priority. His safety — and the safety of everyone in this house — is. I'm moving him elsewhere. Tonight."

She found an unexpected ally.

"It's for the best, Randall," Frances said firmly. "You have enough to deal with getting that ankle healed without worrying about a patient in the house. And you shouldn't trust your staff so blindly. How many times have we been burned by sticky fingers at the cash box? You can't possibly vouch for everyone down there; some of them are quite new, are they not?"

Randall did not reply. Ordinarily this was the part of the conversation where he would walk out of the room. Instead he picked up his book and started reading again.

Bess waved a hand toward the front door. "Off the little guy goes, then!" she said, a bit too merrily. "Let me know if you get a look inside Skippy's house, would you? Ten dollars says she'll take the cage out of your hands before you can get a foot in the door!"

Leigh felt a pang of discomfort. Something was wrong. She took a step toward the dining room. The bird cage was no longer there. "Where did you put him?"

"Out on the front porch, of course," Bess chirped. "You must have walked right by him. He was making such a racket I had to move him somewhere, and Francie absolutely *forbade* me from putting him anywhere else in the house without hermetically sealing it up first. The fresh air helped, though. He calmed down right away. Hasn't uttered a peep since!"

Leigh paled. She swung around, opened the front door, and stepped out onto the porch. She looked at the small table that sat to the right of the door. Its surface and the floor of the porch around it were lightly littered with seed husks.

The cockatiel cage was gone.

"Oh, merciful heavens," Bess murmured behind her. "I can't believe it!"

"What's happened?" Frances called out.

Leigh and Bess returned to the living room.

"He's gone," Bess said weakly. "Cage and all."

"From right off the porch?" Randall asked with disbelief, swinging his feet off the bed and reaching for his crutches.

Leigh waved him back down. "It's too late, Dad," she said sadly. "The bird's gone. He was gone before I got here."

Randall sank back onto the mattress. "But *why?*"

Leigh pulled out her phone. "I wish I knew," she said heavily.

"How utterly ridiculous," Frances said scornfully. "My cookware has a far higher resale value."

All three of them stared at her.

"Well, it does!" she protested hotly, fluffing her covers. "Such nonsense, I tell you…"

"What's up, Koslow?"

Leigh startled at the voice coming from her phone. She hadn't expected Maura to answer. "I'm at my parents' house," she reported. "Somebody snatched the cockatiel from off their front porch. Cage and all."

Maura was silent for a beat. "Holy crap," she muttered. "I didn't really think… hang on. I'm coming over there. Gerry?" she called to the side. "Can you finish burp duty, here? I've got —"

The line cut off. Leigh put down her phone. "Maura's coming over," she announced.

When a knock on the door sounded fifteen minutes later, Bess was still in her kimono and Leigh's legs were still advertising a television show. But Frances was fully dressed with her hair fluffed and her lipstick on, and Randall sat miserably with a rain jacket thrown around his shoulders.

"I'm not wearing this," he protested, grabbing at it. "It's hot. My pajamas are perfectly decent and I'm in my own home."

"Into which you have invited an impressionable young lady!" Frances insisted, pulling the jacket back into place.

Leigh stifled a chuckle. "Impressionable young lady" was not something the six-foot-two-inch, forty-three-year-old policewoman got called every day.

Leigh opened the door and invited her friend inside.

"Sorry to hear about this, everyone," Maura said sympathetically. "I've called the Ross Township PD and they're sending somebody over to take your statements."

"I hope we're not wasting their time," Randall said in his no-nonsense monotone. "Obviously, somebody took the bird from our front porch. But that doesn't necessarily have anything to do with someone cutting through the screen last night. It could just be that some neighborhood kids heard the bird and got curious. They might very well bring him back."

"I'm afraid we can't count on that, Dr. Koslow," Maura said smoothly, accepting the seat offered her on the couch by Bess. "True coincidences are the exception, you know. Most often, what's most obvious is also the most likely."

Her expression turned sober. "I don't know how much of the background Leigh has shared with you so far, but under the circumstances, there are some things I think all of you should know."

Leigh braced herself. She could hardly keep straight whom she had told what, but whatever Maura was about to say was certain not to go over well.

"The cockatiel," Maura began, "and the cat — which I understand is now at Cara's farm — were until Monday morning in the possession of a man named Kyle Claymore. Mason Dublin has known Kyle for some time, because they both play professional poker. In fact, when Mason was looking for a place in town, Kyle told him about the apartment next door to his in Bellevue being available, and that's how Mason came to lease it."

"Mason Dublin has moved to Bellevue?" Frances exclaimed with annoyance. "Who allowed him to do that?"

Maura ignored the question. "Kyle disappeared over the weekend, and on Monday morning Mason noticed that the cat hadn't been fed. He took possession of the bird and the cat, dropped them off at Leigh's, and then left town. His claim is that the cat belonged to Kyle but that he had never seen the cockatiel before that morning."

Frances sniffed. "A likely story."

"Later on Monday morning, someone broke into Kyle's apartment," Maura continued. "On Tuesday night, someone attempted to break in here. On the next night, tonight, someone has taken the bird."

Randall exhaled heavily. "I see what you're getting at."

"I know it seems like a pretty thin link," Maura explained. "But it has to be taken seriously, because Kyle Claymore is wanted for questioning by the state police in conjunction with a murder that took place up in Erie Saturday night."

"Oh, merciful heavens!" Frances shrieked. "I knew that Mason Dublin was up to no good! I told you! I told you all!"

"Oh, s-stuff it, Francie!" Bess blurted, still holding her now-empty glass. "She didn't say Mason had beans to do with it! All she said was that he took care of the man's pets!"

"The long and short of it," Maura continued calmly, "is that we have no idea where the cockatiel came from, who would want it, or why. But given its association with Kyle Claymore, I think you all need to be very careful. Keep your doors and windows locked. And until we have more to go on, don't mention any of this to anyone."

An awkward silence descended. Leigh broke it. "Maura," she said hesitantly. "There's something else. I didn't bring the bird straight here from my house. It spent all day Tuesday at the clinic first."

Maura blinked at her. "Seriously?"

"What on earth difference does that make?" Bess asked with a hiccup.

Leigh took a breath and explained about the petnapping rumors, finding Lucky, and the failed stakeout.

Randall exhaled with a grunt. "You're making too many assumptions," he protested. "There's no reason to believe that whatever's going on with Kyle and the cockatiel has any relationship whatsoever to the petnappings."

Frances's chin dipped. She peered at her husband over her glasses, her lips pursed. "Well, of course not," she drawled. "What could one petnapping in the North Boros *possibly* have to do with another petnapping in the North Boros *on the same day?*"

Randall frowned.

"I'm sorry, Dad," Leigh said sympathetically. "But the clinic is the logical link. That's why I came over here. *Someone* at the Koslow Animal Clinic — knowingly or otherwise — has to be feeding information to the petnapper."

Maura's brow wrinkled. "But the previous petnappings have been motivated by ransom," she noted. "The perp has targeted cats and dogs whose owners had enough of an emotional attachment to cough up a lot of money to get them back. People who would be too scared about their animal's welfare to risk contacting the police. The bird's theft doesn't fit that pattern. Who would pay ransom to get back a cockatiel? What do they cost anyway, fifty bucks?"

The others turned to stare at her. Leigh smirked. "Have you ever *met* a bird person?"

Maura's mouth opened. "Well, I…"

Bess tittered. "Really, my dear. I daresay a petnapper could *specialize* in birds."

"The financial motive would be the same," Randall assured Maura. "But in the case of the cockatiel, we are not the ones who would be paying the ransom."

Another silence descended.

Unpleasant thoughts churned in Leigh's head. Kyle Claymore was in financial straits. Kyle Claymore had been keeping two pets in his apartment this weekend. Had there ever been more?

Her stomach churned with a mental image of Lenna cuddled up in bed with the skittish, three-legged tortie. If the bird was stolen property… what about the cat?

Was Kyle Claymore really MIA, or was it him she had seen hanging through her parents' kitchen window last night? Had he come back for the bird again just now? And what or who was his connection with the clinic?

A loud knock sounded on the front door. "Police!" a man's voice called.

Maura rose and moved to answer it.

Leigh prepared for another sleepless night.

Chapter 14

"Aunt Leigh," Lenna asked speculatively, with no trace of a whine in her usually baby-like voice. "Have you ever heard of anyone suing for pet custody based on abandonment?"

Leigh peered over the rim of her second cup of coffee to study the girl, who was sitting across the breakfast table next to Allison. Lenna, who showed signs of becoming a talented artist, was working on a charcoal drawing of a cat. Closer examination showed that the cat was a dilute tortie with three legs.

Apprehension flared. "I've heard of pet custody cases as part of a divorce," Leigh answered. "But, Lenna... you know that Peep already has an owner."

The girl's eyes narrowed. "Yes, but he doesn't deserve her! She'd have starved to death by now if it wasn't for Grandpa. And she's disabled!"

Leigh's eyes moved to Allison. *Grandpa?* Since when did any of the Pack know that it was Mason who had delivered the pets? Since when did they know anything about Kyle?

Allison sipped her orange juice. Her dark eyes met her mother's without shame, but when she looked at her cousin, her small forehead wrinkled with concern. "You're not going to be able to keep her, Lenna," she said firmly. "Everybody keeps telling you that."

Lenna tossed down her charcoal with a pout. "I don't care what everybody says. She loves me, and I love her. We were meant to be together!"

Allison turned to her mother with a sigh. *Your turn.*

Leigh blinked back dumbly. Words failed her. Clearly, it would take a third cup of coffee to clear the fog from her brain. By the time she'd returned home last night, Warren was already snoring, and before her eyes opened this morning, he was gone again. Whatever sleep she had gotten in between hadn't seemed to make a dent in her deficit.

Thank goodness it was Cara's assignment to haul the boys back down to work at the clinic this morning and to relieve Aunt Bess for day duty. Leigh had assumed Allison would want to go to the clinic also, and was surprised when the girl chose to stay at home. But it was Thursday, a surgery day, and Randall wouldn't be taking any appointments until the afternoon. "And besides," Allison had said with a sour expression, "*Kirsten* is going to be there. And I refuse to watch Matt make a complete idiot out of himself again."

Before Leigh could respond to Lenna's woes about the cat, the girl's personal cell phone rang. Leigh and Warren remained staunch in their belief that eleven-year-olds did not need their own smartphones, but Cara and Gil had different rules.

Lenna picked up the penguin-encased mobile. "Why are you calling me?" she asked, using the particularly peevish tone kids reserved for their siblings. "Why didn't you just text?" She was quiet a moment. "Oh, okay. Here." She stuck the phone out blindly in Allison's direction with her left hand. Her right hand picked up her charcoal again.

Allison took the phone. "You got something?" She listened a moment, then grabbed up a pencil and flipped a page in the notebook in front of her. "Okay."

Leigh leaned back and crossed her arms over her chest. She had been quite deliberate, before the boys left with Cara, to tell everyone an appropriately edited version of last evening's events. The Pack knew that the cockatiel had been stolen, but they were left to believe that in all likelihood, the theft was a random petnapping. All four of them had sat there and listened politely, never bothering to mention that they already knew about Mason's involvement in the matter. How much else did they secretly know?

"Uh huh," Allison replied, beginning to scribble. "And when exactly was that?"

Leigh leaned forward again. Allison's handwriting was as bad as her own, and she could only make out snatches of it, but the story unfolding on the other end — from Mathias, presumably — was evident.

First attempt... screen cut... hacking cough... second attempt... outside. Kyle Claymore — murder suspect?... missing... poker... DEFEND GRANDPA MASON! Stakeout failed due to tipster... clinic?... four PDs... reconnaissance...

Leigh leaned back again with a grumble. Aunt Bess never could keep her mouth shut, even if she wanted to, which she usually didn't. Her refusal to treat children like children had made her the greatest aunt on earth for a young Leigh and Cara, but in the last eleven years, the trait had ceased to endear.

"Okay, got it," Allison said finally. "Thanks. I'll be down later. No, they're still sitting here." Her eyes looked resentfully at the unopened tip letters on the table in front of her. "Still waiting to hear from Aunt Mo. Mom forgot. Okay. Later."

Allison hung up. She sat the phone down again by Lenna, who continued to draw.

Leigh cleared her throat. "Excuse me?"

Her daughter looked up at her innocently. "Yes?"

Leigh frowned. "Did he get everything, or were there any blanks you'd like me to fill in?"

Allison smiled, turned her notepad around, and scooted it across the table. "I don't know, Mom. You tell me."

Leigh's teeth gnashed. She knew it was better, from a college cost perspective if nothing else, to have the children that she had. But some days it really did seem like life would be easier with dumber ones.

Her own phone rang. It was the siren tone.

"Maura!" she exclaimed, answering swiftly. She started to leave the room, but realized the futility of it. "You're up! Thanks for calling back."

The only sound from the other end of the line was a yawn.

"Sorry," Leigh offered. She explained about the two letter-sized envelopes that had arrived at the clinic Wednesday afternoon with Tuesday postmarks and no return addresses. Both had come from the same zip code as the clinic. "There are some people here itching to open them, as you might expect. What do you want us to do with them?"

Maura yawned again. Baby Eddie gurgled happily in the background. "What time does the clinic's mail usually come?" the policewoman asked.

Leigh referred the question to Allison. She might as well use speakerphone.

"Around noon," Leigh relayed. "I'll be taking Allison back down around one, if you'd like me to check for more."

"How about if Master Eddie and I pop down there and meet you?" Maura suggested. "Bring the two letters you already have and I'll take a look at what we've got. I may want to talk to your dad afterwards. And some other people."

Leigh felt a wave of foreboding. She didn't like to think of her father's staff — or even his clients — as suspects in something as heinous as the kidnapping of beloved pets for ransom. But the evidence was compelling.

"Are you on this case?" Leigh asked.

"There isn't one case to be on," Maura replied. "This stuff crosses four local jurisdictions, as you know. I'm still officially on leave till Monday, so you could say I'm providing a little friendly, informal case coordination — but I'd rather you didn't. Just let me see if there's anything in those letters you've got. If so, I'll pass it on to the locals. But right now, there's not enough to kick it up to the county."

"Extortion?" Leigh suggested.

"Lucky came back on his own," Maura reminded. "And no one took the bait. It's not enough."

"We filed a complaint about the cockatiel last night."

"Simple property theft. Unless and until there's a ransom note."

"I get it," Leigh acquiesced. The women signed off, and Leigh poured herself that third cup of coffee.

"Aunt Leigh?" Lenna begged, her tone back to whiny again. "If I have to spend the afternoon at Grandma Frances's, can't I at least spend the rest of the morning at home with Peep? She misses me already, I know it!"

Leigh looked into the girl's giant cornflower blue eyes, which they all knew could turn teary on demand. If Lenna ever decided to study acting, she'd be the scariest of the four. "Sure," Leigh agreed. "I'll pick you up at twelve fifteen."

Shortly after one o'clock, Leigh, Allison, and Randall arrived at the clinic. Lenna had been left with her mother at the Koslow house, pouting at the prospect of being drafted into yet another happy afternoon of cleaning imaginary dirt, and the mood of the family had been somber. No one liked being laid up, having one's home broken into, and then being stolen from. More surprising was that everyone, including Frances, truly seemed to miss the bird.

"I'll check the mail, Mom," Allison offered, flitting off the second they had Randall settled on his stool. His first patient of the day — another emergency visit — was already waiting for him.

Leigh looked across the exam table at a man who was about her own age, but for whom time had apparently frozen in the seventies. He wore a tie-dyed tee shirt, wide-bottomed jeans that dragged the floor, and grungy sandals. His long, graying brown hair was gathered into a thin pony tail, and the glasses perched on his head had giant round lenses framed with tortoiseshell plastic. He reeked of cigarette smoke.

"Hello there, Leonard," Dr. Koslow said pleasantly. "What seems to be the problem?"

Leonard gave a sad grimace, then reached his arm into the carrier on the table. "Come on, Bartie bird," he called with a clucking sound. "Come on, boy."

The bird that stepped onto his hand was one of the most pathetic Leigh had ever seen. It was a cockatoo, and it should have looked very much like the magnificent Zeus that Olan had brought in yesterday. Instead, it looked like a caricature. Its head was snowy white, with a spiky bright yellow crest. But from the neck down, its bumpy pink skin was totally naked, without a single feather. Worse, in the center of its chest was an angry open wound.

"I hate to admit failure, Doc," Leonard said sadly. "But I swear, I don't know what else to do for him. Every collar we've tried drives him absolutely crazy. He obsesses about getting it off, won't eat, bangs his head around till I'm afraid he'll give himself a brain injury. But without the collar, there's just no stopping him from plucking. I've tried every combination of on-time and off-time, and it just doesn't matter. He won't eat till it's off and then he'll start plucking even while he's eating."

Dr. Koslow sighed. "I know how hard you've worked with him Leonard," he said sympathetically.

"Every enrichment I can think of," the man lamented. "Everything that's worked with the others. Toys, physical therapy, bird companions, no bird companions. One-on-one attention... I even hired a pet sitter during the day so he'd never be alone at the house. I've asked around online, and there's only one thing that keeps coming up that might help him, and I can't give it to him."

Dr. Koslow nodded. "Flight."

Leonard blew out a breath and nodded. "My house just isn't big enough, even if he did have the feathers for it. I've got him on the waiting list for an outdoor sanctuary in southern Florida — they've had decent luck with some tough cases." His voice suddenly cracked. "But now that he's opened up that wound again, I'm afraid he won't last long enough to get there!"

Allison rematerialized in the room. Leigh looked down and noticed that she was holding three more envelopes.

"Don't feel bad, Leonard," Randall assured. "You've done absolutely everything you could for him."

Leigh watched sadly as the wannabe hippie lifted his free arm to wipe a tear onto his shirt sleeve.

"There has to be something else," Leonard whispered hoarsely. "I can't just let him die." The cockatoo squawked. Then it bent down its dark beak and nipped at Leonard's hand.

Leonard didn't flinch. He just kept sniffling.

"Allison," Randall said calmly. "Would you go get Morgan? We need to get this wound cleaned up."

Allison nodded and disappeared. Leigh was about to disappear herself when an unexpected sound stopped her cold.

Leonard coughed. A long, drawn-out, hacking cough. A smoker's cough.

It sounded eerily familiar.

"I've been thinking, Doc," Leonard said when he could breathe again. "I know Bart's a long way from flying right now. But... do you think being outside in an aviary could make a difference? Because if you do, I'll... well, I'll call Skippy. We've had our problems in the past, as you know. But if being at her place could help him..."

Leonard's uneven voice trailed off, and Randall nodded. "I think it's worth a shot, yes," the veterinarian answered.

Morgan appeared and slipped behind Leonard to take hold of the bird. "Oh, poor baby!" she cooed. Her pretty nose wrinkled a bit, and her dark eyes narrowed at Leonard. "You *smoke* around him?" she asked disbelievingly.

Leonard bristled. Randall's shoulders slumped with a sigh.

"I do *not* smoke around any of my birds!" Leonard retorted hotly. "I always go outside!"

"They can still smell it," Morgan lectured, swooping up the bird like a pro. She held him out, chest nicely exposed, for Randall's attention. "Bird lungs can be very sensitive, you know. You shouldn't be doing it either. Have you heard that smoking causes cancer?"

The admonishing look that Randall shot at Morgan was stern enough to make Leigh cringe, but Morgan was oblivious. Leonard tried to respond, but succeeded only in bringing on another round of coughing.

Morgan rolled her eyes at him.

Hack, wheeze, hack. Hack hack hack…

Leigh's mind flew back to the night before last. A dark house. No one in sight…

She couldn't swear that the sound was *exactly* the same. But it was amazingly close.

She realized that Allison was at her side, watching her carefully. The look in the girl's eyes showed she had guessed what her mother was thinking.

Leigh took another look at the slim, forty-something man in front of her. If he wore a hoodie that hid his hair… was it possible?

Her brain replayed the brief glimpse she'd gotten of the intruder as he hung over the window ledge, but there were no clues to draw from, no detail. She had seen light skin on his hands — that was all. As for body frame, yes, it was possible. This man was average height, with relatively narrow shoulders. She had assumed the figure to be a younger man, or a woman, but…

"What do you do for a living, Leonard?" Leigh asked pleasantly.

It was a non sequitur, but Leonard appeared to welcome the distraction, even though he probably didn't know who Leigh was or why she was standing there.

"I'm a professor," he answered. "At Carnegie Mellon."

Leigh tried not to look as shocked as she felt. She would have guessed he was a zookeeper. Or the owner of a kitschy vegan restaurant. Or perhaps on lifetime disability for some nonobvious malady. But a professor? "What do you teach?" she asked.

"Biological anthropology."

Leigh was no longer surprised.

Leonard coughed again.

"Mom?" Allison said quietly, tugging on her shirt. "Can I talk to you a minute?"

Leigh registered her daughter's words only with a lag. Her brain was still replaying the cough. She wasn't imagining it. The pitch was a little different, maybe, but it was the same rasp, the same cadence...

She snapped back to alertness and followed Allison out of the exam room and around the corner to the treatment area. "What is it?"

Allison frowned at her. "You know what. You think it was him who broke into Grandma and Grandpa's, don't you? You recognize his cough! I can see it in your face. Shouldn't we call the police? Or at least Aunt Mo?"

Leigh shook her head. "His cough does sound like the one I heard, but that's hardly any reason to sic the police on him. We have no proof of anything, and he's a client. Besides, he's fully employed and obviously knows how attached people get to their animals. What motivation would he have for causing so much heartache and risking his own arrest?"

Allison's small forehead furrowed with thought. "I don't know. But I still think we should call Aunt Mo."

Leigh struggled with her own battling inclinations. Hearing the same cough was downright spooky, but it was only a cough — she could never be certain to the point of testifying. Still, it was worth checking the man out, wasn't it? "Maura's already coming, remember? She should be meeting us here any minute."

"Oh, right," Allison said with embarrassment.

The door from the surgery opened and Kirsten's fluffy blond head appeared. "Hi, Allison! Hello, Mrs. Harmon!" the girl said sweetly, bouncing by them to look around the corner toward the exam rooms. "Ooh!" she exclaimed. "It's the bird professor. Does he have that pretty macaw?"

Allison's scowl was so pronounced Leigh almost laughed out loud.

"No," Allison said shortly.

"Does your cousin really live on a farm in the North Hills?" Kirsten continued. "With a pond and a log cabin and everything?" Her vacuous blue eyes were wide, as wide as they could appear with so much mascara weighing down her lids. The teen hadn't been wearing nearly so much makeup yesterday, Leigh noted.

"Yes," Allison snipped.

"That is so cool!" Kirsten enthused. When Allison made no further response, Kirsten moved toward the exam rooms again. "Well, I'm going to go see the pretty macaw!" she said with a smile.

"Nice to see you again, Mrs. Harmon."

Allison made a low, grumbling noise.

"Hey, everybody!" a husky voice boomed from the waiting room.

Leigh and Allison hurried in its direction, and found themselves surprised. Maura's presence in a small room always had its effects, but usually they were positive. Today the policewoman seemed to usher in a chill. The waiting clients sat as tense as drums, even as they smiled at the dour-looking infant protruding from Maura's chest. With petnapping on their minds, they probably wondered if the detective's appearance at the clinic meant something sinister had happened. Leigh had disturbing visions of the false rumors that could be generated. *A patient must have been snatched from the clinic! Whatever you do, don't leave your pets there!*

"Hey," Leigh called out in her most cheerful tone, gesturing for Maura to come on back. "It's about time you got here. I'm starving. How's Eddie?"

The baby turned his head toward Leigh, looked her up and down, and started to cry.

Maura sighed. "Good going, Koslow."

Leigh's shoulders slumped. "What did I do?"

Mrs. Gregg, who sat by the reception desk without her Maine Coon today, chuckled warmly. "Oh, the poor little tyke," she cooed. "So many new faces! My Jonathan always cried when strangers talked to him."

Leigh fought the urge to argue that she was hardly a stranger. Why advertise the fact that your best friend's baby couldn't stand you?

The door to the far exam room opened, and Leonard appeared with his carrier in hand.

"My man!" Maura called happily, stepping over to extend her hand.

Leonard looked up with a smile and offered his own free hand for a fist bump. "SuperCop!" he replied, only afterwards seeming to notice they had an audience. His smile disappeared as he looked around the room, but upon noticing the baby, he brightened up again. "So here's the new arrival!" he exclaimed, bending down for a closer look.

The baby smiled back at him.

Leigh sighed. Allison giggled.

"I'd say that what's new with me is pretty obvious," Maura chatted. "What's new with you?"

Leonard straightened and turned his attention to the reception desk. "Aw, you know. Same old, same old."

Leigh watched the exchange with curiosity. She didn't realize that Leonard and Maura knew each other; then again, she didn't know Leonard at all. But the policewoman and the professor gave the impression of being old friends.

"Well, I'll let you get back to it," Maura said finally, turning back toward Leigh and Allison and following them out of the waiting room. "Take care, dude!" she called over her shoulder.

The women didn't speak until they had made their way downstairs to Randall's office. Unfortunately, there was no more privacy to be had downstairs. Ethan and Mathias were busily stacking piles of newspapers while Jared pushed a broom, and Paige was attending to a Yorkie that had chewed its bandage off.

Leigh lifted her hands helplessly. "Isn't there anywhere you can talk in this place without being overheard?"

Allison shook her head.

Leigh figured the girl should know. "Let's go outside."

Chapter 15

The women walked up the street a bit and leaned against Leigh's van. "How do you know Leonard?" Leigh asked.

Maura seemed surprised. "We went to school together. He's an Avalon boy."

Leigh explained about the familiar coughing sound. "So I guess you think I'm crazy and that there's no way he could be our petnapper?"

"Well now," Maura said with a smile. "Those are two separate issues. But no, I can't see Leonard risking everything for a few extra bucks. It's not his style; he's too much of a softie. It would take some pretty extraordinary circumstances to make him do something that desperate."

"Aunt Mo?" Allison said plaintively, holding out the handful of letters. Leigh suspected the child was about to burst with curiosity.

"Right," Maura agreed. "Just to be on the safe side..." she dug into the bag slung over her shoulder and produced a pair of gloves and a paper sack. Leigh opened the van and the detective set up a field lab in the back seat. She opened the first envelope and held out a single square of notepaper with block handwriting in blue ink.

> CATCH HIM! Saw his back running off – skinny guy in hoodie.

"That's not much to go on," Allison said disparagingly.

Maura opened another. This note was longer, and produced by a computer printer.

> I'm afraid to go to police but this [expletive] grabbed my cat out of the backyard and made me pay $500 to get him back! Wanted money in can behind elementary school. I heard some woman in Ben Avon had to pay two grand for her dog, but that's all I know. The [expletive expletive]!

"The amounts vary a lot, don't they?" Leigh noted. "They asked $300 for Lucky, but Skippy told me she'd heard rumors of thousands, too."

"Rumors are likely to be exaggerated," Maura commented. "However, the differences are interesting." She thought a moment. "I wonder what the perp is basing his demands on." She opened up the third envelope. This one was handwritten in flowing cursive on flowered stationery.

> I am sorry that I am not brave enough to go to the police. But I almost lost my mind when my precious baby was in the hands of that maniac. I had to take out a second mortgage to get her back – but it was worth it! Please, please, stop him soon!

Leigh sighed. She could only assume that the author was so upset she didn't realize she had offered no helpful information whatsoever. Letter number four was no better. In fact, it was a whole lot worse.

> I heard the clinic was asking for tips. Which is pretty ironic, since you're obviously the ones doing it! I doubt you'll let the police see this, so I'm going to write them too. I mean, who else knows all this stuff? You have all the information on everybody and you know who has money. Shame on you all!

The three exchanged worried glances. "I have to admit, there's some sense to that," Leigh said miserably. "If my dad wanted to make out a hit list, based on who had money and who was most likely to pay up, he would certainly know."

"Sure he would, but people *trust* Grandpa," Allison said loyally.

Little Eddie made a grab at the letter, but Maura pulled it away and dropped it into the sack. "One more."

> They haven't hit us yet, but we're keeping ours locked up. Heard about a dog and a cat stolen but both came back okay. The cat cost $500 but they wanted $1500 for the dog! I heard somebody saw a guy with a ponytail running away from their house. That's all I know. Don't know who got taken exactly, sorry. Nobody wants to say because I guess the ransom notes say that if you tell anybody they'll come back and kill them! I probably wouldn't say anything either if it was me.

A guy with a ponytail. Leigh cast a questioning glance at Maura.

The detective sighed. "A lot of men wear their hair in a ponytail, you know. As well as a lot of women who could be mistaken for men in the dark. Never mind how vague the reference is in the first place."

"I recognized his cough," Leigh said heavily. "I wasn't even thinking about it at the time, but the similarity was so striking it hit me out of the blue."

Maura studied her friend's face. Then she held up her hands. "Fine," she conceded with a sigh. "Let's go pay the professor a friendly little visit. At home."

After a complicated interval of fetching and installing Eddie's car seat in the van and laboriously securing him into it, the foursome took a relatively short ride before beginning the reverse process of getting Eddie back out and into his front pack again. "Are you sure Allison should be here?" Leigh fretted when they at last stepped out onto the sidewalk.

Maura frowned at her. "Koslow, I've known Lenny since we were six years old. If I thought he was in the slightest bit dangerous, do you think I'd be bringing Eddie? I'm only doing this to humor you." She led the way up the front steps of the modest brick foursquare house, which was just over the borough line from Avalon into Bellevue. Even from the street, they could hear birds squawking.

"Has he always been into birds?" Leigh asked.

Maura shrugged. "I didn't know he was into them at all. I usually just run into him at the store or something — I've never been to his house. At least not this one. His folks used to live over on Orchard."

She rang the bell. There was no porch beyond the steps, so Leigh and Allison stood behind her.

Leigh breathed a sigh of relief when the door started to open. Leonard had left the clinic right before they did, and they were hoping he had taken the bird straight home. She wanted to get this over with.

Leonard opened the door just wide enough to peer through the crack. His eyes widened with panic. "Maura?" he said with a gulp.

"Hey again," the policewoman said cheerfully, ignoring his odd behavior. "Listen, can we come in a minute?"

Leonard's frightened gaze darted from Maura to Leigh and

Allison. Then he stuck his head out a little further and looked up and down the block. "Get in quick, then!" he ordered, flinging the door open and practically pulling Maura in by the arm. "Quick! Quick!"

"Okay, okay," Maura said easily. "Chillax, dude! What's the hurry?"

Leigh and Allison filed in quickly also, and after another furtive glance up and down the street, Leonard shut the door behind them. They were standing in a bizarre sort of foyer, the walls of which were entirely formed by beaded curtains.

"I'm sorry," he apologized meekly, pulling aside the colorful beads and gesturing them into the main part of the living room. "Come in, please."

Leigh half expected to see hookah pipes and silk cushions on the floor. Instead she walked into an indoor aviary. Finches and budgies were everywhere, flying from perch to perch, alighting on the sparse furniture, picking through the food that was laid out at several stations around the room, and making a cacophony of clucking, cheeping, and whistling noises.

"Geez, Len," Maura exclaimed, her hands carefully poised to protect little Eddie's exposed head. "I'm guessing you're not into Hitchcock films, are you?"

Leonard was not amused. "Why did you have to come to the house?" he demanded, his hands wringing nervously. "What if somebody saw you?"

Maura's smile faded as she studied him. A green budgie landed on his shoulder.

"Um," Leigh said uncertainly. "We're sorry to intrude, but I found this after you left." She extended the leather glass case that had been in Randall's junk drawer at the clinic since the nineties. A gift from a previous client, it had the image of a macaw burned into it along with the word *Mexico*. Randall had always found it cheesy. "Any chance it might be yours?" she asked innocently.

Leonard stared at the case a moment, his eyes wide. Then he shook his head vigorously. "No, it's not mine." He threw another glance at Maura, then practically crumpled onto the back of his couch, displacing two zebra finches and a pied cockatiel. The man's relief at learning the presumed point of their visit was obvious. Also obvious was the fact that he was scared to death.

Maura stepped over and leaned against the couch back next to him. Baby Eddie was fascinated by the fluttering, colorful animals, and he cooed joyfully while reaching out for any bird he perceived to be within reach. Maura made certain, however, that none were.

"Len," she said warmly. "I didn't mean to scare you. But now that we're here… is there anything you'd like to tell me?"

Leonard shook his head. His weathered face was lined with misery. "No," he said softly. "No, I don't think… that's best."

Then man looked so truly wretched that Leigh began to feel sorry for him. But then he coughed again.

Hack, wheeze, hack. Hack hack hack!

Leigh sucked in a sharp breath and looked meaningfully at Maura. *I'm telling you*, she telepathed. *It was him!*

Slowly and surreptitiously, Allison was moving around to peer into the kitchen and dining room areas that connected with the living room. Leigh figured her daughter must also have seen the pied cockatiel. And wondered…

"Well, you see," Maura said conversationally, scooting over to pull Eddie out of range of a spotted finch. "You're making a problem for me, here. Because we both know that I'm a better detective than you are an actor. Remember that Valley Forge play in the third grade? You totally sucked, man. So I know you're afraid of something. And you should probably just go ahead and spill it."

A hint of a smile played at the corners of Leonard's mouth, but only for a second. Then he looked miserable again.

"How did you know?" he whispered hoarsely, ignoring the two budgies currently scuffling over the space on top of his head. "How did you know to ask me? I didn't say anything!"

Leigh opened her mouth, but Maura threw her a quick warning look.

"Say anything about what, Len? Just tell me. If anybody saw me outside, they've already seen me. You know what I'm saying?"

The professor dropped his face into his hands. "But I can't risk it! I can't lose him again. I raised him from an egg!"

Leigh blinked in confusion. She cast a glance at Allison, who had finished her sweep of the room and returned with a blue budgie on her finger. She gave a slight shake of her head. *Our cockatiel's not here, Mom.*

"Tell me what you mean, Len," Maura repeated patiently.

Leonard was silent for a long moment, evidently contemplating his options. Then, stiffly, he rose. "Come on upstairs," he said with defeat. "I'll show you."

He headed toward another curtain of beads, then pulled them aside to reveal a narrow staircase. He headed up with Maura following, but Leigh hung back a few paces. At the top of the staircase he opened another door, only to have an Amazon alight immediately on his shoulder. "Welcome to South America," he announced. "The cockatoos are in the smaller room that way. I call it 'upper Australia.'"

Leigh's curiosity got the better of her. She climbed the remaining stairs and slipped through the door also, followed closely by Allison. A large, open area that was supposed to be a bedroom contained two free-flying Amazons and a blue and gold macaw, plus a second macaw in a huge cage that took up one corner of the room and a dormer window. "Casper and Goldie don't get along," Leonard explained sadly. "They have to alternate."

"Geez, Len," Maura exclaimed, looking through the myriad bird perches and toys to the sparse human furniture, which consisted of a leather couch and chair. "Where do you sleep?"

He pointed to a short, closed door along the far wall. "In the closet," he admitted sheepishly. "It's the only way I ever get any peace. But what I want to show you is in the bathroom."

Leigh looked over her shoulder to note the quickest exit.

"The bathroom's kind of like an isolation unit," Leonard explained. "Right now the bird in it is… recovering."

"Which bird is that?" Allison piped up.

Leonard opened the bathroom door and gestured them inside.

Leigh looked around. It was an unexpectedly large bathroom, completely covered with white tiles, which weren't nearly as dirty as she might have expected. In fact, considering the number of birds in the house, she had to admit that Leonard did a reasonable job of keeping the place clean. At least he had the sense not to have carpet.

"Opie, boy!" Leonard called. "Come on out! Everybody's a friend, here." He turned to whisper to Maura. "He's still pretty traumatized, I'm afraid."

Leigh watched, breath held, as a white and yellow lutino cockatiel strutted out from behind the toilet and fluttered up to perch on Leonard's hand. "That's my boy," the man cooed affectionately.

The bird cooed back.

Leigh heard Allison's sharp intake of breath beside her. The bird had a dime-sized patch of bare skin in the center of its chest.

Tears formed in Leonard's eyes. "It was so nice outside last weekend. He always enjoys a little time out back. I swear I checked on him every couple of minutes. But one time I looked out, and he was just—" he choked on the words. "*Gone*. Cage and all!"

Maura looked sideways at Leigh, then Allison. Both nodded silently.

"Are you saying this bird was petnapped, Leonard?" Maura asked.

He sniffed and nodded.

Leigh's anxiety grew. It was a nice story, and he was very convincing. But it made no sense. If the bird was his, why was he stealing it from her parents' house? How he could even know it was there? He *had* to be lying!

Leigh stared hard at Maura. They needed to get out of here, before the man started flipping out at a whole new level. However Maura wanted to handle the police part was her problem. But they could all worry about that later. Much later.

She turned to open the bathroom door, but a sound from the hallway outside stopped her.

Hack, wheeze, hack. Hack hack hack!

Her blood ran cold. She whipped around to see Leonard standing quietly in the same place he was before, with the cockatiel still perched on his hand.

He laughed out loud.

Chapter 16

Leigh stared at him, wide-eyed.

"What's so funny, Leonard?" Maura asked calmly.

"The expression on her face!" he chuckled, gesturing toward Leigh. "They do a pretty good job, don't they? That was Ricky you heard, although he's not the only one that does it. It's kind of embarrassing, actually. But they do hear it a lot."

Leigh and Allison exchanged a glance. *The birds?*

As if on cue, Opie sat up straight, puffed up his partially plucked chest, and let loose. *Hack, wheeze, hack. Hack hack hack!*

Leonard exploded into laughter. "He does it better than any of them! Don't you, precious?"

Leigh felt the need to sit down. But the only available surface was the closed toilet lid, and it was speckled with bird poop.

"It was the bird!" Allison breathed, stating a larger truth than was obvious to Leonard.

"Oh, yes," he said proudly. "They're wonderful mimics. Everyone knows that parrots can do it. But cockatiels can do a good job with sounds, too, even if they aren't as skilled at talking."

"But they only do it when they're feeling good," Allison suggested tentatively. "When they're comfortable. Right?"

"That's right," Leonard confirmed.

Maura's sharp eyes connected with Allison's. *Don't say anything else*, the policewoman transmitted.

Allison's return nod was barely perceptible.

"When exactly did the bird disappear, Len?" Maura asked.

His face paled again. "Friday night. There was a note left where the cage had been. It said if I told anybody, they'd kill him!" He gulped. "They wanted three thousand dollars, set out Saturday night at midnight in the park. I got it, and I left it. I expected Opie back the next day, but nothing happened. I hoped maybe that it was just hard to get him back without being seen. You know, with people out in the neighborhood over the weekend. I hoped I would get him Monday. But there was nothing!"

"Why didn't you call the cops? Or me?" Maura asked, sounding slightly hurt.

"The note said they'd kill him!" Leonard defended. "It said that if I told the police even *after* the bird came back, that they'd come find him again — or another bird of mine — and 'wring its skinny little neck!'" He hung his head a moment. "I know I should have. But I just couldn't. This guy means everything to me." He put up his other hand and nuzzled the back of the cockatiel's neck with a fingertip. "Don't you, Opie sweet?"

Maura cleared her throat. "When did you get him back, Len?"

"Not until this morning," he answered gravely. "I looked outside first thing, and there he was. The cage was hanging right where I'd left it. Every day he wasn't returned I worried that something had gone wrong, that maybe he'd gotten away from them somehow... or worse. But I kept telling myself I'd give them just one more day, and *then* I would tell the police everything. Every day I kept hoping for a miracle. And finally, it happened!"

Leigh watched as the cockatiel closed its eyes and leaned into the curve of Leonard's stroking finger. The bird purred happily.

There really was no doubt about it. The cockatiel they had all been pet sitting since Monday was definitely Leonard's bird. Which didn't make Leonard a suspect. It made him another victim.

"Three thousand dollars is a lot of money," Maura said soberly.

Leigh knew what she was thinking. Leonard lived in a modest house in a modest neighborhood with a whole lot of birds. To ask for so much, the petnapper must have known not only that Leonard was emotionally attached to his birds in general, but that he felt strongly about this cockatiel in particular. *And* that he could actually afford such a ransom. Otherwise, the risk of his turning to the police would be too great.

"It was worth it," Leonard insisted, still caressing the happy bird. A tear slid down his cheek. "He missed me, I think."

"I'm sure he did," Leigh agreed sincerely.

Leonard straightened and turned to Maura. "I can't lose him again," he said firmly. "If I cooperate with the police, can you promise me I won't?"

"I'm not God, Len," Maura replied. "But we'll certainly do our best to be discreet. Do you have the ransom note?"

He shook his head. "They wanted it left with the money. But I took a picture of it on my phone."

Maura smiled. "Good work. Can you send it to me?" She pulled a card out of her wallet and gave it to him. "I'll need to explain the situation to the local PDs. There's a couple different jurisdictions involved. But I'll make sure no black and whites come to your house. You can meet the officers elsewhere, if you like. But with your help, maybe we can finally get this guy."

Leonard's answering smile was uneasy. "I hope so."

The ride back to the animal hospital was a quiet one. Leigh was absorbed in her own not-so-pleasant thoughts, and Maura seemed equally contemplative. No one spoke until the van was parked on the street outside the clinic. "You should go back and help Grandpa the rest of the afternoon like we planned, Allison," Leigh advised.

Allison unbuckled her seatbelt, but rather than getting out, she leaned forward between the front seats. "Whoever wrote that one tip letter has a point, you know," she said evenly. "So far the petnapper has a pretty amazing record of targeting owners who care about their pets, who have the money to pay him, and who won't go to the police. Anybody who works at the clinic would know that stuff. *If* they pay attention."

Maura looked at Leigh and nodded. "She's right, Koslow. To look at Lenny or his house, you'd never guess he was a professor at CMU who could come up three grand over a weekend. Ginny cares as much about Lucky as Len does about Opie, but she's been living on social security for years. Three hundred was the most anyone could possibly squeeze out of her. If they asked for too much, she'd have no choice but to go to the police. Our petnapper knew that."

"Even I could come up with a list of good targets, and I'm only there every once in a while," Allison added.

"You wouldn't have to work at the clinic to know those things," Leigh protested, still not wanting to believe that any of her father's current employees could be so secretly cruel. She turned to Maura. "You knew both our victims so far, didn't you? And their circumstances?"

Maura tilted her head from side to side. "Maybe. But I didn't know Len was so gaga about birds."

"I did," Allison insisted. "And I knew he was a professor. I didn't know he was especially attached to the cockatiel, but if I worked down there all the time, I bet I would. He comes in a lot. All the bird people do. All the most devoted clients do!"

Leigh groaned beneath her breath. She really, *really* did not want an employee of the clinic to be involved. What a terrible situation for her father!

"If we are dealing with a petnapper inside the clinic," Maura theorized, "or even just an informant feeding information to somebody else, they'll certainly be aware by now that you and I are looking into it."

Leigh groaned again, this time audibly. The back door of the van opened. Allison was getting out.

Leigh felt a sudden flare of panic. "Allison, wait," she warned. She turned to Maura. "If this person knows we're on to them, should she even be going in there? What about the boys?"

"Who says the perp knows we're on to *them?*" Maura reasoned. "All they know is that you're aware of the petnappings and are trying to get information from clients. If we're lucky, that alone will make them think a little harder before trying it again. But they have no reason to think we suspect anybody inside the clinic. Not yet, anyway. The best thing to do would be to carry on as normal. Wouldn't it look more strange if Allison *stopped* helping your dad now?"

"I suppose so," Leigh grumbled.

"Mom," Allison drawled with typical preteen exasperation, "I'll be fine. I am *not* going to make anybody suspicious of me. They'll never even know I'm listening. You never do."

Maura chuckled.

Leigh frowned. "I'll pick you up at five."

Allison smiled and skipped on into the building, now looking every bit of six years old.

"That child will put me in an early grave," Leigh lamented.

"Well, what are kids for?" Maura quipped, taking a quick look at Eddie in the back seat. He was kicking his tiny legs and drooling on the terry cloth strap covers of the car seat. She smiled indulgently.

Then she turned back to Leigh, and her expression sobered. "I didn't want to say this in front of Allison," she said heavily. "But you do realize that we now have evidence that Mason Dublin handed off stolen property?"

Leigh felt her chest constrict. The thought had been there, at the back of her mind, ever since she'd seen the familiar cockatiel fly onto Leonard's hand. But she hadn't wanted to face it. "He didn't know," she defended. "I'm sure he didn't. He told me himself, that morning, that he didn't know where the bird had come from. That he'd never seen it before."

"That's good to hear," Maura replied. "That's what he told me on the phone, too. But it doesn't change the facts. Kyle had a stolen bird in his apartment. For all we know, the cat could have been stolen, too."

Leigh's angst ratcheted up another notch. *Crap.* "Lenna is head over heels in love with that cat already!" she opined. "I was already dreading having to return it to Kyle. Surely she's not stolen. Mason said that Kyle was crazy about the cat. He must have had it for a while!"

Maura raised one eyebrow. "And of course we have *no reason* to doubt anything that Kyle might say about the pets in his possession."

Leigh sighed.

"We already know Kyle needed money," Maura continued. "Can you think of any link he might have to the clinic, besides Mason?"

Leigh shook her head firmly. "Mason has nothing to do with the clinic. He and my dad get along okay, but they've never been buddies, and Mason avoids my mother like the plague. Up until a few weeks ago, he lived in Jennerstown! As for Kyle Claymore, I'd never heard the name before all this started. Living in Bellevue, he could be a client, but I don't know. You'd have to ask my dad."

"I suspect the police will do just that," Maura said thoughtfully. "But under the circumstances, I'll see if I can get them to interview him at home, rather than at the clinic." She cleared her throat. "As for Mason, he told me he'd likely be rolling back into town sometime tomorrow. For his sake, I hope he does."

Leigh felt slightly sick again. "I mean it, Maura," she repeated. "I really don't think Mason had any idea that the bird was stolen. I know he's an ex-con, but he's got a good heart. He wouldn't have anything to do with a petnapping ring. I know he wouldn't."

Maura's baby blue eyes shone with sympathy. "If it makes you feel any better, Koslow, I don't think he had anything to do with it, either."

Leigh exhaled with relief.

"But it's not my call," Maura added ominously. In the backseat, Baby Eddie squalled. "Nap time," she announced. "Would you mind running us home?"

Leigh dropped off Maura and the baby at their house, her thoughts drifting in an unpleasant fog as she drove away. She *did* believe in Mason's innocence. But that didn't mean he wasn't in trouble. And trouble, for an ex-con, always came with a capital T.

Without conscious thought as to where she was going, Leigh found herself parked back outside the animal clinic. The phenomenon was an oft-rehearsed one. From the day she had gotten her first driver's license, her father's clinic had been her port in a storm.

She got out of the van and walked inside.

Chapter 17

Leigh went in the back door of the clinic and waited outside the exam rooms for a chance to catch her father alone. When she saw Allison head out of the room to fetch something, she scooted inside and found a chow and its owner just leaving.

"Dad," she asked swiftly. "Important question. Do you remember a patient that's a youngish shorthair cat, dilute tortie, with its left front leg amputated?"

Only after she asked the question did she notice that her father was standing up on one leg, leaning against the table. He looked tired and a little pale.

"Dad!" she chastised. "You're supposed to be keeping that foot elevated."

Randall exhaled loudly. "I know, I know. I just get so tired of sitting all the time."

"Sorry," Leigh said genuinely. It would be a tough couple weeks for Randall, who was used to working long hours in his veterinary domain, then escaping to his basement workshop at home to putter. Enforced rest and excessive togetherness with an equally incapacitated Frances would surely take their toll. Leigh resolved to take him out for a long drive over the weekend.

"To answer your question," Randall replied, "no. I can only think of two feline amputees that are living now. One's a Persian that had cancer and the other is a black shorthair that got run over by an ATV. But as I told Allison, one of the other vets could have seen the cat."

"Allison?" Leigh asked. "When did she ask you about it?"

"A couple days ago."

Of course she had. Most likely Allison had also already asked the other vets about Peep, *and* checked the computer to see if Kyle Claymore was in the client database.

Paige entered from the waiting room leading an older woman who carried a geriatric dachshund wrapped in a blanket. Leigh nodded a farewell to her father and scooted out the other exit, just passing Allison as the girl hurried back to the exam rooms with a new box of syringes. Leigh walked down the stairs, hoping to find some relative quiet in her father's office. She passed by the refrigerator and nearly tripped over a pair of legs sticking out in the floor beside it. "Ethan?"

The boy sat up. He had been wiping down the side of the fridge with a rag. Leigh smiled to herself. "Jared getting near the end of his list, huh?"

Ethan rolled his eyes. "I hope so. Jared's a nice guy, but geez. He's as bad a clean freak as Grandma!"

Leigh chuckled. That was a strong statement, indeed. "What's Matt doing?"

"Wiping out the bottom of the freezer," Ethan answered. Then his face soured. "Man, is he in a mood."

"What happened?"

Ethan's eyes rolled again. He lowered his voice to a whisper. "*Kirsten*, of course. Her boyfriend picked her up. *In a car.*"

"Ouch," Leigh agreed, feeling her nephew's pain. With good looks and a rich family to his credit, Mathias was ultimately unlikely to suffer much in the romance department. But there was only so much a guy straight out of the eighth grade could do when his competition had a driver's license.

"Carry on," she advised, moving into Randall's office. She plopped down in her father's chair and closed her eyes. *Kyle Claymore.* He lived in an apartment in Bellevue and played professional poker. She got the impression from Mason that he was young, maybe in his twenties. She'd had the same impression of the guy who broke in the kitchen window. Mason said he was in financial straits, perfect motive for moonlighting as a petnapper. But how had he known that the cockatiel was at her parents' house? Mason hadn't even known.

Kyle had to have some connection to the clinic. Most likely, a willing accomplice.

Leigh went over the payroll in her mind, starting at the top. Her father's two associate veterinarians, Dr. McCoy and Dr. Stallions, were above suspicion. Both women had been with her father for over a decade, and both were in their forties and married. She also ruled out Jeanine, who had been with Randall since the dinosaurs roamed. Nora, the other longtime technician, was also above suspicion, even if she hadn't been on vacation the last week. And of course Jared was innocent. He was far too honest to cooperate with such a scheme willingly, and anyone trying to pry information out of him by trickery was doomed to disappointment. Jared had the importance of privacy drilled into him at an early age by his overprotective little sister Nicki, and any question he deemed the slightest bit suspect was met with a firm and mechanical, "I've got nothing to say about that."

There hadn't been a business manager in house for months, and they were down one part-time receptionist as well. That left the two veterinary assistants, Paige and Morgan, and the full-time receptionist, Amy.

Leigh picked up a pencil and tapped it on a notepad. Paige was over thirty, but the other two appeared to be somewhere in their twenties. None of them were married; any of the three could be dating — or at least consorting with — the likes of Kyle Claymore. Paige had been with the clinic a few years, but the younger girls were both relatively new hires. Leigh could consider all the other youngish staff who had worked at the clinic at one time or other and still occasionally dropped by, but then she would lose her mind. There were far too many of them. Besides, whoever had told Kyle that the cockatiel was headed for Dr. Koslow's house in West View must have been in the clinic on Tuesday.

Even then, Leigh thought with frustration, as much as one lutino looked like another, how could they possibly be sure that the bird Leigh had brought in was the same bird Mason had taken from Kyle's place? Maybe the kids were talking about "Grandpa Mason" and were overheard. Or maybe someone recognized the cage.

A shiver slid down her spine. If that was the case, the informant wasn't just passing along random tidbits on clients and their proclivities unawares. They must have actually *seen* the stolen bird while it was in Kyle's possession.

Leigh set down the pencil and pulled over the keyboard and mouse of her father's ancient desk computer. She typed in his personal password (which had been the same for years), pulled up a search engine, and typed in Kyle Claymore's name. It was a relatively uncommon one, and she zoned in quickly on the most likely prospect.

Kyle Claymore had a Facebook page. Although it hadn't been updated in ages, some basic information was readily attainable. He had started community college in Butler County, but never finished his degree. He had played online poker all through his late teens and early twenties, and when that industry was shut down, he had moved into casinos. He was not into posting pictures of himself, but preferred screenshots of poker plays. He was a man of few words who would now be in his late twenties.

And other than the Facebook page, he had not left much of a footprint online. At least not under his real name.

Leigh pulled up the clinic software and ran a quick search on his name in the client database. There were no hits. She logged off the computer and began tapping with her pencil again.

Paige, Morgan, and Amy. Could it really be one of them?

It seemed unlikely. Yet she could not rule any of them out.

A tall, solidly built man with a full head of blond hair and bright blue eyes appeared in the doorway. "Hello, Leigh Koslow."

"Hello, Jared," Leigh responded.

"It's dirty in here, Leigh Koslow."

Leigh looked around. Now that he mentioned it, there was an unusually thick layer of dust over her father's office. She knew that Jared had been forbidden to touch Randall's files or disturb things on his desk, but surely he still cleaned around them?

"Dr. Koslow told me to leave this room alone, Leigh Koslow. I don't clean in here anymore."

Leigh considered the odd instruction, then smirked. Perhaps, with clean freaks constantly scouring both his home and his clinic, Randall had decided he needed one oasis of human normality. That explained the filthy files, anyway.

"Jared," Leigh inquired, changing the subject. "Have you heard anybody around here mentioning the name Kyle lately?"

"Yes, Leigh Koslow," he said immediately.

She straightened. "Who?"

"Allison and Mathias and Ethan."

She slumped back in her chair again. "Oh. Do you know anyone named Kyle?"

He blinked at her a moment. "I've got nothing to say about that."

Leigh sighed. "Thanks anyway, Jared."

He whirled on his heel and walked away. Leigh's eyes rested on the file cabinet where her father kept his personnel records. She knew she shouldn't, although that technicality had never stopped her before. Still, what good would it do? None of the unmarried women were going to list a significant other's name on their employment applications. Then again, they could list an emergency contact...

She rose from the chair and moved toward the cabinet, only to notice that the drawer in question was sticking out a little. She pulled on it. It was empty.

Frances.

Leigh's phone rang. She answered. "It's me," Cara's voice said apologetically. "Look, if you're home working, do *not* worry about this. But your mom really seems to want the contents of the bottom file drawer in your dad's office. She's muttering about 'organizational continuity' and she's gone absolutely bonkers with those color-coded folder labels she sent Aunt Bess out for—"

"No problem," Leigh resolved. "I'm in the office now, actually. I'll drop them by." *And maybe look at some of the others while I'm there?*

Leigh finished the call and looked around for a box to transport the contents of the bottom file drawer. The prospects had already been picked over, and she found nothing until she got to the freezer room in the back corner of the basement, where one limp, oversized box sat on top of the recyclable bin, waiting to be crushed. She grabbed it and left the room, opting not to speak to Mathias, who muttered darkly to himself as he wiped out the deep freeze.

Leigh loaded up the desired files, slipped out the basement door, and climbed the steps to the parking lot. Allison was there, waving as a car pulled away. It was the elderly woman who had brought in the dachshund, and Leigh assumed Allison had helped her to get her pet back into the car. Leigh studied her daughter thoughtfully.

"Allison," she asked quietly, setting down the box. "You don't happen to know whether Amy or Paige or Morgan are dating any mystery men that might be our friend Kyle, do you?"

Allison smiled smugly. She took a quick look around for listening ears. "Paige has been living with a guy named Steve for, like, years. Amy and Morgan don't have boyfriends, but Morgan goes out a lot." Her dark eyes sparkled with enthusiasm. "Anything else you want to know?"

Leigh's teeth gritted. "Have you found any link between Kyle and anybody at the clinic?"

Allison shook her head. "Not yet."

Leigh picked up the box again. She wasn't sure what to say. "Carry on" would be too permissive. But "be careful" was too... well, too *Frances*.

"I'll... uh, see you later," she said lamely. She drove the files back to her parents' house and parked in the street again. She was beginning to feel like she'd done nothing all week but drive in circles.

Probably because she hadn't. The few hours she had spent staring at real work from Hook, Inc., her advertising agency, had been next to worthless. Her mind was hopelessly distracted, and she was relieved that she had scheduled herself so lightly this week. Although she'd had no premonition of the current level of chaos, the prospect of Frances's bunion surgery alone had been daunting enough to plan for a mental health break.

She walked into her parents' living room to find her mother more deeply buried in paperwork than ever. The bed itself was now covered with stacks of files, as well as the card table and the floor. Each stack was aligned relative to the others with perfect symmetry, the labels making a pleasing spectrum of color.

"Oh goody!" Frances said delightedly, looking at the box in Leigh's arms. "Now everything will be complete!"

Leigh set the box down in front of her mother, and Frances rubbed her hands together. Leigh slowly backed away.

"I'm afraid to go back in there," she whispered to Cara when she reached the kitchen. "I'm afraid she'll start explaining what she's doing."

Cara smiled tiredly as she wiped down the spotless countertop. "Your fear is wise."

Leigh's phone made a siren sound. She looked down to see a terse, three-word text from Maura, asking for Leigh's location. She answered, but received no further response.

The exchange did not bode well.

Leigh looked up at her cousin, and her anxiety increased. Cara's normally peachy complexion seemed flushed. "Are you okay?"

"What?" Cara stared at her a moment, then shook her head. "Sorry. I guess I'm not feeling so great, actually." She paused a moment. "Mom finally got around to answering my texts."

Sensing an issue, Leigh dropped into a kitchen chair, and Cara immediately sank down beside her. "What's up?" Leigh asked.

Cara sighed. "I don't know. She hardly said anything. It seems like she's so busy — or preoccupied — that she can't be bothered."

Leigh remembered having the same impression when she'd answered the call from Lydie earlier in the week. She waited.

Cara sighed again. "I guess I'm just having trouble dealing with the fact that she doesn't trust me."

"Trust you?" Leigh repeated, confused.

"Well, why else would she insist on keeping her romantic life such a huge secret?" Cara whispered. "Does she really think I couldn't control myself from running off to tell Aunt Frances? Why can't she just be honest with me? Throughout my entire adult life I've kept asking her if she isn't lonely, if she doesn't miss having a significant other..." Cara's voice broke. Her face was etched with hurt. "She knows I'm not judgmental about... that sort of thing. So why can't she talk to me?"

"I don't know. I don't understand it, either," Leigh replied. But she did have a theory. "I bet it's not really about your reaction, or even my mom's, so much as how your mom feels about herself. You know the history — she went completely postal when Mason was running from the law, and the excuse she always gave for covering the whole thing up was that she said she didn't want you to suffer the stigma of being a criminal's daughter. But it was really about her overcompensating because she felt like she'd failed you as a mother."

Cara nodded. "I know that's probably the root of it. But her feeling like she has to be perfect all the time just to keep from disappointing *me* is so damn irritating."

Leigh smiled. "Yeah? Try having a mother who expects *you* to be perfect all the time."

Cara chuckled, even as her eyes glistened with moisture.

Leigh felt another wave of dread. She needed to tell both her mother and Cara that the cockatiel was home with its real owner and that all was well — at least from the bird's standpoint. But telling them that the bird had been petnapped originally would implicate Mason as an accessory, which would upset Cara all over again. Never mind subjecting her to Frances's predictable reaction.

An unpleasant noise from the second floor delayed the issue. "Lenna?" Cara said worriedly, rising. Leigh followed her cousin up the stairs to discover a miserable-looking Lenna hanging over the bathroom sink. The poor girl had been sick. And she was still sick.

"I told you I wasn't faking it, Mom," Lenna gasped.

Cara felt her daughter's forehead. "You're feverish."

Leigh stepped up and put her own hand on Cara's flushed forehead. "So are you," she announced. "I bet you've both caught that bug Gil brought home from Houston."

Cara nodded with unhappy acquiescence.

"Take Lenna home," Leigh instructed. "I'll stay here."

"But I was supposed to make dinner for everybody," Cara protested weakly.

"I'll manage," Leigh lied, wondering if her favorite Chinese place delivered this far south.

"The chicken is already in the marinade," Cara instructed, "and for the vegetables, all you have to do is —"

Cara looked like she was about to imitate her daughter.

"On second thought, just relax," Leigh ordered. "I'll call Gil to pick up the both of you."

A half hour later, Leigh waved goodbye as Gil's Lexus pulled away from the curb with two unhappy passengers holding plastic trash bags in their laps. Neither she nor Frances commented on the risk of the bug spreading any further in the family. Under the circumstances, it was too horrible to contemplate.

Before Leigh could close the front door, Maura's car pulled up into the space Gil's had just left. The policewoman unfolded her long legs from the too-small car and walked over.

"Where's Eddie?" Leigh questioned, her anxiety increasing.

"Asleep," Maura answered, reaching her. "Neighbor's watching him." Her eyes flickered toward the house, and Leigh let the half-open door swing shut. This wasn't good.

"What's happened?" Leigh whispered.

"It looks like we've been barking up the wrong tree," Maura said soberly. "It couldn't possibly have been Kyle Claymore who broke into this house last night."

"And why not?" Leigh asked.

"Because he's dead," Maura answered. "He was murdered four days ago."

Chapter 18

"Come on, kiddo," Bess said affectionately, putting a hand on Leigh's arm. "Let's go sit outside a minute and cool down. It's hot as Hades in here."

Leigh shut the dishwasher door and punched the start button, then looked over her shoulder at the crowd gathered around the kitchen table. Mathias had talked her parents into joining the kids in a game of Rage while Leigh and Bess cleaned up the dinner dishes. Everyone knew that Mathias was not so much interested in entertaining Randall and Frances as he was in avoiding going home to a sick mother and sister, but whatever his motivation, Leigh was glad. The group was laughing and having a good time, and she felt like anything but.

"Come on," Bess repeated, heading toward the front porch.

Leigh followed. She was feeling very kindly disposed toward her aunt at the moment. As soon as Cara reported her illness, Bess had come to Leigh's rescue, picking up the crew at the clinic, making dinner for everyone, and then offering to stay another night. "You have kids," Bess had insisted with a dismissive wave of her hand. "I only have the cats at home, and as much as I'd like to believe otherwise, the creatures are horridly self-sufficient. Ever since I got the automatic feeder they barely bother to yawn when I come home." Leigh doubted the truth of that statement, but hadn't argued. Since the cockatiel was no longer in residence at the Koslow house, Bess had brought her dog Chester along, which Leigh knew would be helpful on two counts. One, because Bess wouldn't feel guilty about the elderly Pekingese mix being alone so much, and two, because his profuse shedding would give all of Frances's caretakers something real to clean.

The women settled on the steps of the porch and found that the evening air was indeed cooler than the stuffy kitchen.

"What's bugging you, kiddo?" Bess asked. "And don't tell me nothing. You know how poor a liar you are, although Lord knows I've tried to train you better."

Leigh smiled sadly. Ever since Maura left, she had debated with herself over how much, when, and with whom she should share the disturbing new information. As yet, she had made no decision. She wanted the Pack out of the matter entirely, but since they were already in it, that was easier said than done. It was one thing for the children to muse about the identity of a local petnapper. Involving them in a state police investigation of the murder of two professional gamblers was another.

Maura's news had been grim. Kyle Claymore had been in attendance at an illegal poker game up in Erie County, along with several notable lowlifes, when their play was interrupted by accusations of cheating. Shots were fired, and a man was killed. Whether the original victim was the accuser or the accused was still unclear, but the theory of the state police was that Kyle, a relative unknown in the group, had witnessed the murder. He had most likely attempted to flee from the scene, but he had not gotten far. His car had been found abandoned in a ditch off an isolated road a few miles away, and his body was found in some nearby woods three days later.

It wasn't impossible that Kyle himself was responsible for the first murder. But for reasons Maura wouldn't get into, the state police didn't think so. The boy had owed some loan sharks somewhere a whole lot of money, and he was desperate to win some back. But he had been playing out of his league.

Leigh didn't even want to think about Mason's potential involvement. If he had done anything illegal — if he'd had anything at all to do with the murderous gamblers — the family would be devastated.

Leigh didn't know what to tell anyone. She wanted to discuss the issue with Warren, but tonight was the big closing dinner of his conference, and he wouldn't be home until late.

What to do?

"I miss my husband," Leigh said wistfully, answering Bess's almost forgotten question. "There's just so much going on. I'm thinking of pulling a Scarlet O'Hara and ignoring it all till tomorrow."

"Works for me," Bess said simply, stretching out her legs. "Lydie will be back tomorrow, and we'll all be delivered. I may fall prostrate and kiss her feet."

Leigh grinned, but her smile quickly faded. "Cara's upset. About her mother being so secretive… again. She feels like Lydie doesn't trust her."

"Hogswaddle," Bess said immediately. "It has nothing to do with trust. Lydie trusts me, and I don't have a clue what the hell she's up to." Bess pursed her lips thoughtfully. "But she's definitely up to something, I'm sure of that."

Leigh leaned in and lowered her voice still further. "Aunt Bess," she began uncertainly, "Cara and I were wondering… Do you think there's any chance that her friend Cynthia… I mean, that maybe Lydie and she…"

"Oh, no," Bess said sharply. "No, no, no."

"What?" Leigh argued. "You don't think it could happen in this family?"

Bess laughed out loud. "Oh, heavens, no. It isn't *that*. Why, your Great Aunt Myrtle was gay as a maypole. Lived with her 'friend Ruth' out in Sharpsburg for fifty-seven years. And don't you remember our cousin Byron? The one who moved to Florida?"

Leigh thought. "The musician?"

"He was a church organist."

"Oh."

Bess chuckled again. "Lydie likes men, kiddo. I'm quite sure of that."

"Then who the heck has she been seeing?" Leigh demanded.

"Damned if I know," Bess lamented. "She's always been miserably secretive, that one. After everything that went down with Mason, she felt so guilty it's like she chose to be a nun, just to punish herself. Sister Lydie has a serious martyr complex, if you haven't noticed. Puts everybody else's happiness first. Now that she's finally gotten up the nerve to do something for herself, she's too chicken to admit it. Honestly, kiddo — I don't even think Francie knows who she's been seeing."

The landline rang inside the house, and Leigh jumped up. If she didn't get there quickly enough, her father would attempt to answer it. She raced around to the kitchen and pulled the headset off its wall cradle just as Randall reached for his second crutch.

"Koslow residence," she answered.

A strange, high-pitched male voice caterwauled on the other end. "I need to speak to Dr. Koslow!"

"Who is this?" Leigh asked as politely as she could. The person was practically sobbing as they spoke.

"It's Olan! Please! Put him on, now!" A hysterical gulping noise followed.

"Okay, okay. Just a second." Leigh pulled the headset down to her chest. "Dad, it's Olan. He sounds really upset."

Randall reached for his crutches again. Leigh looked at the coiled leash on the ancient phone with a sigh. It was long enough to stretch to her mother's cooking area, but not all the way to the table. "Just sit," Leigh ordered. "I'll get the other phone."

She jogged upstairs to the master bedroom, grabbed the portable phone she had given them for Christmas years ago and which they never used, and returned to the kitchen. She could hear Olan sobbing on the other end as soon as she turned it on. "Here," she said breathlessly, handing the phone to her father. She really did need to exercise more.

"Hello. This is Randall," her father said calmly.

She could hear Olan squalling even with the receiver to Randall's ear. The rest of the crowd at the table, including a returning Bess, stopped what they were doing and stared.

"Calm down, Olan," Randall said after a moment. Then he paused for another long interval while the tinny screeching continued unabated. "Olan!" Randall said finally, his voice firmer. "You shouldn't be calling me. You should be calling the police."

Leigh's eyes sought her daughter's. She found Allison looking right back at her. *Another petnapping!*

"You need to think about why they told you that," Randall explained evenly, his voice no different than if he were explaining how to trim a nail. "They don't want anyone to contact the police precisely *because* once that happens, they know they'll be caught."

More screeching followed. "Olan," Randall continued, "they are aware of all that. They will work with you to make sure no one knows you've contacted them. That's part of what they do." He paused a moment, then grimaced. "No, that will *not* help. Do you want an innocent person hurt? Skippy could go to jail for that."

"Oh, merciful heavens!" Frances interjected. "Tell him to call the police, Randall!"

Randall nodded to her with a raised palm. "Olan, I'm going to give you a phone number. You know Maura Polanski? Right. Chief Polanski's daughter. You're going to call her, and she's going to walk you through what you should do. She understands the situation, and she'll make sure—" A particularly high pitched squeal vibrated through the phone, and Randall lowered it briefly, closing his eyes with a sigh. "Olan, listen to me. Maura knows all that. No sirens, no flashing lights. You have to trust the police, Olan. You have to. For Zeus's sake."

Allison's eyes met her mother's again. *Zeus!* The magnificent cockatoo was Olan's pride and joy. He had said as much when he was in the clinic just the day before yesterday. *I would die if I lost Zeus, Doc! I would just die!*

"That's right, Olan. Good man. You have something to write with?" Randall looked up at Leigh. She nodded and told him Maura's number, which he repeated into the phone. "You're doing the right thing, Olan. Yes, I'm absolutely sure. Okay, Olan. Goodbye, now."

Randall gave the phone back to Leigh and picked up the hand of cards resting on the table in front of him. "Whose turn is it?"

His question was met with groans. "For pity's sake, Randall!" Bess chastised. "You have to tell us what the man said!"

Randall looked at the uniformly expectant faces around him and sighed. "His favorite cockatoo disappeared from its cage on his back porch. There was a ransom note threatening him not to tell the police. He's understandably upset. But he agreed to call Maura. Now, is it my turn?"

The veterinarian would say no more, and one by one the card players picked up their hands and resumed the game.

Leigh drifted back into the living room. Her mind was reeling again, but as her gaze fell on Frances's perfectly symmetrical color-coded stacks of files, she recognized her window of opportunity.

"I have no idea what you're doing," Bess whispered as Leigh began rifling through the stacks. "But something tells me Francie wouldn't approve, so can I help?"

"I need to sneak a peek at the personnel files," Leigh whispered back. "While keeping an eye on the kitchen!"

Bess winked back conspiratorially, and the two began the hunt. Within a minute Bess tapped Leigh on the back with a folder. Leigh turned and took it, then flipped through its contents with a smile. She nodded silently to Bess.

"I'll make sure you're not disturbed," Bess whispered, facing toward the kitchen. "But you have to tell me what you find!"

Leigh's eyes roved over the papers hurriedly. It sounded like the card game was fast nearing its conclusion.

Paige Smyth was 34 years old and lived in an apartment in Avalon. Her emergency contacts included her parents in Irwin and a Steve Hawley, about which she had given no information other than a phone number. She listed her hobbies as animals, skiing, and snowboarding.

Morgan Childress was 24 years old and appeared to still be living with her parents in Mount Lebanon. Her resume went on forever about her bird experience, including the Pittsburgh aviary. She had obviously misunderstood several of the questions. Under "hobbies" she had written "blue" and for "career goal" she had listed some random woman's name and phone number.

Leigh shook her head and moved on.

Amy Washburn's personnel forms were equally instructive. She was 62 years old according to her listed birthdate, she gave herself as her own emergency contact, and she supplied her high school name and graduation date in three different places — the latter information serving, at least, to confirm Leigh's suspicion that her true age was somewhere between 21 and 23. She lived at an indecipherable address in Bellevue that included a 12-digit zip code.

Clearly, the last two had been hired when Randall had no business manager.

Leigh slapped the file closed and handed it back to Bess. "Worthless," she murmured.

Bess slid the folder back where it belonged and looked at Leigh expectantly. "So, what were we looking for, exactly?"

"I don't know," Leigh whispered back. "I'd take anything that would make me suspect one employee over the others."

Bess's heavily made-up eyes widened. "Suspect them of what exactly?"

"Colluding with the petnapper," Leigh confided uncertainly. She still had not managed to completely process Maura's news about Kyle. Opie the cockatiel had been stolen from Leonard's house last Friday night. Kyle Claymore had left for Erie sometime on Saturday and had never come back. Mason had found both animals early Monday morning and brought them to her. But Kyle's apartment had been broken into *after* that, after Kyle was dead and the animals were gone. Why? Was it the loan sharks Mason had mentioned, looking for Kyle... or was it Kyle's own accomplice, trying to retrieve the bird?

Leigh shuddered. There was no doubt about it — Kyle had to have an accomplice. And that accomplice must have been the one to petnap Lucky, and to steal back the cockatiel, and now to take off with Zeus. But if one of the clinic employees was in league with Kyle, they had to know by now that he was dead, or at least be worried about his disappearance. Yet as far as Leigh could tell, none of the staff seemed in the least upset.

It made no sense. Could there possibly be an entire ring of petnappers, of which their clinic informant was only a part? Was the employee in question not emotionally involved with Kyle at all? Or was she a full-blown sociopath?

Leigh shuddered again. Her past experience with sociopaths had not been pleasant.

"What are you thinking?" Bess demanded.

They could hear chairs scooting back from the kitchen table. The card game was over.

"I'm not sure," Leigh replied miserably. All at once she felt very, very tired. "But whatever it is, I'll think about it tomorrow."

Chapter 19

Tomorrow came entirely too soon. Warren didn't straggle home until nearly midnight and he fell asleep within seconds of lying down. Leigh hadn't the heart to wake him, and so had spent much of the night staring at her ceiling again, wondering how anyone at the clinic could be cold-hearted enough to conspire in a petnapping scheme, and wondering further how Mason Dublin could be such a terrible judge of character as to consider Kyle his "buddy."

She came up with a variety of answers. She didn't like any of them.

She had finally dropped off in the wee hours of the morning, then woke to find Warren's side of the bed empty again. Thank goodness this was the last day of his conference. She could have used his help in the speech she was about to give the children, but unfortunately, she had to face them alone.

She took a long drag on her second cup of coffee and looked across the kitchen table at the twins. Ethan was deep into a bowl of sweetened cereal; Allison nibbled on some organic whole grain bread that looked like it was covered with birdseed, one of several healthier (a.k.a. more expensive) food items the girl was now demanding thanks to the influence of her Aunt Cara the earth mother.

"I think it's best," Leigh began firmly, "if you guys don't go in to the clinic today."

Allison's head shot up, her dark eyes radiating annoyance. Ethan merely shrugged and dug back into his cereal.

"We weren't going to anyway," he said. "We finished up Jared's stuff yesterday."

Leigh studied her son. His mop of red hair was standing straight up in the middle of his forehead, and she made a mental note to get it cut again. "I thought that Mathias talked Grandpa into paying you guys to do some work outside tomorrow. That's what you said at dinner."

Ethan shrugged again. "Matt changed his mind."

Allison's eyes rolled. "What he means is that Matt only

suggested it because he wanted to see *Kirsten* again. When he found out she wasn't coming in tomorrow, he lost interest."

Leigh perked an eyebrow. The Pack usually got along well, considering the difference in age between Cara's son Mathias and the younger three. But last evening, she had noticed a distinct chill in the air between Matt and Allison. Could the living Skipper doll be the cause of it?

"You have a problem with Mathias liking Kirsten?" Leigh inquired.

Allison merely glared.

"Allie thinks she's, like, a total fake," Ethan chimed in. "Matt thinks Kirsten likes him. And she *has* been flirting with him and stuff. Allie told him Kirsten was only doing it because he was related to Grandpa, and Matt got ticked."

"He *asked her out*, Mom," Allison said, her voice uncharacteristically bitter. "He's like, living in a parallel universe or something."

"She said she'd think about it," Ethan interjected.

Allison rolled her eyes again. "Sure she will." Her gaze fixed back on her mother. "Why can't I go back to the clinic today? You said I could help Grandpa all week."

Leigh cleared her throat. "I know. But your Aunt Mo has found out some new information that makes me think we should all back off a bit. It may not be completely safe for you guys to be hanging around down there asking questions. Not if anyone starts to suspect—"

"What new information?" Allison demanded.

Leigh sighed. She suspected that most mothers did not regularly have awkward conversations with their children regarding family member involvement in murder investigations. She hoped those mothers appreciated it.

"Kyle Claymore is not our petnapper," she explained. "At least, he's not the only petnapper. He was killed last weekend up near Erie. The police think he was murdered by some people engaged in illegal gambling, and his death may have nothing whatsoever to do with the petnappings down here. But until we know that for sure — that no one at the clinic is associated with that kind of violence, even accidentally, I want you guys to stay away."

Allison stared darkly at her mother. "Seriously? Some guy gets murdered all the way up in Erie and that makes it too dangerous for me to spend the day with Grandpa?"

Leigh braced herself for yet another battle where she was forced to defend herself from uncomfortable accusations about how she didn't trust them, how they weren't little kids anymore, how she was as bad a worrier as Grandma... yada yada yada. "I have enough to worry about taking care of your grandparents all day today," she said firmly, trying to short-circuit the usual argument. "I don't need to worry about you guys, too. And I *will*, whether you think your involvement in all this is dangerous or not."

Allison's brown eyes stared back at her, the young brain behind churning with heaven-only-knew what thoughts. After a long moment the child appeared, oddly enough, to concede. "If Kyle's dead, what happens with Peep?" she asked finally.

Leigh relaxed a little. "I don't know. I haven't talked to Grandpa Mason about it yet. I think he's coming back today."

Allison leaned forward and took a slow sip of orange juice.

Leigh waited for more protestations, but Allison went back to nibbling at her birdseed bread, and Ethan poured himself a second bowl of cereal.

Leigh tried to dismiss the vague, unsettled feeling in her gut. "Your Aunt Cara still isn't feeling well," she explained. "So your Uncle Gil is going to work from home today. Call him if you need anything, but try to stay away from Lenna until she's completely better. We don't all need to get sick."

"How long will you be gone?" Allison asked.

Leigh's feeling of disquiet niggled again. "I have to get Grandpa to the clinic in time for his shift, then I'll be staying with Grandma until whenever your Grandma Lydie comes home. You two want to come over there with me?"

Both kids shook their heads. "No. We're good," Allison answered.

"Your dad will probably beat me home," Leigh continued. "His conference ends today."

"No problem. We'll be fine," Allison assured in the super-mature tone that, paradoxically, always made Leigh more nervous. At nearly twelve, the twins were perfectly capable of entertaining themselves on a nice summer day with their uncle right next door.

But still.

Leigh continued to battle an unpleasant mixture of guilt and nervousness as she drove herself back down to West View to collect her father. She had no choice but to hang out at her mother's house today. Cara was out of commission and Bess had stayed over three nights already. Frances was doing better with the walker and could scuffle about on her heels without too much discomfort, but she still needed someone within shouting distance. And after his shift at the clinic today was over, so would Randall.

She arrived at her parents' house to find Randall ready and waiting on the front porch. He said nothing about his haste, but Leigh could hear Frances muttering to herself in the living room about imprudent behavior, and a quick peek revealed Bess, still in her kimono, passed out on the couch with her mouth open.

Leigh chose not to go inside.

She delivered her father to the clinic and settled him on his preferred stool. There were no regular surgeries on Fridays, and with only two vets working and none of the teens hanging around, the practice seemed eerily quiet. Dr. Koslow was early, and his first patient had not yet arrived. The silence was eventually broken by the ring of the office phone, followed by Amy popping open the connecting door to the waiting room.

"Dr. Koslow?" she chirped, her freckled face looking confused. "Birds get rabies, don't they? I mean, I've never heard of a bird getting rabies, but I've heard of bats getting rabies, and bats are birds, right?"

The veterinarian's shoulders slumped. "No, Amy. Bats are mammals. Only mammals get rabies, not birds."

The receptionist's vacuous eyes widened with alarm. "Uh oh. I told him birds get rabies. Because bats are birds."

"Do you know why the person was asking?" Randall inquired.

Amy shook her head. "I'll check." She turned toward the waiting room, then whirled back again. "Should I tell him bats aren't birds?"

Randall sighed. "Yes. And then ask whomever it is if he needs to talk to me. I'm perfectly free at the moment."

Leigh knew she probably shouldn't, but she mentally struck Amy's name off her suspect list. The girl just wasn't smart enough to be an extortionist. Gullible enough to take advantage of, maybe, but far too likely to accidentally screw things up. Orchestrating a series of petnappings didn't necessarily require criminal genius, but there had to be a decent brain operating somewhere in the mix.

Amy burst back into the room. "He said he's going to walk over!"

Randall blinked at her. "Who is?"

"The policeman! He said it all happened just down the street!"

Leigh and her father exchanged a glance. "What happened?" Leigh demanded.

Amy pressed her face against the window a moment, but drew back disappointed. "I can't see anything. It happened just down the street, the policeman said!"

"What—" Randall began.

"This woman got attacked by a bird!" Amy reported. "Like it just flew at her for no reason, like it had rabies or something! But birds don't get rabies, right?"

They could get no more information from the receptionist. She flitted back and forth between the lobby and the exam room repeating herself in an endless loop until a uniformed officer with the Avalon police stepped through the front door.

"Oh, come on back here!" Amy twittered, leading him to the exam room. "Dr. Koslow's right back here!"

The officer walked in, and Leigh pointedly shut the door behind him. Thanks goodness no clients had arrived yet.

"Is there a problem, Russell?" Randall asked mildly.

The policeman gave his head a shake. "It's a weird one, Doc, I got to tell you. Ms. Adams, up on Jackman, says she looked outside earlier and saw a huge bird on the ground under her bird feeder — some kind of bird she'd never seen before. She said it had blood on it, and she figured it must be injured, so she went outside to see if there was anything she could do for it. Well, then she says she got about four or five away and the thing just lunged at her. Came at her with its beak snapping, looking to fight. Didn't break the skin or anything, but scared her near to death. She went back in and called us, but wherever it went to, we can't find it now." He shook his head again, lifting a hand to scratch the back of his neck. "I never heard of anything like it. If we shoot the thing, you want to take a look at it?"

Randall stood up on his good foot. "Did she tell you what the bird looked like?"

The officer shrugged. "She just said it was white. And really big. One of the guys thought maybe it was an egret."

Leigh's heart pounded in her chest. She caught her father's eye. *Zeus!*

"Don't shoot it," Randall ordered. "It may be somebody's pet bird that's escaped. That would explain why it wasn't afraid of the woman. If it's upset, it could very well attack again." He looked down at his cast with a grimace of annoyance. Then he hobbled over and punched a button on the intercom. "Morgan? Can you come up here?"

"You think it could belong to that woman up in Ben Avon? The one with the aviary?" the policeman suggested. "Or maybe it was stolen?"

"Maybe," Randall said noncommittally. Leigh was heartened to know that the officer was aware of the petnappings, even if he had not yet gotten word of the perp's latest conquest. She couldn't remember exactly where Olan lived, but most likely, it was in another jurisdiction.

"You should check in with Maura Polanski," Randall suggested. "Tell her I said that this could be the bird that was stolen from McKees Rocks last night."

The officer turned to speak into his radio.

"Should I call Olan?" Leigh whispered. It was only a chance, but it seemed like a pretty darn good one. If Zeus had indeed escaped from his captors, the rest of the mystery bird's actions were perfectly in character.

Randall nodded. "He might be the only one who could recapture him safely."

"What's up, Dr. Koslow?" Morgan asked from the doorway, looking nervously at the policeman.

Paige stood right behind her, doing the same thing. "Did something happen?"

"A large bird is running loose, and we think it might be somebody's pet parrot," Randall answered. "It could be injured. Or it could injure somebody, if they try to catch it and don't know what they're doing."

"I'll go with you," Morgan said immediately, stepping up to the officer. "Where is it?"

The policeman looked relieved. "They're still looking for it now.

But I can take you where it was seen last."

"Take some gloves and one of the carriers from the basement. And a blanket, just in case," Randall directed.

Morgan nodded and headed for the stairs. Paige drifted back into the treatment room.

Leigh found a phone and called Olan. A few minutes later, she found herself tagging along as the policeman led Morgan up the block to a small but well-manicured backyard along Jackman Street. Leigh knew she should get back to her mother's house, but she wanted to know if the bird in question was really Zeus. She wasn't familiar with Ms. Adams, and she didn't want to draw any conclusions about the petnappings only to find out that the woman had been frightened by a loopy pigeon.

They arrived to find three other officers scanning the nearby trees, two with binoculars. Leigh studied Morgan, and found that she, too, was looking up. Leigh struck another name off her suspect list. Surely Morgan wasn't *that* clever an actress. If she suspected they were looking for Zeus, she would be looking down, not up. She had helped to clip the bird's flight feathers three days ago.

"Morgan," Leigh informed thoughtfully. "It may be Zeus we're looking for."

The girl looked back at her with surprise. "How would Zeus get here?"

"He was petnapped from Olan's last night," Leigh admitted. There was little point in keeping the secret when Olan himself would be arriving shortly.

Morgan stared at Leigh for another moment, then quickly began scouting out suitable cover at ground level. She located their quarry within minutes. The bird was hiding only one backyard over at the base of a rhododendron bush.

Morgan peered in at the bird from a distance, then quickly withdrew and stepped back. "Don't go any closer," she told the gathering crowd, holding out her arms protectively. "He's really agitated. You poke in there after him, and he'll take your face off."

Those same, disturbing words had met Leigh's ears way too often lately. "Is it Zeus?" she asked.

"I think so," Morgan answered. "I can't see him all that well, but it's definitely a cockatoo."

"Is that as far as the bird got?" asked a policeman whose uniform identified him as the chief. He was relatively new to the position, and Leigh didn't know him.

"If their wings are clipped, they can't fly," Morgan explained. "They can only flutter around a bit. He probably just walked over here looking for a place to hide."

"Did you see any blood on him?" Leigh asked worriedly.

Morgan's dark eyes widened. "No. Why? Has he been injured?"

"My baby!" shrieked Olan, running towards them from the car he'd double-parked haphazardly by one of the police cruisers. "Oh my. Oh dear. Oh my. Where is he? Is he okay?"

"He's over here," Morgan called out, seeming to decide she was in charge now. She gestured impatiently to the policemen and other neighbors who had gathered around. "Everybody else back up!" she ordered. "Let Olan in here alone."

As Olan chugged toward them breathing like a freight train, the policemen obliged without comment.

Olan ran straight to the bush, leaned down, and parted the branches. "Zeus, baby?" he called. "Are you here, boy? Don't worry. Daddy won't let anything happen to you!"

A loud squawk erupted from the center of the bush.

"That's my boy!" Olan cried. "You're okay. Come to Daddy!"

He reached into his pocket, pulled out a plastic bag, and dropped some small orange chunks at his feet. "I brought your favorite! Come and get it. It's okay, baby…"

Olan continued crooning to the bird, and within a few moments the cockatoo walked out from under the bush and began pecking at the fruit on the ground.

The assembled crowd let out a collective sigh, but their relief turned quickly back to concern. The bird's white breast and forewing were splattered with blood.

"Oh, precious," Olan moaned, bending down slowly toward the parrot. "What happened to you?"

Morgan took a step closer. "If you can hold him, I'll take a look," she suggested.

When the cockatoo had consumed all the available fruit, it willingly hopped onto Olan's arm. He carefully circled its neck with his fingers, cooing all the while, until he had the bird under his control. Morgan slipped up and gently examined the bloodied breast and wing. "He doesn't act hurt," she said curiously.

"No," Olan agreed hopefully. "He doesn't, does he?"

After as thorough a look as Morgan could take without upsetting the bird, she stepped back with a frown.

"You know," she said, planting a hand on one cocked hip. "I don't think that's *his* blood."

The policemen looked at each other. "No?" the chief asked.

Morgan shook her head. "I think he nailed somebody."

"You *would* do that, wouldn't you, my precious?" Olan said proudly, moving the bird slowly towards the carrier Morgan had brought. Morgan pulled the plastic bag back out of Olan's pocket, then tossed the remaining fruit in the back of the carrier. "Thank you, dear," Olan replied, lowering the bird towards the opening.

The bird struggled in the direction of the fruit, and Olan gently released him as he moved inside. Olan then closed the door behind the bird and wiped weepy eyes with his sleeve. "He's okay," he murmured, looking weak with relief. "He's okay."

"This bird was stolen from you?" the chief asked.

Olan nodded. "Last night. There was a ransom note. I—" He hiccupped. "I couldn't believe it. I couldn't believe anyone *could* take him. He won't let just anybody touch him. But then I saw the fruit on the ground. By his cage on the patio." Another hiccup. "Zeussie just can't resist mango!"

"Chief?" one of the policemen interrupted, pocketing his radio as he walked up.

The older officer turned. "Yeah?"

"Polanski requested some non-urgent assistance over at her house. You want me to check it out?"

The chief nodded. "I'll be by in a few." He turned back to Olan. "Would you mind coming down to the station? We'd like to get some more information from you."

Olan did not look thrilled at the prospect, but he nodded in acquiescence.

Leigh watched the younger officer stride toward his squad car. Assistance at the Polanski house?

Maura's duplex was only a few blocks away.

Leigh started walking.

Chapter 20

Leigh could hear the commotion as soon as she turned the corner. Some kind of crowd had gathered — and was still gathering — in front of Maura's house, along the sidewalks, and out into the street. It wasn't an unruly crowd, but the people she fell into step with as she neared were clearly on a mission. People of all ages and an assortment of pets appeared to be assembling for some sort of event.

As Leigh walked closer she could see Maura standing on her front porch while little Eddie gazed out over the crowd from his belly pack. The much shorter figure standing by Maura's side had been gesturing for the crowd to come closer, and as Leigh complied along with the rest, a husky voice began to speak.

"Come on up, everybody," Skippy called with authority. "There's nothing to be afraid of. We all know what's been going on around here lately, and we all know it's got to be stopped. I don't know about you people, but Skippy Titus don't let *anybody* mess with her birds! And you're not going to let some cowardly scumbag mess with your pets anymore either, are you? Well, I say, *are you?*"

"No!" a woman shouted from near to Leigh. "I've had enough!"

"Nobody's messing with my animals, I can tell you that!"

"Mine either!"

"No way!"

A chorus of determined voices ensued, mixed with a smattering of enthusiastic applause, and Leigh's heart warmed.

"We let this happen!" Skippy continued when the noise died down. "Because we were all too damn scared to say anything. And what's that got us? Nothin'!"

Again the crowd applauded, and many voices cried out in agreement.

The officer Maura had summoned made his way slowly up onto the porch, and to Leigh's surprise, the crowd cheered him, too.

"Police can't do dip squat to protect our pets if we won't talk to 'em!" Skippy railed. "You'uns know me and I ain't no cop lover, but we got to do what we got to do, you know what I'm sayin'?"

There were more hoots and applause.

"This scumbag's been terrorizing us — all of us — for weeks now, and we've not only put up with it, we've helped the bastard! We've helped him by doing exactly what he says, by being quiet. Well, I say that's over! No more divide and conquer! Scumbag's got to deal with *all* of us now!"

Cheers resounded.

"He can't take everybody's pets!"

"We got to all stand together!"

"He don't stand a chance then!"

The commotion only grew louder as the officer, Maura, and Skippy conferred among themselves. Finally Skippy turned to the crowd again and raised her hands in the air. "So here's what we're going to do!" she yelled. "Instead of nobody talking, we're *all* going to talk. Every person here's going to come up and get a sheet of paper, put down your name and number, and write down what you know. Whatever you've seen, whatever you've heard. If you don't know nothing, then write that. Don't matter! Copper here's going to pick them all up and call the people who need called. Then they're going catch this bastard and put his scrawny behind in jail where he belongs!"

The crowd erupted with enthusiasm, and as Maura and the officer began distributing sheets of paper and pencils from the porch, people pressed forward to participate.

"Isn't it wonderful!" piped up a voice at Leigh's elbow. She looked down to see Mrs. Gregg, the waiting room's nearly permanent occupant, smiling from ear to ear. "People have been talking about doing something like this, but who would have thought Skippy would be the one to get it done?"

Leigh confessed that she had not, and wondered to herself if the kidnapping of Olan's bird last night might have spurred Skippy into action. She could easily picture Olan calling up his supposed rival and bawling out his grief over the phone. They were both bird people, after all. They might disagree on method, but they understood each other.

"It's so lovely to see one's community come together in times of crisis," Mrs. Gregg beamed.

"Yes," Leigh agreed, smiling herself as she watched everyone move up to the porch in an orderly manner, collect their papers and pencils, then move out of the way to find someplace to write. Car hoods were popular, as were nearby concrete porch railings, the sidewalk, and other people's backs.

"Everybody take a sign, too!" a cheerful voice called out from near the porch. When Leigh moved close enough, she could see that Ginny Ledbetter had set up a card table in Maura's front yard. In front of her were photocopied sheets of bright yellow paper adorned with thick black marker. On the top of each was a copy of the skull and knife drawing that formed the signature on Ginny's ransom note. "Hey, Bonehead!" the signs proclaimed. "We're watching YOU!!!"

"It's a little crude," Ginny said apologetically as Leigh approached the table. "My grandson did it. But it gets the point across, don't you think?"

"Perfectly," Leigh agreed, reaching down to pat Lucky. He sat on the grass by Ginny's side, attached to her wrist by a leash.

"I brought him home," Ginny said proudly. "We're not going to let that weaselly fiend scare us anymore!" She leaned in toward Leigh and lowered her voice. "Besides which, the Jack Russell was a terror and my sister thinks she can cook." She rolled her eyes toward heaven. "Mercy, I've never had such indigestion!" Her voice got louder again. "Everybody take a sign!"

Leigh took a sign, figuring she would put it up at the clinic as a show of solidarity. Then she gradually made her way up onto the porch towards Maura. Baby Eddie was kicking up a storm, energized by the buzz of activity around him. He stared out at everyone with a look of fascination until Leigh approached and smiled at him, at which point his expression turned dour.

"Hey, Koslow," Maura greeted. "What do you think?"

"I think it's great," Leigh agreed. "You think it will work?"

"Can't hurt. It'll certainly make the perp think twice about picking another victim from this area. And between these tips and what's been coming into the clinic, we could get lucky."

Leigh staked out a spot on the porch and waited until the crowd had dispersed and the Avalon policeman had taken his stack of tip sheets back to the station. Although several clusters of citizens remained nearby, talking and making plans for sign postings, Leigh did finally manage to steer Maura far enough out of anyone else's earshot to speak privately.

"I was there when Olan came for his bird," Leigh said, figuring the other officer had already filled Maura in on the basics. "Morgan found it, actually. But unless she's a better actress than I think she is, she didn't know *what* bird we were looking for until I told her."

"What makes you so sure?" Maura asked.

Leigh explained how Morgan had helped to clip Zeus's wings.

"Interesting," Maura replied, playing absently with Eddie's feet while she mulled the thought over. "What's more interesting is how a flightless bird ended up there in the first place. Olan lives in McKees Rocks. However the bird got loose, it didn't fly over the river. Somebody snatched it there and drove it over here, then lost it. And it was found wandering not two blocks from where you found Lucky — which was right outside the clinic."

Leigh groaned. "I do not like the way that sounds."

"Neither do I. But it's bound to cause talk." Maura's forehead furrowed with thought. "Do you think anyone at the clinic is aware that they're being considered as a potential suspect?"

Leigh considered. "I don't think so. I haven't noticed anyone acting paranoid. But we did get that one accusatory note in the mail, and after it gets around where Zeus was found, more people could start to wonder. Then the staff are bound to get sensitive and start looking over their shoulders."

Maura nodded in agreement. "McCleary said there was blood on the bird?"

Leigh's stomach soured. She didn't like thinking about bloody feathers. No matter whose blood it was. "Yes, but the bird didn't appear to be injured. Zeus is a pretty aggressive cockatoo. I've seen him take stabs at people before. My guess is that whoever kidnapped him got a little more trouble than they bargained for."

Maura considered. "Olan believed the bird was tempted from its cage and into a carrier with a food lure. He didn't think anyone else would be able to handle it otherwise."

"I'd say he's right," Leigh agreed. "Maybe after they stole the bird, they tried to move it to another cage, and it attacked. That could explain how it got away."

"And Lucky," Maura added. "The kidnapper most likely tried to lure him off the same way, then made the mistake of trying to pick him up."

He'll take your face off. Leigh remembered the colorful warning associated with both animals. "So the petnapper had both animals in his control, at least for a while, then was startled by a surprise attack and lost hold of them. Lucky ran off and headed towards home. But the bird couldn't go far even if it did know which way to go. It was just wandering around, scared and looking for food."

"Which means both animals were being held at some point near the clinic."

Leigh shook her head. "Not necessarily. I saw Lucky's paws. He had run a long way."

Maura's lips pursed. "It will look bad for the clinic, just the same."

"Fabulous," Leigh said with a sigh.

Maura's phone buzzed, and she looked down at the number. "Hang on, Koslow," she ordered, answering it. "Hey there, deputy! What's up?" She listened a moment. "Well, as a matter of fact, we have had a few developments. Olan's bird wandered into somebody's backyard here in Avalon this morning. The bird's back with his owner now, safe and sound. Can't say as much for our petnapper. The bird evidently had some secondhand blood on its feathers."

As Maura described the scene Leigh had just described to her, followed by an accounting of the community gathering, Leigh wondered to whom Maura could be talking. Was the county sheriff's office involved now, too? The many and overlapping divisions of law enforcement in Pittsburgh were beyond mind-boggling.

"No, haven't had a chance to look into that yet," Maura continued. "But I'm definitely not ruling it out." Leigh puzzled over Maura's tone, which was warmer than her usual detective voice. "Oh, really? Not sure about that. You want to ask your mom? She was there."

Leigh stiffened. *Allison?* Maura had been talking all this time to *Allison?!* She fixed the detective with a glare even as she reached for the phone.

Maura handed it over with a smirk.

Leigh took it. "Allison?"

"Hi, Mom. Don't freak out. I just wanted to know if any other pets had been stolen… or anything. You could have told me Zeus was okay," Allison added with a touch of hurt. "I was worried about him too, you know."

"I know," Leigh defended. "I'm sorry. But I came straight over here afterwards and wound up in the middle of a citizens' rally. You would be proud of Skippy. She was brilliant."

"Can you get me a sign?" Allison asked. "And also, I was wondering, did Olan say what kind of food the petnapper used to lure Zeus out of his cage last night?"

Leigh perked an eyebrow. When Allison started asking weird questions Leigh didn't understand, trouble generally followed. "Fruit. Why?"

"What kind of fruit?" Allison persisted.

Leigh considered. "Mango, I think. Why?"

"Just wondering. Can you put Aunt Mo back on?"

Leigh's teeth gritted. "Not until you tell me what you're thinking."

"I'll explain it all when you get home," Allison assured, "but I really need to talk to Aunt Mo again."

Leigh debated.

"Mo-om!" Allison begged. "I'm sitting here at the house, and I'm not going anywhere, and I'm perfectly safe, and so is Ethan. We're not stupid. But if Aunt Mo can use some help, shouldn't I at least be able to *talk* to her?"

Leigh blew out a breath and handed the phone back to Maura. She hated it when her kids played the logic card.

Maura listened a moment, her brow furrowing. "Is that right? Well, that is interesting."

Leigh tapped her foot nervously. Maura's end of the conversation was mostly silence.

"It's possible. You know that for a fact? I see. Okay. No, probably not. The news about Zeus's recapture will be all over town by nightfall — too many people involved to have a prayer of keeping it quiet. Okay, you see if you can confirm that. Call me if you do. Right. Thanks, Allie."

Maura hung up and pocketed her phone. Baby Eddie looked at Leigh and made a gurgling sound.

"Lydie come home yet?" Maura asked, changing the subject with infuriating nonchalance.

Crap! Leigh thought miserably. She was supposed to relieve Bess ages ago. It was a wonder her aunt hadn't sent a stream of obscene texts already. "Not yet," she answered. "I've got to get back over there."

Maura played with Eddie's feet again. He looked back up at his mother and made a sound suspiciously like a giggle. "Tell your mom I owe her a housecleaning sometime this weekend," Maura offered.

"Oh, you do *not* want to do that," Leigh warned.

"Why not?" Maura insisted. "She certainly helped me out enough times when I was on bedrest. My house hasn't been as clean before or since."

"There *is* nothing to clean in my parents' house," Leigh explained. "A certain minimal amount of dirt has to accumulate before it becomes visible to the naked eye. My mother never lets that happen. The dust is all in her mind."

Maura chuckled. "Well, that should make things easier for me. Gerry's off Saturday; I'll give her a call."

Leigh shook her head. "Your funeral." She held her friend's eyes a moment.

Maura sighed. "Koslow, will you stop worrying about nothing? Allison's a smart girl, she's very observant, and she has good ideas. You know I'd never encourage her in anything that was dangerous, any more than I would little Eddie, here. But she'd be a lot happier if you stopped actively *discouraging* her."

"I don't want her to go into police work," Leigh said flatly.

"She's not signing up for the academy," Maura argued. "She's only trying to use her brain on an otherwise dull summer day. She has great instincts, you know."

Leigh frowned. "I have good instincts. About... you know... crime stuff."

Maura's eyes flickered with amusement. "I didn't know this was a competition, Koslow."

Leigh's face flared with heat. She opened her mouth to fire back the perfect snappy retort, but the perfect snappy retort eluded her.

She shut her mouth and started back down the street.

Chapter 21

Leigh was just pulling up at her mother's house when her cell phone rang.

"Hey there, kid," said a tired-sounding voice. "Can we talk?"

"Oh, we are most definitely going to talk," Leigh replied, getting out of the van and shutting the door behind her. "Where are you, Mason?"

"The airport," he answered. "Where are you?"

"My parents' house. I'll be here all day. Can you come over?"

He hesitated.

"My mother will not bite you," Leigh said irritably. Her head was still whirling with the events of the morning, and the week, and every time she thought of him spending that time gambling merrily away on the high seas, her jaws clenched. Now her teeth were sore.

"You sure about that?" Mason asked skeptically.

"Just get over here," Leigh ordered. "I'll meet you out front if you like."

A beat passed. "Okay, kid," he agreed. "I guess I owe you that much."

You think?

Leigh hung up before she could say anything she would regret later. She knew that Mason had nothing to do with the petnappings, much less the murders, even if he did consider Kyle a friend. But she wasn't above resenting the mess he'd gotten her — and by extension the Pack — into. A mess that surely could have been straightened out earlier if he hadn't been so out of touch.

Leigh thought with trepidation of poor Lenna, who was at this very moment probably lying in bed cuddling the three-legged cat she had fallen in love with. But had Peep been stolen from her real owner, too? There was no question that Kyle had been up to his neck in the petnapping operation. What was strange was how little his demise had seemed to affect it.

Leigh stomped up to her mother's door. She dreaded the earful she was about to get from Bess, and she had come prepared with a credible-sounding explanation. She was surprised, upon entering, to discover that it wouldn't be necessary.

Bess was still passed out on the couch, snoring. Her Pekingese mix lay sprawled across her stomach. The dog was snoring, too.

"Pathetic, aren't they?" Frances called from the kitchen table, which was now completely covered with paperwork. "I told her she was drinking too much. And she stayed up too late besides. Watching some ridiculous movie on that device she calls a phone up until the wee hours of the morning... I mean, *really*. On a Thursday night! At her age!"

Leigh chose not to comment. "Have you talked to Aunt Lydie?"

"She's guessing she'll get here between seven and eight this evening," Frances reported. "Depending on the Turnpike traffic."

"I see," Leigh replied, stressing over the prospect of providing another dinner. She couldn't possibly ask Bess to cook again, and Warren deserved a quiet evening at home. Perhaps she could guilt-trip Mason into bringing something?

She smiled. Now *that* would be justice.

Frances began muttering something about "utterly ridiculous credit extension," and Leigh removed herself to the living room so that she could keep an eye out for Mason through the front window. When his banged-up old Corolla pulled to the curb, she called to her mother. "I'm going to sit outside for a bit. If you need anything, just yell."

Frances harrumphed. "You'd hear me before Bess would, I'd wager."

Leigh cast a glance at her still-prone aunt, whose only response to the women's voices was to snort, turn sideways, and pull the little dog against her chest. Leigh made sure the front window was open, then walked outside and closed the door behind her.

She met Mason on the sidewalk and they leaned against the side of the Corolla. He was dressed in clothes equally dapper to those she had seen him leave in, except that this outfit was rumpled. He seemed haggard, as well.

"You don't look so good," Leigh noted, thinking she sounded about as tactful as Morgan.

"I've been better," Mason said sadly. "They told me about Kyle this morning."

Leigh felt a strong twinge of guilt. It hadn't occurred to her that Mason would be upset about the murder, but of course it should have. "I'm sorry," she commiserated.

Mason nodded. "He was a good kid. A mess at the end, but a good kid."

Leigh puzzled over the statement. "You do know that the cockatiel in his apartment was stolen from a man in Bellevue? Kidnapped for ransom?"

Mason shook his head. "Kyle wouldn't have anything to do with something like that."

"Oh no?"

"No," Mason repeated. "I know he was desperate for money, but Kyle just wasn't wired for a life of crime. He was a computer geek, for God's sake!"

"Seriously?" Leigh asked with surprise.

Mason nodded. "He started playing online poker when he was a teenager, and he was amazingly good at it — a natural talent. But just when he started to make some real money, the industry got shut down. He turned his hand to live play, but at first he was terrible. Learning to read other people, being up close and personal with your opponents — it's a whole different game. But he and I traded some secrets, and we both got better. He just never got quite good enough."

"And he got into debt," Leigh declared.

"He was an idiot with money," Mason explained. "Always risking too much, never seeing the consequences if he lost. He was all about statistics and calculations, but he never really seemed to grasp that just because the odds are with you doesn't mean you're *going* to win, eventually or otherwise. Improbable stuff happens. And it kept happening to him."

Leigh sighed. "So he borrowed money from the wrong people, and then he got scared."

Mason nodded solemnly. "They were just messing with him. They might have roughed him up a bit, but they wouldn't have killed him — all they wanted was their money back. But he was terrified. And convinced that he could win it all back with one really good, high-stakes game. So he went illegal, despite my warnings," Mason's face crinkled with pain. "And that did kill him."

"I'm sorry," Leigh repeated, feeling more like a heel by the second.

"I tried to help him," he continued. "I made good on his rent a couple times, but I've been down this road before — you can bail water all day and night, but you can't keep a man's boat from sinking if he keeps poking holes in it."

Leigh studied Mason's face. It was obvious that he really did care about Kyle. Which made her wonder how objective Mason could be about his friend's character, now that Kyle was dead.

"Did he have a girlfriend?" she asked tentatively.

Mason chuckled sadly. "Um, no. Kyle was a little shy around women. You could say he had some 'social anxieties.'"

Leigh frowned. This conversation wasn't tying things up nearly as neatly as she'd been hoping. In fact, it wasn't helping at all.

"If Kyle wasn't involved in the petnappings," she insisted, "why would he have a stolen cockatiel in his apartment?"

Mason shrugged. "Maybe he was keeping it for a friend. He liked animals."

"Keeping it for a friend?" Leigh repeated skeptically. "How would you word that request, exactly? 'Hey bro, I've decided to kidnap pets for ransom, but I ran out of space. Could you keep this one for me until its loving owner pays up?'"

Mason's expression was patient. "How about, 'Hey, Kyle — I'm getting paid to watch my buddy's bird, but my girlfriend's allergic. Can you keep him over at your place for a couple days? I'll pay you what he's paying me.'"

Leigh's lips pursed. Mason was right. Bad as it looked, a guy like Kyle *could* have gotten the bird from just about any acquaintance and still been clueless as to its origins. It was possible.

But not likely.

"One way or the other," Leigh maintained, "there must be some link between Kyle and the petnappings. Maybe you can help the police find it."

Mason frowned. "And why would I do that? Kyle was a good kid, and now he's dead. I'm sure his family has enough to deal with without the cops trying to label him as an extortionist, too."

"The suspicion is already there," Leigh argued. "Finding the real petnapper could help clear Kyle's name. In addition to stopping all the anguish!"

"All right, all right," Mason conceded quickly. "They're already lining up to harass me, you know. I've got three phone messages to return, and I haven't even been home yet."

He stood up as if to leave, and Leigh realized how many questions she still wanted to be answered.

"What about the cat?" she inquired. "Lenna is hopelessly in love with her. What if Peep is stolen, too?"

"She isn't," Mason said flatly. "Kyle got her from a rescue place when she was just a kitten. She'd gotten her leg caught in an illegal trap. I told you he was crazy about her. I guess... well, I'll have to see if anyone in his family wants her. They may already be attached."

Leigh didn't want to think about Lenna's having to give up the tortie. Never mind that it would have been inevitable if Kyle had returned as planned.

"Well, I'd better get going and answer these calls before a black and white shows up at my apartment," Mason said grimly, straightening.

"That reminds me," Leigh interjected, straightening also. "Why *did* you move to Bellevue? And why keep it a secret?"

Mason's eyes flickered with an unexpected light. For a moment, he looked like the cat who ate the canary. He turned away from her. "That's a long story that's going to have to wait a few days. I need to get home."

Leigh hadn't asked him nearly as much as she wanted to. She still wanted to know why he had lied to his daughter about where he was going this week. But before she could reason out a non-accusatory way of asking the question, her phone rang in her pocket. She recognized the tone, and it proved serendipitous. "Wait a minute," she told Mason. "It's Cara."

"Hey Cuz," Leigh greeted.

"Hey," Cara said roughly, her voice hoarse. "Mom says she'll be there to relieve you by eight."

"I got the same message from my mom," Leigh responded. "Thanks. You better?"

"Much," the voice rasped. "It really does seem to be a twenty-four hour thing. But, Leigh..."

A pregnant pause followed.

"Yes?"

"There was something weird," Cara continued uncertainly, "about Mom's message. She left it early this morning, but I couldn't figure out why it bothered me until a little while ago, and then I listened to it again. It was the noise in the background. I swear I heard seagulls."

"Seagulls?" Leigh repeated. "In Hershey?"

Mason gestured to her that he needed to leave. She gestured again for him to wait.

"That's what I thought," Cara replied. "She said they might go visit some of Cynthia's family nearby, but I wouldn't call the coast 'nearby.' Neither is Lake Erie. Where else could she drive from the middle of the state to find seagulls?"

Leigh pondered the question. "Nowhere comes to mind, but they could be migrating or something. I've heard about them swarming inland parking lots, looking for food."

"I suppose," Cara responded, obviously unappeased. "Well, I guess we'll find out soon enough."

Mason stepped away. Leigh gestured once more, but he merely waved.

"I guess so," Leigh agreed hastily. "You take care." She hung up.

Mason was already getting in his car, and Leigh waved back a disappointed goodbye. All the secrets were beginning to get to her, and Cara had to feel even worse. Both Mason and Lydie were hiding things from their daughter.

Leigh turned back toward the house, then froze in her tracks.

Seagulls?

She spun around. Mason was starting up his car. She darted out almost in front of it and waved her arms like a mad woman.

Mason stared at her through the windshield, then cut the engine and rolled down the passenger side window. "Yeah?"

Leigh moved to the passenger door, but instead of leaning in the window she opened it and sat down. She looked deeply into his sharp, blue-green eyes and found what she was looking for.

His trademark mischievous twinkle.

"You sly old dog, you," she accused.

The corners of Mason's mouth tipped up slowly. It was the grin that sold a thousand steak knives. "Who are you calling old?"

Leigh shook her head and stared at him. "All this time?"

He shrugged.

"And you haven't said anything, but—" she recalled his half-hearted lie about the pawnbrokers' convention. "You wanted me to figure it out," she concluded.

Mason smiled smugly. "Denied."

"But," Leigh stuttered, still disbelieving, despite the perfect sense it made. "All this time…"

"You said that already," Mason interrupted.

"But… Lydie always… and you—"

"I've loved Lydie since the first day I saw her," Mason declared. "Standing there at her parents' front door. Looking so pretty and so perfectly, horribly *bored*. I looked into those gorgeous brown eyes of hers and I could see it, plain as day. She was an adventurer. Same as me. And she could see it, too."

Leigh resisted the urge to give her head a shake. "Lydie? An adventurer?"

"You know the mother and the aunt," Mason insisted. "I know the girl. And the woman. I broke her heart and ruined her faith in me, and that wound took a long, long time to heal. I'm still not sure it's gone, though God knows I've tried everything I can think of to make it up to her."

"But she," Leigh began helplessly, "she always acts so uncomfortable around you!"

Mason nodded. "She is, when the family's around. She knows how Francie feels about me, and she thinks everyone else will think less of her for… well, for still caring about someone like me. After everything I put her through."

"She put you through a lot too," Leigh said automatically, thinking of how rigid Lydie had been when Cara was growing up, refusing to allow Mason any part in his daughter's life, letting Cara believe he had abandoned them both. It was understandable, but it hadn't been right.

"We worked through that," Mason said softly. "After I came back. I won't say there weren't times when I was furious with the woman — because I was. But I always loved her. I never wanted to let her go." He settled himself into the car seat with a sigh. "We've been in touch all along, you know. More than anybody realized — including Francie. About a year ago, it finally happened."

He smiled again, and the sparkle in his eyes made Leigh's own heart melt. "She finally decided to let herself fall in love again," he said softly. "And we've been very happy. Except for the obvious."

Leigh considered. "The secrecy. She didn't want anyone to

know."

"Not just anyone," he said sadly. "Francie. She's spent her whole life trying to keep the peace with that twin of hers. But she knows Francie'll never approve of me, and she's afraid it will change things between them. Forever."

"That's not fair!" Leigh protested. "Lydie deserves to be happy, no matter what my mother thinks. She's punished herself long enough. And you. You were young! You both did stupid crap. Life moves on."

Mason grinned at her. "Yeah, I knew you'd be okay with us. And a part of me did wish you would figure it out. Hell, I've wanted to shout it from the rooftops. But Lydie made me promise. She wanted to tell Cara herself and she wanted to do it in her own time. I couldn't argue with that."

"But it's been months!" Leigh protested. "And Cara *knows* Lydie's been seeing somebody!"

"You're preaching to the choir here, kid. I've said all that till I'm blue in the face. Cara's going to be happy about us. I know she is. And she won't give a damn what Francie thinks — no one else in the family will. But Lydie's just kept dragging her feet, figuring if she told Cara she'd have to tell Francie, and all of a sudden here we are, and now she's afraid of how upset Cara will be just because she's waited so long."

Leigh huffed out a breath. "Well, that's valid. Cara's going to be furious with her mother for keeping all this from her. But when she gets over that, she's going to be happy." Leigh smiled at Mason. "Ecstatically happy."

He smiled back. "I hope so. Lydie's finally agreed that the sneaking around has to stop. This week was a kind of turning point; that's why I couldn't miss it. I've been promising Lydie an ocean cruise for more years than Cara's been alive, and thanks to my little card-playing hobby — which, by the way, is entirely legit — I finally saved up enough to take her."

Leigh averted her eyes and grinned. "I see." And she did see. The lies about both conveniently timed conferences. The mystery apartment in Bellevue. Why neither he nor Lydie had been responding to texts all week, and why calls were so expensive. She recalled her aunt's claiming that half of where she would be staying was "underground."

"I never knew Lydie was such a smooth liar," Leigh marveled.

Mason smirked. "There are a lot of things you don't know about her, Kid. Truth is, she's a great actress. Smart as God makes them, pretty as a picture, and handy with the power tools, too. She's an amazing woman all around."

Leigh looked at the abiding love for her aunt that was written so plainly on the man's face, and her eyes filled with tears. She reached across the car seat and gave him a hug, then wiped her eyes to prevent the overflow.

"It's going to be okay," she choked out. "But Lydie had better tell Cara the truth now, or I will. Don't worry, I'll insist I figured it out for myself and I won't say anything to my mother. But Lydie can't keep lying to Cara like this. I won't let her."

Leigh got out of the car, and Mason started the engine up again. If she wasn't mistaken, his twinkling eyes looked a bit moist, too.

"Thanks, kid," he returned.

Chapter 22

When Leigh returned to her parents' living room, she was surprised to find the couch occupied by Frances instead of Bess. Her mother's walker was nowhere to be seen. "How did you get back in here?" Leigh asked.

"I hobbled," Frances said shortly. She patted the cushion next to her with a glare. "Sit."

Leigh hesitated. "Where's Aunt Bess?"

"Upstairs getting dressed."

"Oh," Leigh mumbled mindlessly, still standing in the doorway. "She woke up?"

"I sat on her." Frances patted the cushion again. "Now, come here."

Leigh shuffled forward. She was fairly certain that her mother couldn't hear well enough from inside the house to eavesdrop on her conversation with Mason. But if Frances had been on her feet, she certainly could have seen them both out the window. "What's up?" Leigh asked tightly, perching by her mother's side.

"Do not 'what's up' me," Frances rebuked. "What exactly did Mr. Dublin have to say for himself this time?"

Leigh inhaled deeply. "He said he doesn't think Kyle had anything to do with the petnappings. He thinks he was just keeping the bird for somebody else."

Frances's eyes narrowed. "Oh, of *course* he was."

"It's possible, Mom," Leigh defended. "You don't really think Mason would intentionally hand off stolen property to me or the Pack, do you?"

"Well, of course he would."

"No, he wouldn't!"

Frances's lips pursed. "You do not know the man like I do, Leigh Eleanor."

Leigh's face grew hot. She was fairly certain that her mother had not carried on a single civil conversation with Mason in forty years — if then. But Leigh's losing her temper wouldn't help the situation. They'd had this same argument before and it never got her anywhere. Frances's mind was made up.

Leigh stood. "I have to go."

"Go where?" Frances said skeptically. "We need to discuss this situation. In light of what's happened, I think it's time for another family conference. That man should not be allowed to continue influencing the moral development of my grandchildren. I shall bring up several points for discussion, including—"

"Sorry, Mom," Leigh said, looking around for inspiration. "I can't do this now. I have to... um... clean something."

Frances's chin dipped to her chest. She glared at Leigh over the rims of her glasses. "Oh?"

Inspiration dawned. "Ethan left bubble gum stuck to the bunk bed."

Bullseye.

Frances's whole body stiffened. "You saw chewing gum? *In my house?*"

Leigh nodded enthusiastically. "I should go get it off, don't you think?"

The color had all but drained from Frances's face. "*Where* on the bed?" She shifted on the couch and threw a determined look at the stairway.

"On the wooden supports underneath the top bunk," Leigh continued. "It's hard to see. Probably been there for years. It's blue, and it has stuff stuck in it. You know. Like corgi hair. And lint. And—"

"Leigh Eleanor Koslow!" Frances shrieked. "You get up there and dispose of that horrific substance right now!"

Leigh hid a grin. "Okay, Mom."

She hustled up the steps. She would be alone with her mother all afternoon; it was pretty unlikely that she could avoid the topic of Mason Dublin indefinitely. But she could try.

Bess popped out of the upstairs bathroom just as Leigh reached the hall. Bess was fully dressed, but bleary-eyed and clearly hung over.

"Thanks again for staying last night," Leigh said. "You're free now. Mom will be fine long enough for me to pick up Dad, and Lydie will be back by eight."

Bess's eyes focused slowly. Her forehead wrinkled. "You talk loud."

"Sorry," Leigh whispered. "Rough shift, huh?"

"Let us never speak of it again," Bess replied, passing by her and heading on down the stairs.

Leigh grabbed a roll of paper towels and some wood cleaner from the "auxiliary cleaning cabinet" in the hall and slipped into the guest bedroom. She made her gum-removal task take as long as humanly possible, then lay down for a nap besides.

The effort was fruitless. She had too many loose-ended thoughts tickling her brain. What "good ideas" had Allison come up with for Maura? And if Kyle *wasn't* involved in the petnappings, how could they ever find out who was? Was there necessarily a man involved at all, or was Leigh being subconsciously sexist? Did she have any real reason to assume that the figure she'd seen hanging in the kitchen window was male, other than that it was wearing a hoodie and jeans and doing something criminal? Maybe the scheme was being perpetrated entirely by women. Maybe every female on her father's staff was in a conspiracy, and the newbies were only acting dumb. Was it possible?

Leigh couldn't decide. She knew it was important to keep her mind open, but seeing Amy in particular as being a covert evil genius was impossible.

Her cell phone rang. The call was from her cousin-in-law, and she swooped it up immediately. He was supposed to be watching the Pack. "Gil?"

"Hey, Leigh," he boomed back, sounded self-assured as usual.

Leigh relaxed. A little. "Something wrong?"

"Nothing serious," he answered. "Cara's better, but she's sleeping. And Lenna's fine; the virus seems to run a pretty short course. I just wanted to ask you a question."

A twinge of angst had worked its way into his tone, and Leigh got nervous again. "Yes?"

"Do you have any idea what's going on between Matt and Allison?"

Leigh closed her eyes and exhaled. "I might. Have you heard the name 'Kirsten' being bandied about, by any chance?"

He was quiet a moment. "Possibly. I haven't heard much of what they're saying. Matt mainly just texts. But twice now, Allison's come over here and then left again in a huff. The second time, which was just now, the two of them practically had a shouting match out in the yard."

"Oh." That did not sound good.

"So what's going on?" Gil asked. "Matt won't tell me a thing, and I've never seen the two of them go at it like that before. Matt and his sister, yes, but not him and Allison."

"No," Leigh agreed. "You're right." She could accept the fact that Matt wasn't a child anymore, but the realization that growing into teenagers would inevitably send the Pack their separate ways was depressing at several levels. "I'm pretty sure it's about a high school girl Matt met at the clinic. He likes her, but Allison has known her longer and can't stand her. How that equates to shouting at each other in the yard, I don't know... Probably Allison's annoyed that he's not taking her advice."

Gil chuckled with relief. "Oh. Well, I guess clashes like that are inevitable. Matt's growing up, all right."

Inevitable. Leigh really didn't want to think about that. "Don't worry about it," she advised. "I'll talk to Allison tonight." And talk they would. Allison was used to having the rest of the Pack — and even various detectives — take her opinions seriously. But she might as well learn now that lovestruck teenagers never listened to anybody.

They hung up, and Leigh felt slightly more at ease. Fighting with one's older cousin, at least, was an entirely age-appropriate activity for an eleven-year-old girl.

A loud knock sounded from below. Leigh hastened down the stairs.

She looked out the front window and blinked in surprise at the sight of a tall, extremely burly man standing on the front porch. Only after he moved a little did she realize that her father was standing beyond him. A third person flanked Randall's other side. Leigh saw the top of a frizzy blond head and recognized Paige.

"We do have a bell," Frances sniped from the kitchen as Leigh raced from the window to the door. *"Really!"*

Leigh reached the door just as it popped open. "Dad!" she exclaimed. "Why are you back so —"

She didn't need to finish the question. The greenish tint to his face and all-too-familiar odor drifting up from his pant legs told the story.

"Oh, no," She breathed.

"Whatever is the matter?" Frances's voice called out.

"He upchucked," Paige said unnecessarily, holding out a hand to steady Randall as he hobbled over the threshold and into the house. The giant man with her moved quietly back a step. "He said some other people in the family had a bug, so we figured he had it, too."

Randall moved past Leigh and straight towards the half bath.

Leigh cast another glance at Paige, who was today wearing bright purple feather earrings with a tight pink and orange scrub shirt that barely covered her midriff. "He must feel really bad," Leigh said worriedly, "to agree to come home early."

Paige scoffed. "Agree? Are you kidding me? Dr. Stallions and Jeanine practically had to drag him out! He only gave in after they started to make him feel guilty — telling him he was endangering clients by spreading viruses everywhere." She shook her head with frustration, but her voice held respect. "You know the doc. Everyone's allowed to get sick but him!"

Leigh watched as her father made it safely into the powder room and shut the door. An unpleasant sound followed.

"Lift the seat first!" Frances screeched from the kitchen.

Leigh winced. "Thank you for bringing him home."

Paige shrugged. "Oh, it was nothing. Steve was coming to pick me up anyway. Have you met my boyfriend?" She turned and gestured to the man behind her, and Leigh felt an odd sting of disappointment. Had she been hoping that the mystery boyfriend would turn out to be skinny and shortish?

She had. "Hello, Steve," she said pleasantly, feeling hypocritical. "Nice to meet you."

"You too," the man answered politely.

"What do you do for a living?" Leigh blurted.

Oh, was that ever smooth, she chided herself. *Sheesh!* She was no better than Morgan.

"I'm a civil engineer," he answered, not seeming offended.

"Awesome," Leigh replied, feeling further disappointed.

"You need me to help the doc get upstairs or anything?" he asked.

Leigh considered. Randall would doubtless be more comfortable upstairs, and Steve could probably swoop him up and haul him up the steps like a baby. But Randall would hate that. Besides which, how would they get him down again?

"No thanks," Leigh replied. "It'll be easier if he stays down here. Thanks again, though."

The couple waved off her gratitude and departed towards Steve's car, a recent model Honda SUV with a moon roof. Leigh's disappointment was complete. Paige might not be making a fortune as a veterinary assistant, but her boyfriend appeared to be doing fine — making it unlikely that either would risk jail time to moonlight in extortion.

Leigh closed the door and leaned back against it with a sigh. So much for her suspect list.

She had to be missing something.

Could their zeal to find a common link associated with the clinic be leading them astray? What if Kyle really was nothing more than a patsy, approached by an acquaintance and offered money to warehouse the bird? Kyle needed money, and it was easy work. How many questions would he ask?

Leigh tried to put herself in the mind of the petnapper. Most likely, he or she lived in Avalon or Bellevue, not too far from where Zeus had been found. They had stolen dogs, cats, and birds, after which they had kept them for at least one day — until the next nightfall. But where were the pets being hidden in the meantime? A backyard? A basement? Wouldn't neighbors notice a sudden series of unfamiliar barks and meows? The longer they kept the pets, the higher their risk of discovery.

Leigh had never really considered the logistics. The cockatiel was loud. Zeus was even louder. If any of the neighbors were suspicious types, the squawk of an unknown bird would be a dead giveaway. Which meant it made perfect sense for the brains of the operation to farm the animals out to unsuspecting third parties. At least the noisier ones.

Leigh frowned again. The realization was interesting, but did it help anything? Kyle was dead. They had no way of finding out, now, from whom he had gotten the cockatiel. His apartment could have been broken into by the loan sharks who were threatening him, but it seemed more likely that the culprit was actually the petnapper.

Leigh sucked in a breath. It made sense. All the petnapped animals she knew of had been returned on time except Opie, the cockatiel. He was stolen on a Friday. Kyle left for his poker game on

Saturday, fully intending to return that night or the next morning. The victim, Leonard, set out his money on Saturday night and expected the bird to be returned on Sunday, as the note indicated. But the petnapper couldn't reach Kyle on Sunday and had no idea where he was, which was a problem. The longer the petnapper waited to return the bird, the greater the chance that Leonard would break down and call the police, figuring he had nothing to lose. And once *any* victim cooperated with the authorities, the petnapper's days of easy money would be numbered. Hence, by Monday morning, the petnapper was desperate enough to break into Kyle's apartment.

He would not have been pleased to discover that the bird wasn't there.

The sound of the bathroom door opening broke Leigh's concentration. Her father emerged and headed towards the bed. "You need help, Dad?" she offered.

He waved her away.

She didn't blame him. It was lousy enough to be sick without adding crutches into the bargain. From the kitchen, Frances barked out a series of admonitions and suggestions to Randall regarding the proper way to throw up, then turned her attention to her daughter.

"Leigh," Frances called. "You'll need the antibacterial cleanser to decontaminate the powder room. And don't forget to put on gloves! All your materials should be disposed of in a plastic bag — the thick ones, not the kitchen bags, and you'll have to —"

Leigh tuned out. She watched her father make his way to the edge of the inflatable mattress. He was steadier on the crutches now, at least. He leaned them against the wall, then collapsed on the bed with a groan, causing a half dozen of Frances's perfectly symmetrical file stacks to converge into a heap.

Leigh walked over and sat on the couch. Her mother continued to make fussy proclamations from the kitchen, none of which Leigh took in. Her brain was otherwise occupied.

When the petnapper broke into Kyle's place on Monday, he had found no bird. Maybe he realized that Kyle's own cat was gone too, and maybe he didn't. Either way, he couldn't have known that Leigh had them. But by sometime on Tuesday, he had figured out that the cockatiel was at the veterinarian's house. And even after a narrow escape from the police that night, the petnapper had been bold enough to return for the bird on the next evening, Wednesday. And he had taken the bird straight back to Leonard that night.

If the petnapper *didn't* have an informant working inside the clinic, how could he have known where to find the bird? How could he have known that the ransom set out for Lucky was a sting?

Leigh caught herself clenching her teeth again. Maybe her father was right. Maybe that critical information could have been obtained just as easily from *outside* the clinic.

All one had to do was watch.

The house's landline rang, and Leigh jumped up to get it.

"Where are your gloves?" Frances demanded as Leigh swung through the kitchen doorway. Leigh picked up the phone. "Koslow residence."

"Hey," Maura's voice greeted. "I saw your dad take off. Sorry he's feeling bad."

"We're all sorry," Leigh agreed. Then the detective's words penetrated. "You saw him? Where are you?"

"I'm at the clinic," she answered. "He gave me permission to cross-check our new list of petnapping victims with the clinic database."

Leigh felt a sick feeling in her stomach. *Oh no, you don't,* she ordered herself grimly. *You cannot catch this damnable virus, too. You just can't!*

"Your dad made it clear that he wanted to know the results. That's why I'm calling." Maura paused a beat.

"And?" Leigh prompted.

"He's not going to like this," Maura said soberly. "But we've identified victims now in five different police districts. The petnapper's targets have been spread out all the way from West View to Sewickley and across the river into McKees Rocks. But they all have one thing in common. Every one of them is a patient of his."

Chapter 23

Leigh had never endured a longer Friday afternoon. The endless bonanza of scrubbing and sanitizing necessitated by Randall's sickness was interrupted only by Frances's periodic need for help in reordering and restacking six bankers' boxes' worth of clinic files. Leigh had followed her mother's directions like a zombie, grateful that Frances had been distracted from her plan to call a family conference about Mason. Leigh could only hope that the next time her mother thought about it, Leigh wouldn't be around.

It was past dinnertime now, but there was no dinner. Randall was nowhere close to eating again and Frances had declared that she would be satisfied with cottage cheese and an apple. Leigh was concerned that her mother might be coming down with the virus too, but other than the light meal, Frances showed no signs of deceleration. Leigh dug into her own bowl of cereal and tried not to feel sorry for herself. Warren had dropped by on his way back from town with the intention of bringing the kids over and fixing dinner for everyone, but Leigh had been forced to intercept him outside the door. Three family members down sick was enough already; odds were, there would be more. Warren's absence all week had given him a good shot at escaping it, and Leigh was determined that he would.

No matter how much she would love one of his homemade enchiladas.

She swallowed a spoonful of granola and realized that her mother was staring at her.

"I daresay it will not be good for business if anyone in your father's employ is involved in these petnappings," Frances proclaimed.

"No," Leigh agreed solemnly, "it will not."

There had been no further developments in the investigation — at least not so far as Leigh knew. Randall had insisted on talking to Maura over the phone himself, and a couple hours later, he had also had a discussion with the Avalon Chief of Police. Both encounters seemed to drain the veterinarian significantly, and Leigh was consumed with curiosity about their content — particularly the second one. But as Randall had ended each call either succumbing to nausea or drifting off to sleep, Leigh hadn't the heart to interrogate him. She was more annoyed that she'd been prevented from eavesdropping by her mother's untimely monologues on the virtues of sodium hypochlorite and hanging file folders, respectively.

Which is why Frances's bringing up the subject now was curious.

"I think we should do something about this," Frances announced.

"We?" Leigh inquired.

Frances's lips pursed. "The family, of course! We'll already be conferencing to discuss the Mason issue. We might as well brainstorm a solution to your father's PR problems at the same juncture. Although I daresay the timing is abominable. We'll have to wait until the sickness has passed to prevent further infection."

Leigh resolved to get sick herself if it would delay such a debacle. "I really don't think Lydie would want Mason to be the topic of a family conference."

Frances scoffed. "He's been the topic of enough of them over the years, that's for certain! But Lydie will agree with me on this one. The children must be protected."

Leigh bit back any comment and took another look at her watch — for the fortieth time that day. Lydie should be back soon. And when she arrived, Leigh had every intention of intercepting her in advance as she had Warren. First off, because it was the right thing to do to offer to stay overnight and spare Lydie the risk of contracting the virus herself. Never mind that there was zero chance Lydie would take her up on it; both twins were inordinately proud of their ability to fend off bugs that laid everyone else low. Secondly, Leigh refused to let another day pass without Lydie's knowing that the jig was up. Cara deserved to know the truth about her parents being a couple again. And Frances could not be allowed to put Mason through the indignity of a family conference when the poor man's only crime had been to respect Lydie's desire for discretion.

Leigh had just finished her last bite of cereal when she heard the slam of a car door close by.

"Lydie's home," Frances said with certainty.

Leigh rose and put her empty bowl in the dishwasher. She fetched her mother's cell phone from the recharger on the counter and sat it down on the table next to her. "I'm going to talk to Aunt Lydie and see if she wants me to stay tonight. I'd hate for her to get sick."

Frances nodded her approval, knowing as well as Leigh did that Lydie would be coming over regardless. Leigh looked around the counter again, then frowned. "Where is Dad's phone?"

"He took it with him this morning," Frances answered.

Leigh walked into the living room and looked around where her father was sleeping. Then she checked the powder room and everywhere in between. "He must have left it at the clinic again," she said, returning to the kitchen.

Frances frowned. "If he would only leave the thing in his pocket! But he hates wearing it while he's working." She threw up her hands. "Well, I'm afraid you'll just have to go down there and fetch it. Some clients have that as his emergency number. He may not care a whit at the moment, but if he wakes up in the middle of the night and realizes he doesn't have it, he won't sleep a wink."

Leigh promised she would take care of the matter, even as she hastened out the back door. Lights had come on inside Lydie's house. She crossed the short distance and knocked on her aunt's door. "It's me, Aunt Lydie," she called.

The door opened to reveal Lydie offering the same unconditionally loving, uncomplicated smile that had soothed Leigh all her life. Leigh and Cara, naturally, had never thought their mothers looked identical, despite what others said. Leigh could see how both twins would have been attractive girls, with their dark brown eyes, pert noses, and wavy brown hair. They were still attractive, despite the Morton female curse of being shaped like a pear. But they were rarely mistaken for each other anymore, since only Lydie dyed her hair and the pear curse was more pronounced with Frances. For Leigh and Cara, though, the most obvious difference between the women had always been their smiles.

"Hello, dear," Lydie greeted, ushering her inside. "You look exhausted. Don't worry, I'll be over in a jiffy. I just wanted to get my things out of the car."

"No rush," Leigh replied. "I only wanted to catch you up on a few things." As Lydie moved around putting her things away,

Leigh explained about Randall's illness and made the expected gesture of offering to stay over.

"Oh, don't worry about me," Lydie said with a dismissive wave of her hand. "I never get those things. I'll be fine."

Leigh couldn't help but note that her aunt looked unusually happy. Unusually… relaxed.

"How was your drive?" Leigh asked, not even thinking until that moment that the whole "tooling down the Turnpike" thing was probably just part of the scam. For all she knew, her aunt had been cooling her heels in the Pittsburgh airport all day. She had left three days earlier than Mason as well. Where had she spent all that time?

"Long," Lydie replied with sincerity. "Too much construction. As usual."

Leigh frowned. She understood the reasoning behind the deception. Still, it hurt to believe that her aunt could lie to her so easily. "Where were you, really?" Leigh asked softly. "Before and after the cruise with Mason, I mean?"

Lydie stopped what she was doing and whipped her head around toward Leigh. Her face reddened, but she said nothing.

"I figured it out for myself earlier today," Leigh explained. "Don't blame Mason. He only confirmed it."

Lydie still said nothing. Her expression was perfectly stoic.

"I didn't tell anyone," Leigh continued. "But I really wish you would." She offered a smile. "I think it's wonderful. And Cara will, too. We already love the man."

Lydie's eyes moistened. Then they sparkled in a way Leigh had rarely seen before. Lydie took her niece's hand and led her to the living room couch to sit down.

"I can't tell you how happy I am to hear that," Lydie said quietly. "And I'm sorry for lying to you. But it's all so terribly complicated."

"No, it's not," Leigh insisted. "Whatever ideas you've had over the years about how you didn't deserve to be happy or he didn't deserve to be happy or whatever other nonsense you've been telling yourself… it's all just that. Nonsense. Everyone who loves you believes you both deserve to be happy."

Lydie's answering smile was brief. Her eyes misted further. "Not everyone."

Leigh sat forward. "Yes, *everyone*. My mother doesn't think Mason *will* make you happy. But she's wrong about that."

Lydie shook her head slowly. "She might want me to be happy, but she couldn't care less what happens to him. Even after all this time, she... she hates him, Leigh." One tiny tear escaped Lydie's left eye.

Leigh's stomach churned. Her aunt had never been the crying type. "My mother," Leigh responded forcefully, "does not hate *him*. She doesn't even know him. Not anymore. She only hates what he did what to you, because she's nothing if not loyal. She sees herself as a soldier for your cause, and she'll defend you to her dying breath. She would defend me, too, although I don't think she'd enjoy it as much."

Lydie chuckled. Another tear rolled down her cheek. "Don't be silly."

"I'm not being silly," Leigh argued. "I'm being real. I'm not like my mother; I'm more like Aunt Bess. Mom loves both her and me dearly, but she'll never stop trying to improve on us, because we'll never *be* her. We'll also never be *you*."

Lydie looked at Leigh curiously.

"My mother's standards of perfection are high," Leigh explained. "Frances herself is the gold standard for women everywhere, of course. But you're the next best thing, with Cara coming in a close second. The only thing you ever did that she didn't approve of was to marry Mason, and in her mind, that ruined your life. She sees his influence as the antithesis of her own. In the black and white world of Frances Koslow, he is an evil that it is her job to vanquish... and she is determined not to fail you."

Lydie winced. "Good Lord, that's dramatic."

Leigh grinned. "You know I'm right."

"But what can I do?" Lydie shot back. "Other than choose between them? *Again?* That picture you painted doesn't leave much room for compromise."

"That isn't your problem," Leigh insisted. "She doesn't get to decide who you love. You make that decision; her job is to deal with it."

Lydie huffed. "She won't deal with it. She's absolutely refused to spend any time with him since he's come back. She can't be bothered to get to know the man he is now."

"So give her a reason to!" Leigh fired back. "Stand up to her. Tell her that Mason is a part of your life now, whether she likes it or not.

Then she'll have no choice but to make the effort!"

Lydie drew in a long, tired breath.

"You do *not* need to choose between them," Leigh finished gently. "The only choice is my mother's. She has to decide whether being your sister is more important than being Mason Dublin's enemy. And we both know what she's going to pick."

Lydie looked up with a guarded expression.

"Eventually," Leigh added.

Lydie smiled back. "I hope you're right."

Leigh stood. "So," she pressed playfully. "Where *have* you been all day? And all last weekend? You went to quite an effort to pull off this ruse."

Lydie grinned. "You have no idea. Our daughter is too smart by half and must be part bloodhound. We've had more than a few narrow escapes."

Leigh smirked. The thought of Mason climbing out her aunt's window and sliding down the drainpipe as Cara walked in the front door calling, "Mom! The kids are here!" was really too funny. But that had probably never happened. Having Frances living next door 24/7 must have scaled back the couple's options considerably.

"I did go to the historical symposium," Lydie defended. "For the weekend, anyway. I flew out of Harrisburg to take the cruise, which is why I had to drive back down the Turnpike just now."

"And the pawnbrokers' convention?" Leigh asked.

"It's been happening in Las Vegas all week. But I'm afraid Mason never had any intention of going."

Lydie's tone held just enough smugness that Leigh wondered if her aunt didn't actually enjoy the sneaking around... just a bit. Mason had called Lydie "an adventurer," and as Leigh studied the twinkle in her aunt's eye and the pinkish flush to her cheeks, she knew he was telling the truth.

It was disturbing how long one could know a person without really knowing them. Or rather, without seeing them as someone else might.

"Well, take your time coming over," Leigh offered, moving toward the door. "Relax, unwind."

Lydie looked like she was trying not to laugh. After a moment, Leigh realized why. Her aunt had never looked more "unwound" in her life.

Chapter 24

It was past dark when Leigh finally made her way out the door of her parents' house, setting off to drive yet another West View/Avalon loop before heading back up to the North Hills and home. The fact that she could make the drive in her sleep was fortunate, because doing so might be necessary. She yawned as she parked her van across the street from the clinic, hopped out, and made her way toward the basement door.

She didn't carry keys to the clinic. Since the last break-in a decade ago, no one did, except her father. After-hours visits were always made through the basement door, where a staff key was cleverly hidden in a slot behind an electrical box. Randall didn't worry that an intruder would find the key, because unless he or she proceeded immediately to the security panel upstairs and punched in the proper code, the police would be arriving shortly. And the code itself was changed on a regular basis by Jeanine, who would write each new creation down on a special card she inserted into the veterinarian's wallet. The system worked brilliantly as long as Randall remembered to check the card.

Tonight, doing so had been Leigh's job, and she repeated the numbers in her brain as she jogged down the stairs, unlocked the door, and replaced the key. *8258, 8258...* She slipped inside and locked the door behind her, then headed up the stairs. *8258...*

Leigh didn't pause to switch on the lights, as she could see well enough by the emergency lighting and was anxious to get to the panel in time. She had made way too many mortified calls to the Avalon PD over the years explaining how a false alarm was the result of her either forgetting the code, tripping on the staircase, or chasing a wayward young twin across the parking lot.

8258. Leigh reached the security panel and pressed in the code. It took her several seconds to realize that the monitor screen was blank. She frowned and looked at the power light, which generally glowed green.

It was dark.

Leigh swore and looked around her. She saw no evidence of a

power failure. The autoclave light was on and the refrigerator was chugging.

Well, that's just friggin' fabulous, she muttered to herself. The last thing Randall needed to worry about tonight was a problem with his security system. The timing was wretched in any event, with the police definitively linking the petnappings to the clinic. If word got out about a security failure on top of that grim note, no one would ever leave a pet overnight again.

Leigh continued to mutter as she flipped on the lights and scouted the treatment room and pharmacy countertops. Her father could have taken the cell phone out of his pocket anywhere, including the bathroom. Surely someone on staff had noticed it after he left? In which case, where would they put it?

She flipped off the lights in the back and turned on those in the reception room. Randall's cell phone was not on the main desk, or in its drawers, or even in the secret cash compartment under the ledgers. Leigh slammed the last drawer shut again. She felt uneasy, and that annoyed her. It was ridiculous for her to be afraid of being in the clinic alone at night. Her father did it frequently, as had she herself countless times before. So what if the security panel was down? All the doors were locked. And she would be out again in a matter of seconds.

Provided she could find the damn phone.

She raised her head and looked around the waiting room. She opened her mouth to direct a question to the empty yellow chair in the corner, then chuckled at herself. Mrs. Gregg's chair might as well have her name on it, as often as the woman was in residence. No doubt the lonely widow knew that Randall had gone home sick today. She might actually even know where he left his…

Leigh froze. Her gaze remained fixed on the chair. It was the nearest chair to the reception desk. It was also the closest chair to the door of exam room #1, where Randall had parked himself since his injury.

Was it possible?

Her mind quickly ran through the information their petnapper needed to know — information that *could* have come from watching the clinic from the outside.

Or, Leigh thought with a sharp pang of anxiety, *it could have come from sitting right there.*

Mrs. Gregg? A petnapper? It was inconceivable. Partly because she was too darn sweet. Partly because she had no motive. And partly because her hair was in a bob and her short, roundish body could under no circumstances have been the intruder Leigh saw hanging through her parents' window.

But did all those "partlies" add up to a whole? Mrs. Gregg could have been the accomplice. The informant. The one who knew which clients were vulnerable and how much each had to spend. The one who knew that Lucky was headed back home again. And that the cockatiel was going to Randall's house.

It was possible. But was it likely?

Leigh searched her mind for everything she knew about the woman. Mrs. Gregg was somewhere in her fifties. She lived within walking distance of the clinic. She was always spoken of fondly by others, although it was often in a hushed, empathetic tone because her husband had died young of cancer, and their only son had gone to —

Crap!

The memory galvanized her instantly. She moved into the exam room and flipped on the lights. Where *was* that dratted phone? Had her father been in here when he got sick? If so, it was probably still sitting on the counter...

She searched the room with a growing sense of urgency, even as she willed herself to remain calm. She was in no immediate danger. She just needed to find the phone and get back to her father.

The phone wasn't there. Leigh swore out loud again, then quickly checked the other exam rooms. The clinic always felt eerie when it was quiet, and tonight it seemed deathly so. The two cats in their cages in the recovery room had taken no notice of her as she passed by, nor did whatever rabbit, ferret, or guinea pig was sleeping in its nest box in the kennel on the floor. Dogs usually barked when someone came in at night, but at the moment there were none to oblige.

Leigh headed back down the stairs. If someone else found Randall's phone, perhaps they would put it on his desk in the basement. She moved quickly down the steps, around the corner, and past the row of extra-large dog runs that led back to her father's office. A relic from the bygone days when the clinic had doubled as a boarding facility, the runs had more space than most sick pets needed and were now used mainly for storage. The last run held old newspapers for the cage bottoms, and Leigh noticed as she passed it that Jared's usually ordered stacks were jumbled. Blaming Ethan and Mathias, she made a mental note to question them later. But she didn't stop walking. She wanted to find the blasted phone and get out of here.

Mrs. Gregg's son, she pondered, switching on her father's office light. She could remember the woman mentioning him just a few days ago, when Maura was in the waiting room. *My Jonathan*, the widow had said fondly. *He always cried when strangers talked to him.* Somehow, when Mrs. Gregg said those words, Leigh had thought of a shy little toddler.

Aha! Leigh pounced on the phone on her father's desk with glee. It was sitting right in the middle of the newly cleared workspace, and she berated herself for not checking his office first. Her father might not be able to get down here himself on crutches, but it was still a logical place for someone on the staff to put his belongings.

She pocketed the phone, flipped off the light, and turned to leave. Then she heard the sound of a key turning in a lock.

She stopped her breath. The sound was coming from the far side of the basement. From the same door she had come through.

She heard the pop of a metal door opening. Then the swish of rubber weather-stripping sliding along the concrete floor.

Footsteps.

Leigh released her breath as quietly as possible. There was no reason to panic. Whoever had walked in obviously knew where the key was hidden and was probably supposed to be here. They would be heading up the stairs any second to punch in the code, and once they were overhead, Leigh would hasten herself out. That way she would be covered on the extremely small off-chance that said person *wasn't* supposed to be here.

The footsteps moved slowly. They stopped now and then. Whoever had entered seemed in no rush to get up the stairs.

Did they know that the security system was down?

Leigh shivered at the thought, but could not rule it out. The petnapper did seem to know everything else about the clinic... and its clients.

Thanks to dear, sweet Mrs. Greg, Leigh thought to herself miserably. *That poor, lonely woman whose only son had gone to jail...*

The beam of a moving flashlight reflected off the ceiling outside Randall's office.

...for beating his girlfriend to death with a shovel.

Chapter 25

Leigh remained still. The irony was great, given how frequently the chorus of barking in the basement could break an eardrum, that it was now so quiet she feared to move.

She tried to come up with a nonthreatening explanation.

Maybe Jeanine or Dr. Stallions had noticed a problem with the system when they locked up. They had called the company and a friendly technician had just arrived.

Nice try. No way would anyone on staff do such a thing without notifying Randall, or at least asking Frances to do so. But no one from the clinic had called all afternoon.

The narrow beam continued moving, and Leigh's heart began to pound. Strike two. Anyone with authorization to be here, including a technician, would have no reason to use a penlight. They would simply flip the wall switch.

Jonathan Gregg.

Leigh had never met him. She would not remember who he was now had his conviction not been front-page news at the time. Everyone at the clinic had felt terribly for his mother, who had seemed both heartbroken and bewildered. *Maybe if his father were still alive*, the gossipmongers had theorized. *But she couldn't control him. Poor Mrs. Gregg. Poor, poor woman.*

The light moved away again. Leigh began to relax, then heard the sound of a cage door clanging.

She tensed all over again. This was no burglar out for drugs or cash. The intruder was looking for something in particular. Something he expected to find in a cage?

Leigh conjured a mental picture of Mrs. Gregg. Short, frumpy, sweet-natured. She had seemed as happy as anyone when Skippy rallied the community to catch the petnapper. Could her warm smile and slightly dim manner be an act? Was she desperate to help a son paroled — or possibly escaped — from prison? Was he giving her any choice?

The footsteps came closer again. Leigh's breath shuddered. From what reflections she could see, the flashlight beam seemed to be drifting over the empty dog runs.

What animal was he looking for? Leigh hadn't noticed any patients in the basement earlier. The surgeries had all gone home now; the sick animals were kept upstairs.

Was he looking for an animal at all?

Leigh struggled to control her breathing. It sounded like she was wheezing.

Wait. Was that her breathing? Or was that tinny, muffled, TV-volume-down-all-the-way sound coming from *him?*

A creak sounded at the bottom of the stairs, and Leigh's taut shoulders slumped with relief. She was only imagining things. The intruder wasn't closer; he was farther away. He was climbing the steps now.

And as soon as he was up them, she would be free. She would run for the door and call the cops the second she was safe. She didn't need to understand what was happening; she only needed to get the hell outside.

If only he wouldn't notice her on the way up. When he reached the halfway point, he would technically be able to see her, but she consoled herself with the fact that she was in darkness. The dim glow of the emergency lights only lit up the steps and the exit route. She would be able to see him as he came up the stairs, but he shouldn't be able to see her.

Unless, of course, he decided to shine his light right at her.

Don't breathe!

The figure moved into view. Leigh willed her heart to stop thumping so loudly. It disobeyed her.

Step. Step.

She saw his face first. And she really wished she hadn't. His hood was down, and the strange light made his skin glow a yellowish orange. His dark hair was long and pulled into a band at the base of his neck. His lower lip was swollen and the whole right side of his jaw looked puffy. His chin and neck bore multiple scratches. His left nostril was an amorphous blob of swollen tissue and dried blood.

Leigh choked back a cry of horror. *Don't shine the light here, don't shine the light here…*

The figure passed. The footsteps stopped; the doorknob at the top of the steps squeaked slightly. Leigh swore she could hear the man breathe again.

The door swung open. Footsteps moved on into the treatment room. Leigh allowed herself one good drag of oxygen. Surely he would head straight for the kennels now. She prepared to make her move.

As soon as his footsteps moved from the doorway overhead she tiptoed the first few feet out of the office and into the corridor between the staircase and the dog runs.

She heard a noise and stopped again. Another door had just swung open.

The basement door that she was headed for.

One of Maura Polanski's favorite curse words echoed inside her head.

Leigh looked to her right and left. It was hopeless. Scarface, whoever he was, was most definitely not supposed to be here. But the person who'd just entered wasn't either. And this one didn't even have a penlight. The basement door had popped open as quietly as it was possible to pop it, and the few footsteps that followed had gone nowhere. Criminal Number Two, as far as Leigh could tell, was doing nothing but standing quietly by the door.

She could not run out of the basement. She could not run up the stairs. She could not make the slightest sound, and she could not stay where she was. If the silent doorman decided to move, he would spot her as soon as he rounded the corner. She could backtrack into her father's office, but if anyone bothered to search it they were bound to find her, because there was absolutely nowhere inside of it to hide.

Could she hide anywhere else? An idea formed in her mind just as the sounds started up again. The ceiling creaked as the man upstairs walked, and the footsteps across the basement began to move as well. Leigh didn't bother thinking through the rest of her plan. She used the cover of other sounds to pivot and slip through the door of the paper run.

A rough hand grabbed her and covered her mouth; another coiled around her waist.

She decided it was okay to panic now.

"Don't scream!" a male voice hissed in her ear, just as she freed a hand to poke at the nearest eyeball. "We're the police! It's a sting!"

Holy hell. Leigh's muscles sagged with relief.

"Can I let go of you?"

Leigh nodded emphatically, and the man's arms gradually loosened.

"Just hold still and be quiet."

Leigh wanted to protest that she wasn't an idiot, but since there was some evidence to the contrary, she kept her mouth shut.

The door at the top of the steps creaked. Footsteps started down. The policeman tried to muscle his way in front of Leigh, but their movements made a rustling noise. Leigh winced as the figure on the stairs stopped suddenly.

He had heard them.

Crap.

The tinny, muffled sound came again, and now that Leigh stood mere inches away she realized the policeman was wearing an earpiece. It was clearly not a great one, but the Avalon PD was no SWAT team, either. "He's got it," she heard the voice squeak. "Move in!"

The overhead lights switched on. The officer beside her hustled out of the run in a flash. Leigh stood still and watched as the figure on the steps hesitated a moment, then started up, only to be confronted by another policeman at the top of the steps. "Put your hands up!"

Scarface was carrying a kennel in one hand. He made a feint as if he would jump off the staircase and run, but his cause was clearly lost. There were policemen at the top and bottom of the stairs and another by the basement door. "Put your hands up!" all three shouted.

Scarface swore. He dropped the kennel and kicked it viciously the rest of the way down the steps. The officer at the bottom sidestepped the missile and charged just as the other at the top descended. Scarface offered no further resistance as the two cuffed him and hustled him down to solid ground.

"We got him," the officer by the door reported into his radio.

"Got her too," another one reported from the other end.

Leigh crept out of her hiding place. *Her, too?* The officers began to frisk their suspect, and Leigh moved down the corridor on shaky legs. The carrier Scarface had kicked had bounced down the stairs, struck the door of the staff bathroom and careened toward her. The policemen seemed wholly unconcerned with it. But Leigh was not.

"Whatcha doing wandering around a vet clinic, boy?" the police chief questioned their captive. Leigh realized he must have been the man stationed upstairs; most likely hiding somewhere in the kennel room. The carrier Scarface had picked up was the one Leigh had seen sitting out in the floor, holding some kind of sleeping small mammal.

No sound came from the carrier now. No evidence of movement.

"Well?" the police chief repeated.

The accused said nothing. In full light, the injuries to his face looked even more gruesome than in the dark. He also looked considerably younger than Leigh had assumed.

"What happened to you?" the chief continued. "Did you get in a fight with a pair of scissors?"

"It was a beak," Leigh blurted, unable to restrain herself. The policeman seemed to have forgotten she was there. She was only a foot away from the dropkicked carrier now, and still she could hear nothing from within. She felt a certain amount of empathy for the boy with the ravaged face; his torn nostril would leave a scar for sure, and though the rest of his injuries would heal, they would be painful in the process. But her empathy only went so far.

"The beak of a cockatoo," she repeated as all four men stared at her. "And its claws. Most likely also a puncture or two from the teeth of a friendly mutt named Lucky."

"Friendly?!" the boy protested, evidently forgetting his plan to stay quiet. He followed up with a string of rather unimaginative four letter words. "That dog's psycho!"

"We're bringing her down," a voice over the radio informed.

Leigh cast a nervous glance down at the carrier. Through the slats on its sides she could see a tuft of soft brown fur. It was motionless. "You're the psycho, Jonathan," she hissed.

"Who the hell is Jonathan?" he snapped back.

Footsteps pounded down the staircase outside.

Leigh squatted by the carrier, opened the door, and braced herself to look in. Wood shavings had scattered everywhere. The dome-shaped plastic house in which the animal had been sleeping was upended in the rear of the kennel. The mass of fur was lying on its side in the front. Leigh put in a hand and gently felt it.

It was cold and stiff.

It was also completely synthetic. Leigh's heart skipped a beat as she pulled out a stuffed rabbit with large plastic eyes that somehow looked vaguely familiar.

"Aw, man!" the boy roared, staring at the object in her hands with disgust. He followed up with a few more vulgarities just as a fourth policeman walked through the door, guiding in front of him a cuffed accomplice. Her face was partly obscured; wisps of her bountiful, flyaway hair were stuck in the tears that streamed down her cheeks.

It was Kirsten.

Chapter 26

The fourth policeman was followed down the steps by a very self-satisfied looking Maura Polanski. She shot a look at Leigh that was part castigation, part amusement, then threw both hands up in the air. "I knew it would be you," she said with a smirk, walking over. "They told me an unidentified female had jumped out of a van and sashayed right into the clinic, and I told myself, 'Of course that's her. Who else would knowingly barge into a sting operation?'"

Leigh's face flushed. "*Knowingly?* What am I, psychic? I just came to get my dad's phone!"

Maura blinked at her a moment. "Your dad didn't tell you?"

Leigh groaned. "My dad has been either throwing up or unconscious the entire afternoon!"

"Oh," Maura said with surprise. "*Oh*," she repeated heavily. "Sorry about that. Both the chief and I talked to him, and you were right there with him at the time, so we assumed... I mean, the doc sounded pretty good to me. I had no idea he was that bad off."

Leigh blew out a breath. "It's what he does. Like a wounded gazelle on the Serengeti — he can show no weakness. I'm sure he did his best to sound perfectly normal to you, then collapsed as soon as he hung up. He hasn't said a word to me or my mother all afternoon!"

Maura reached up and scratched her head. "Well, that explains that, I guess."

"Why didn't the police just tell me when I got here?" Leigh questioned.

"The guy watching the lot didn't recognize you," Maura answered. "By the time they figured out who you probably were, the perp was at the door."

"So they figured they'd just let me stumble into some potentially homicidal maniac?" Leigh asked, irritated.

Maura smirked again. "You weren't in any danger. There was no indication the perp was armed, and if it looked like you were getting into any trouble, they would have intervened. But as long as you stayed out of his way, they figured they might as well see how far he'd go. They had him on breaking and entering at the door, but when he picked up the rabbit cage, that clinched it."

The boy swore again. The police officers had been reading him his rights while Maura and Leigh talked, but he appeared to be listening more to Maura. Now his grisly face swung toward Kirsten.

"It was a setup, you idiot!" he yelled.

"Well, how was I supposed to know?" Kirsten screeched back.

Leigh looked down at the stuffed bunny she still held in her hands.

"That's Eddie's," Maura said proudly. "Cute little thing, isn't it? Very realistic."

Leigh considered. It all made perfect sense... in retrospect. Kirsten's appearances at the clinic might be sporadic, but when present, she did have access to all that happened therein. She had been somewhere in the back when Paige treated Lucky's bleeding nail and she had been in the room when Olan said he would die if anyone ever stole his prized cockatoo. Even more telling, she could have seen the cockatiel cage at the clinic on Tuesday and known that Randall planned to take the bird home.

But she was just a kid!

Leigh looked at the sobbing blonde. The teen appeared mortified. But apparently she was not so cowed that she wouldn't try one last-ditch effort to save herself, even if it meant throwing her boyfriend under the bus. As Leigh watched, Kirsten looked from one policeman to the other and then suddenly assumed a hurt expression. "You never told me you were going to *steal* the animals!" she accused, blinking at Scarface through mascara-smeared lids.

The boy's eyes rolled.

"I didn't know what you were doing!" Kirsten protested, her attempt to sound innocent so fake it was cringeworthy. "You never told me!"

"Yeah, right," he spat back sarcastically. But then his thin shoulders slumped in resignation. "*Whatever*, Kirsten."

"All right, you two," the chief ordered. "Let's head back up the stairs. Going to take a little ride to the station now. You can call your parents from there."

Kirsten sniffed.

Scarface spouted another vulgarity.

The policemen marched them both up the stairs.

"Well, good job Koslow," Maura said magnanimously, giving her a hefty clap on the shoulder.

Leigh barely remembered to brace herself. She looked up at her friend with skepticism.

"No, I mean it," Maura said, smiling. "You could have screwed the whole thing up completely. As it was, you were only a pain in the ass."

"Thanks," Leigh said dryly.

Maura laughed. "No, really. You stayed quiet and stayed out of it. What more can the Avalon PD ask of a private citizen?"

Leigh continued the skeptical look. Her friend had been possessed by disturbingly good cheer ever since she realized she was going to have a healthy baby at age 43. Leigh kept expecting that the euphoria would wear off eventually, but so far it had not. "I can't believe you're smiling," Leigh said cautiously, "when you know this means my name will appear on yet another police report."

The detective shrugged. "Hey, at least I don't have to write it. I'm not even on duty yet, remember?"

The one other officer remaining in the basement approached Leigh. "Sorry about the… er, manhandling," he said sheepishly. "We were hoping you'd want to keep out of sight, but if you'd bumped into me in that kennel I suspect you would have been too startled to stay quiet."

"You assumed correctly," Leigh agreed. "No problem."

"Can I get a quick statement from you?"

Leigh not so patiently answered the officer's questions as Maura prowled around the remainder of the clinic. When the technicalities were concluded, the last policeman left and Leigh dropped down on the staircase, scattering wood chips in the process. "Jared will not be happy about the state of this place," she said tiredly as Maura sank down beside her.

"Au contraire," Maura said cheerfully. "He's just like your mother, you know. He'll clean it right up and then spend the rest of the day telling everyone what a mess it was."

Leigh smirked. "You know, you're right. He'll be thrilled."

"I'm always right," the detective said smugly.

Leigh scowled at her. "You could have *told* me you suspected

Kirsten."

Maura perked an eyebrow. "Me? I never gave the girl a second thought. I barely knew she existed."

Leigh frowned. "Then how —"

Maura made the annoying smirk again. "Okay, so I'm not *always* right. Myself. But I'm usually right, because I know who to listen to. Who's in the right place at the right time noticing all the right sorts of things."

Leigh considered. "Allison?"

"Incredible instincts, that girl," Maura praised. "She had Kirsten pegged as a phony from the get-go, but she didn't leap from that to petnapper. Not immediately. But when we were looking at people inside the clinic, Allison didn't automatically rule her out just because she was young, pretty, and innocent-looking, either."

Leigh groaned. She herself *had* discounted Kirsten, albeit subconsciously, for no better reason than that the girl was so close in age to her own kids. As if a child's actions, by definition, could be of no consequence. Had Kirsten not been standing right there when Olan mentioned the mango? Allison had remembered that.

"I've got to give her credit," Maura continued. "Allie didn't like the girl, but she didn't jump to conclusions because of that. She waited, and she watched. And when I told her you guys had found Zeus wandering around Avalon, she had a different take on it than we did."

"Oh?" Leigh asked, growing annoyed that it was Maura, and not herself, who had been the recipient of her daughter's musings.

Maura nodded thoughtfully. "We assumed that Zeus had escaped, just like Lucky did. Most likely because he got aggressive with his captor."

"Well, looking at the guy's face, that's pretty obvious, isn't it?" Leigh insisted.

"Well, yeah, but Allison was thinking more about how the animals came to be wandering around free afterwards. With Lucky, it makes sense. Kirsten would have known that the dog hated being picked up, and would have certainly told her boyfriend to avoid that. But you know Lucky... he's good at lulling people into a false sense of security. The petnapper could have lured him with food, put a leash on him, and convinced him to jump in a car. But then what do you do with him? What if he wouldn't get out of the car?

What if he got progressively more nervous and refused to go in a strange house? What if the petnapper used up his treats? You can imagine the guy forgetting all about the warning and just grabbing the dog to hurry it along. Then *whammo*, got your face. You know what I'm saying?"

Leigh nodded. It was easy enough to picture. "So then Lucky's free, and he trots right down the Boulevard and back home. Where does Romeo live, by the way?"

"Other side of Bellevue," Maura confirmed. "But with Zeus, Allison wasn't buying it. She didn't believe he'd gotten away."

Leigh's brow creased. "Why not?"

"Because he would have been in a cage. Or a carrier. Or something. Olan found fruit on the ground and figured the perp had put fruit in the destination cage, opened both doors, and voila. The bird moved from one to the other and the perp slammed the door."

"Yeah," Leigh argued, "but he could have gotten away easily enough the second the door was opened again. They would have to feed him or give him water or something, and he would almost certainly attack."

Maura smiled. "Exactly. And Allison insisted that Kirsten would know that. That she would know *better*, particularly after what had just happened with Lucky. No one had to open the door at all. It would be easy enough to slide food through the bars and hang up a water bottle."

"So what did happen?" Leigh asked, irked that whatever it was that must have occurred to her daughter still hadn't occurred to her.

"Allison's theory was that Zeus was intentionally let go," Maura explained. "Which, if you think about it, could be even riskier than keeping him in the cage."

Leigh pictured someone putting the carrier on the ground, opening the door, and backing away a few feet. *Yeah, right...* she thought grimly. *Good luck with that.*

Cockatoos weren't stupid. And they had long memories.

"But why on earth would they let him go?" Leigh asked. "After taking such a huge risk to capture him?"

"Because they knew that Olan had spilled the beans."

Leigh mulled the thought. "They couldn't have. Olan called my dad at home Thursday night. There was no conversation about it at the clinic; the clinic was already closed. And Kirsten didn't even come in Friday. She couldn't possibly have overheard anything!"

Maura shook her head. "She didn't."

"Then how could either of them have known that Olan squealed? Kirsten heard him say he would *die* if anything happened to the cockatoo — I was there. I wouldn't have guessed he'd take the chance, either. I still don't think he would have if my dad hadn't talked him into it."

"Kirsten knew that Olan called your dad," Maura replied.

"How?"

"Texting," Maura answered. "Another thing that comes more immediately to Allison's mind than it would to yours or mine. I mean, we text, sure. But teenagers —"

"I *know* how much teenagers text," Leigh grumbled. The picture became clearer. "It was Matt, wasn't it? He was texting Kirsten, probably about five times a minute all week."

Maura nodded. "Yep."

"So he just happened to tell her that Olan called, and that Zeus was stolen, and that the police were going to get involved. And here Kirsten and Scarface —" she stopped and looked at Maura. "What is his name?"

"Shawn."

"And here Kirsten and Shawn are sitting with a cageful of unhappy, screaming cockatoo that everyone in the North Boros is soon going to be looking for."

"Exactly."

Leigh blew out a breath. "So they let him go. Drove him somewhere dark in the middle of the night and just opened the cage door. They wouldn't have cared if he lived or died at that point, as long as he couldn't be traced back to them." She considered some more. "It makes sense, but it's hardly proof. The bird *could* have attacked while they were feeding it or moving it from cage to cage."

"Yes," Maura agreed. "But even so, it was unlikely they would attempt such a thing *outside*, as loud as the bird could be."

"Shawn would have been bleeding like a stuck pig," Leigh argued. "It could have gotten away from them somehow, whether they intended it or not."

"Absolutely true," Maura agreed. "I wasn't convinced, either. Not until I ran a check on the boyfriend. Turns out he's a dropout just shy of eighteen, with a juvey record. So Allison proposed a sting operation."

"Why didn't she tell me any of this?" Leigh protested. "Why didn't you?"

"She told me that you insisted this morning that you had enough to worry about just taking care of your parents."

Leigh frowned. She made a mental note never to say anything like that to Allison ever again.

"And as I explained already," Maura continued, "I thought your dad told you everything else."

"Fine," Leigh conceded. Then she remembered Gil's reporting to her that Allison and Matt had been arguing all day. "Matt didn't want to believe that Kirsten was involved, I bet," she theorized. "He also wouldn't want to admit that he'd inadvertently leaked critical information to the petnapper. Allison would have a field day with that."

Maura grinned. "I believe the youths had words, yes."

Leigh shook her head. "But she convinced him to try a sting?"

"She did," Maura confirmed. "Matt texted Kirsten that the security system at the clinic had broken down, and that your Dad was upset because it couldn't be fixed until Saturday morning. Matt also told her that Lenna was freaking out because her bunny was down there, and she was afraid it wasn't safe."

"Why would a pet rabbit be in the clinic over a Friday night?"

Maura shrugged. "Who knows? Who cares? The point is, Matt told Kirsten it was there. He also bragged to Kirsten that if the petnapper *did* steal it, it would be a real windfall, because Lenna's dad was super rich and would pay anything to get his baby girl's precious bunny back, and Randall *couldn't* report it because once word got out that a pet had been stolen from the clinic, he'd be ruined."

Leigh blew out a breath. "My God, that's brilliant. Far out, but brilliant."

"Well, they bought it," Maura declared. "Not only that, but they decided — like the teenagers they are — that such a ridiculous risk was actually worth it. With the community banding together and sharing information, the next pet they targeted was almost certain to be their last. But I think the easy money had gone to both of their heads. The bait Allison dangled was just too perfect to resist.

Harmless bunny. No security. Rich Daddy. Strong motive for silence. Shawn probably figured he'd do just this *one last job*, and then he could go out a winner."

Maura shrugged. "And if not, well, the sting would give the Avalon PD a little something different to do on a Friday night. We had a guy watching the drop-off point for Zeus's ransom too, just in case. But of course nothing happened there." Maura smiled. "Because your brilliant daughter was right all along."

Leigh smiled sadly. "She is brilliant, isn't she? I just wish she wasn't so secretive."

"You know," Maura suggested tentatively, "she would have talked to you, if you'd talked to her." She rose from the steps and offered Leigh a hand. "Just saying."

Leigh took the hand and got up. She looked over her shoulder, then sighed and dusted the wood shavings off her butt. "I'm only trying to keep Allison safe," she defended. "It's my job as her mother. She may be smart, but she also has a natural inclination to get herself into trouble."

Maura smirked. "Yes, Frances."

Chapter 27

"So the security system's back on now and everything's buttoned up," Maura assured Randall, whose green complexion and mussed hair belied his attempts to feign normalcy. At his request, Maura had followed Leigh back to West View to explain the evening's events in person. But the best the veterinarian could manage when the detective arrived was to prop himself up in bed, and even then, his eyes occasionally lost their focus and drifted toward the powder room.

Maura's summary had been succinct.

"Well, I suppose that's the last of the teenage volunteers," Frances announced bitterly. "Really!"

Randall started to shake his head, but stopped. "We've had a hundred kids through the clinic, Frances," he said instead, closing his eyes. "This was just a fluke."

Frances's lips pursed. "We'll discuss it later."

Randall sank down in his pillows, obviously spent. Maura hastened a polite exit, and Leigh walked her out to the street.

Maura got into her car. "I'd better get a move on. There's a little man at my house that probably has the big man at my house at the end of his rope about now."

Leigh chuckled. Lieutenant Gerry Frank was one proud papa. Maura's college-age stepkids were thoroughly enamored of their little half-brother as well.

"I should get home to Allison," Leigh admitted. "She's bound to be anxious to know what happened. Unless she's already found out?"

Maura grinned. "She's sent me a couple of texts, yes. But I told her she'd have to ask you."

Leigh smiled. "Thanks."

Maura started up her car and began to pull out, but had to wait for a van to pass by. A van which then pulled to the curb by Lydie's house.

"Looks like you're on, Koslow!" Maura laughed as she pulled away. "Enjoy!"

"Thanks," Leigh repeated. They had both recognized the van as Cara's. They both also knew that Allison was very likely to be inside it.

Leigh's daughter popped out of the back seat and sprung onto the sidewalk, looking after Maura's departing car with obvious disappointment. Lenna and Matt followed and their parents emerged from the front.

"What happened?" Allison begged her mother. Barely a pace behind, Matt stared at Leigh with equal intensity.

"Um..." Leigh began uncertainly, studying Cara and Lenna. She was relieved to see that both of the sicklings looked back to normal. "It's kind of a long story."

"Come inside!" Lydie called pleasantly from her front porch. "You too, Leigh and Allison, if you'd like."

Leigh was beginning to get the idea that delivering Allison was not the March family's primary goal.

"Mom asked us all to come over," Cara explained in a whisper, her eyes burning with an equal mix of excitement and worry. "I think she has some kind of announcement. Please stay, if you can."

Leigh looked at her daughter. "Ethan's sick," Allison offered, answering the unspoken question. "Dad's with him. He told me it was fine to get out of the house for a while."

Leigh's shoulders slumped. Poor Ethan. Another one down. And an exhausted Warren left alone with him! They were all doomed now.

"Come on, Leigh," Cara urged. "You can explain what's happened to all of us."

Leigh nodded in agreement, and a few minutes later they were all assembled comfortably in Lydie's small living room. The windows were open, assuring that assistance for Randall and Frances was only a shout away, but without an extra person constantly in the house, the Koslows could at last return to some measure of peace and privacy.

"Yes, please do explain things, dear," Lydie suggested amiably, even as she kept glancing toward the street out the front windows. Leigh couldn't help but notice that the new twinkle in her aunt's eye, so obvious earlier in the afternoon, seemed even brighter now. Still, the flush in Lydie's cheeks and her slightly hurried speech betrayed anxiety.

Leigh started her tale with the discovery of Zeus under the rhododendron, filling in the blanks for Gil and Cara as needed. She made sure to give Allison all the credit she was due, with the exception of whatever methods the girl had used to get her besotted cousin to see reason. Sensitive to Matt's potential embarrassment, Leigh painted the sting as more of a mutual effort, and she was gratified to see that Allison made no contradiction. Accidentally aiding and abetting the enemy was one thing; being both used and cuckolded by your first significant crush was a whole other level of humiliation.

"How could Shawn not suspect somebody was in the clinic already?" Allison asked astutely when Leigh completed her rundown. "You must have had the lights on when you were wandering around upstairs."

"I did," Leigh answered. "But Maura said they parked his car in a parking lot off the Boulevard, over the hill. They climbed up through the woods and couldn't even see the clinic till they got there. Kirsten was supposed to stay back until Shawn came out with the rabbit, but one of the policemen spotted her and took her into custody before she could warn him."

"So how did the guy who got murdered get hold of the cockatiel in the first place?" Matt asked. "Did he have anything to do with the petnappings?"

"Probably not," Leigh admitted. "Kyle was Shawn's cousin; most likely he agreed to keep Opie for a few days without having any idea what was going on. Shawn lives in the basement of his parents' house in Bellevue, and the police are guessing he was able to keep most of the animals there, but the birds would have been too loud. They're not sure yet who Shawn planned to con into watching Zeus, but the cockatoo wouldn't have been there for long in any event. Once Kirsten told Shawn that Olan had called the police, Maura thinks he probably released the bird on the edge of the hollow between Avalon and Bellevue. Probably hoped it would stay in the trees and not be found for a while. If ever."

"The whole idea is just horrible," Cara said with chagrin. "The bird could have died."

"Kirsten does really like animals," Allison admitted begrudgingly. "I don't think they ever intended to hurt any of them, physically, no matter what the ransom notes said. They're just both kind of stupid."

"Kirsten's a ditz," Mathias said dismissively, not looking a bit sheepish. "Anyone can see that!"

"Sounds like it," his father agreed cluelessly.

Leigh and Allison exchanged a glance.

Men!

A knock sounded on the front door, making nearly everyone jump. Only Lydie seemed unsurprised as she smiled and walked over to open it.

"Grandpa!" Lenna squealed, jumping up to wrap her arms around her grandfather's waist. "I didn't know you were coming!"

Mason hugged his granddaughter back. "Well, I didn't either until a little while ago." He cast a questioning glance at Lydie, but she kept her eyes averted.

"Hi, honey," Mason said to Cara, leaning down to give his daughter a kiss on the cheek. He smiled warmly at Leigh and Allison, then turned to the men of the family. "Hey, Matt. Gil."

They acknowledged his presence with friendly nods. "You missed all the excitement, Grandpa," Matt proclaimed. "Allison and I helped the Avalon PD with a sting operation. They caught the petnapper!"

"Really?" Mason returned. "Who was it?"

"Kyle's cousin Shawn," Leigh answered. "Eighteen. Skinny. Short. Long brown hair. You ever see him?"

Mason shook his head slowly. "Doesn't sound familiar. Not too many visitors came to Kyle's place. But I know he has a big family." He looked at Leigh hopefully. "So does this clear the boy's name?"

Leigh smiled. Mason really did care about the unfortunate, poker-playing geek, no matter what grief he'd caused his ex-con friend with the police. "I believe it will," she answered.

"Grandpa!" Lenna begged, still clinging. "Did you talk to Kyle's parents yet?"

He looked down at her adoringly. "I did, darlin'. And they said they'd be forever grateful if you'd keep Peep with you and love her as your own."

Lenna squealed again, literally kicking up her heels. "Really, Grandpa? Oh, Dad, can I? Can I?"

Gil looked helplessly at Cara. She smirked back at him. "Don't even try the allergy thing. That cat was in the house three days before you heard her, and only *then* did the sniffles start. Face it. You're busted."

Gil frowned. "Dander accumulates over time, you know."

"You can take shots, Daddy!" Lenna informed gleefully. "Mom said so!"

Gil shot a withering look at Cara, but she only laughed. "I thought the prospect of shots might be just as effective as not knowing the cat was there. Same concept, really."

"Are you saying it's all in my head?" Gil accused.

Leigh's eyes rolled. Gil was an intelligent man, objectively, but being devoid of a sense of humor did keep a person a beat behind.

"Come on, Dad," Mathias said impatiently. "We all know you're going to let her keep it. Can we just get the screaming over with already?"

Gil sighed. "All right, Lenna. You can keep the cat."

They all kept their ears covered for a full ten seconds. When Lenna finished expressing herself, she made a rush at the door. "Can we go home now so I can tell her we're her new forever home? Please? Please? Please?"

"Wait a second, sweetheart," Lydie interjected. "I haven't... told you what I need to tell you yet."

The intent tone of her voice made all eyes turn immediately in her direction. Even Lenna calmed herself and drifted back into the center of the room.

"What is it, Mom?" Cara asked tenderly, shooting a glance at Leigh. "We're all family, here. You know you can tell us anything."

Leigh watched the strong emotions flickering in Cara's eyes, and noted that the predominant one was angst. Cara wanted her mother to come clean about her mysterious social life, but it was out of character for Lydie to choose to do so in a public forum.

Lydie cleared her throat. "Well, I... I know this is all a bit awkward, but I thought maybe explaining it all at once would be best. And... well... it would make it harder for me to chicken out, too."

Leigh cast a surreptitious glance at Mason. He was trying to smother a sigh.

"There's something that I've been... well, hiding from all of you," Lydie admitted, her obvious discomfort with the topic making everyone else squirm along with her. "I figured it was my business, and it was at first, but now it needs to needs to be everybody's business, so I have to say what I have to say."

Leigh winced. Her aunt had never been one to make speeches. She didn't even like to talk much. Growing up with Frances attached at the hip, it had never been necessary.

"You see," Lydie pressed on, balling her hands into and out of fists as she talked. Her face and neck were beet red. "I've led you to believe that... Well, I always just thought it would be best if... You know, under the circumstances, with the children being so young..."

"We're not so young any more, Grandma," Mathias pointed out.

"I know that," Lydie assured. Now she was wringing her hands and shuffling her feet besides. "I just don't know how you'll take it, and I don't want you to think less of me. But you shouldn't, because that would mean... and there's nothing to be ashamed of. Not anymore. It's just that's it's been so long... and I'm afraid you'll all be... well..."

"Lydie!" Mason said firmly. "Please. You're making this way too difficult for yourself."

She looked at him helplessly.

He exhaled and closed the distance between them. "Cara, kids," he proclaimed, looking at his progeny. "It's like this."

He reached out an arm, wrapped it around Lydie's waist, and pulled her to him. She gulped slightly with surprise, but made no resistance as he put both arms around her, leaned down, and kissed her.

The collective breath in the room seemed to stop as the kiss went on. And on.

And on.

"There," Mason said finally, releasing Lydie just enough for both of them to face the crowd again. "Any questions?"

Cara stood up. Her face glowed as red as her mother's. "This week," she whispered raggedly. "Where—"

"Cruising in the Bahamas!" Mason said with enthusiasm. "And it was divine, thank you."

The kids were all staring at the couple, their eyes wide with amazement. Lydie met their gazes and took a breath. "We're getting married," she said quietly. "Again."

"Oh," Cara breathed, her shock finally giving way to the joy

Leigh knew was exploding inside her. "Oh!" She stumbled forward and practically threw herself at her parents, enveloping them in an exuberant three-way hug. "I'm so happy for you!"

"Yay! Me, too!" Lenna and Matt declared, coming forward to make it a group hug. Allison and Gil both hung back a moment, though each was smiling from ear to ear, and when finally the huddle broke up a bit they each came forward with their own congratulations. As Lydie's anxiety turned to relief, she began to tear up, and within seconds there wasn't a dry eye in the house.

"You scoundrel," Cara chastised her father, hugging him tightly. "How could you possibly manage it? Do you have any idea how hard I've tried to catch—"

Mason laughed. "Oh, yeah. You've come damn close, too."

Cara's blue-green eyes widened. "That one time, when Aunt Frances and Uncle Randall were out of town and I came over and–"

Mason's eyes twinkled devilishly. "Yeah, that was me."

Cara smacked him playfully on the shoulders. "You're terrible!"

The landline rang. Leigh had a creeping sense of premonition and looked out the window toward her parents' house. Their lights were all still on, but she saw no one standing at the windows. She gestured to Lydie and went to pick up the phone herself.

"Dublin residence," she said formally, hoping she was wrong.

"Leigh Eleanor," Frances scolded, "What in the devil is going on over there? We can hear hooting and hollering and everything else but can't understand a word. What's happened?"

"Hang on, Mom," Leigh replied without enthusiasm, lowering the phone. Lydie was watching her, and Leigh cringed to see her aunt's glow of happiness begin to dampen. *What should I say?* Leigh mouthed.

Lydie stood still a moment, looking fraught. Then Mason stepped over and clasped his arm firmly about her shoulders. "You want me to come with you?" he offered.

"No!" Lydie said reflexively. But as she leaned into her fiance and looked up at his face, she quickly reconsidered. "I mean, *yes*. Yes, I do." She straightened and looked around the room. "In fact, I want all of you there. Let's walk over and do this right now."

"Are you sure?" Mason asked, even as his face showed his delight.

Lydie nodded and smiled at him. "Completely sure." She turned to her niece. "Leigh, tell her we're coming over."

"Will do," Leigh agreed.

Three minutes later the crowd walked out of Lydie's front door, crossed the short distance to the Koslow's front porch, and reassembled just beyond its steps. Frances had insisted on speaking with everyone outside so as not to disturb Randall, and Leigh had helped her hobble out onto the porch and settle into a patio chair.

"Oh, bother," Frances had muttered to Leigh as the procession began. "What is *he* doing here?"

Leigh didn't need to ask to which "he" Frances was referring.

"He's family, Mom," she replied.

Frances tutted. "He's not my family."

Leigh felt a distinct twinge of foreboding. Her aunt was doing the right thing, and now was as good a time as any. But that didn't mean it would be pleasant.

"What's this?" Frances said more good naturedly as the six happy faces beamed up at her. "Did someone win the lottery?"

"In a manner of speaking," Cara said cheekily.

Lydie shot her daughter a warning look. Then she looked at Leigh. They both knew that however intense Frances's reaction, she would not erupt in front of the grandchildren. She would hold in her feelings and let them brew, gathering force for some later, greater explosion. Lydie's announcement tonight only marked the beginning of what promised to be a long and thorny process. But at least it was a beginning. The lies and the sneaking around were over. And for everyone else, at least, it was a joy that deserved to be celebrated.

Leigh nodded her encouragement.

Lydie swallowed and nodded back. "Frances," she proclaimed, her voice admirably steady. "I know I told you I've been seeing Cole Harbison again, but that was a lie. He's engaged to someone else now. I only said that because you were hounding me so, and I didn't want you to—"

"Cole Harbison is marrying someone else?" Frances interrupted. "But he was so fond of you! And you know I always thought—"

"I told you I didn't love him."

"Well, that's hardly all that matters!" Frances lectured, seeming to forget that the two of them were in the midst of a crowd. "But if you're happy being alone, you know that's fine with me. I wasn't trying to push you into marriage at your age. It's just that Harbison is such a *stable* man, and I thought it might be prudent to—"

"Oh, to hell with it," Lydie murmured. She turned around to where Mason stood behind her, threw her arms around his neck, and kissed him.

She kissed him passionately. In fact, she kissed him so passionately that all three kids and Gil found it suddenly necessary to avert their eyes. When at last Lydie released the man, only Cara and Leigh were still watching, frankly unable to look away.

Mason himself was stunned speechless. No one else moved.

Lydie wiped her swollen lips gingerly with the back of her hand, then took a step forward to face Frances. "We're in love and we're getting married. The sooner the better. And you can scream and fuss all you want, but it's still going to happen. I hope you can make peace with it, because I'd really like to have you there. At the wedding, I mean."

Leigh braved a look at her mother. The only apt description for her mother's face was "apoplectic." For a long time, Frances didn't move. She hardly even seemed to breathe. Her skin was deathly pale and her eyes bugged. Lydie continued looking at her, and Frances looked back. The twins' eyes seemed to lock in an endless round of unspoken communication Leigh couldn't begin to interpret.

Then finally, slowly, color began to suffuse back into Frances's face. Her jaw moved slightly. She blinked.

The crowd all stared at her, motionless with anticipation.

Frances cleared her throat loudly, making them all jump. Then she swallowed and sat up straighter. Her thin lips pursed. She made her response.

"Well. We'll see."

The crowd breathed a collective sigh of relief, and nearly everyone smiled again. Even Cara took the words as the equivalent of "Fabulous! I'm so happy for you!" But as Lydie withdrew from the porch, she and Leigh exchanged a knowing look.

The battle was far from over.

"Let's celebrate," Gil suggested, stepping over toward the van. "How about if I run out and bring back some ice cream?"

Lenna practically jumped up and down. "Oh, yes, Daddy!"

Lydie let out a huge breath and smiled. It was a smile at all of them. A smile of pure joy. "That sounds perfect!"

She called back to her twin. "You're welcome to join us," she said pleasantly. "Shall we bring some chairs out and have a lawn party?"

"Don't trouble yourself on my account," Frances said shortly. "It's late. I need to turn in." She began to struggle up, and Leigh leaned in to assist her.

"Come on, Mom," Leigh cajoled in a whisper. "Just *look* at her! I can't remember ever seeing Aunt Lydie so happy."

Frances looked. For a moment, the lines of her face seemed almost to soften a bit. But then her lips pursed once more.

Leigh helped her mother through the door and back to her walker. "I can manage perfectly well from here," Frances insisted. "You go on home, now. You've fussed over us enough."

"All right," Leigh agreed. She started to say something else, but thought better of it. Some things just took time.

Leigh waved a pointless goodbye to her sleeping father and opened the door. "Tell your Aunt Lydie," Frances called out suddenly after her, "that she can bring me some ice cream later."

Leigh smiled warmly. "I'll do that."

She returned to Lydie's house just long enough to deliver the message, enjoy another round of hugs, and collect Allison. They had ice cream in the freezer at home, and she was anxious to check on Ethan and spend some time with the man she married. Tonight, the Harmon family would have its own celebration.

Allison didn't argue as they buckled themselves in the van and drove off.

"Did you know, Mom?" Allison asked after a moment. "About Grandpa Mason and Grandma Lydie?"

"Not until earlier today," Leigh admitted.

Allison sighed dreamily. "I can't believe no one saw it. It was so obvious tonight. And I thought I was good with reading people, you know?"

Leigh smiled. "You are very good with reading people, Allison. I was proud of you tonight."

The girl swung her head toward her mother with surprise. "Really?"

"Really."

"I just thought you'd be mad. You always get mad."

Leigh sighed. "It's not that I don't think you have valuable skills to offer in these situations. It's just that I'm your mother. My first priority is always to keep you safe."

"Mom," Allison protested sternly. "When have I *ever* done anything in the slightest bit dangerous? What did you think I would do? Run right out and burst into the middle of a sting operation?"

Leigh's face reddened. She shot a sideways glance at Allison. The girl was grinning.

Smart aleck. And she was only eleven. In a year and a half, she would be a teenager.

God help them all.

"If you really were proud of me tonight," Allison suggested, "then maybe next time something like this comes up, you can tell me what's going on and let me help without me having to sneak around. Okay?"

Leigh tensed at the thought. "Well, we're not going to have to worry about that," she replied. "This was a highly unusual situation. It's not like we're ever going to find ourselves caught up in another police investigation."

"Oh, Mom!" Allison giggled, stifling a snort. "Sure, we will."

About the Author

USA-Today bestselling novelist and playwright Edie Claire was first published in mystery in 1999 by the New American Library division of Penguin Putnam. In 2002 she began publishing award-winning contemporary romances with Warner Books, and in 2008 two of her comedies for the stage were published by Baker's Plays (now Samuel French). In 2009 she began publishing independently, continuing her original Leigh Koslow Mystery series and adding new works of romantic women's fiction, young adult fiction, and humor.

Under the banner of Stackhouse Press, Edie has now published over 25 titles including digital, print, audio, and foreign translations. Her works are distributed worldwide, with her first contemporary romance, *Long Time Coming*, exceeding two million downloads. She has received multiple "Top Pick" designations from *Romantic Times Magazine* and received both the "Reader's Choice Award" from *Road To Romance* and the "Perfect 10 Award" from *Romance Reviews Today*.

A former veterinarian and childbirth educator, Edie is a happily married mother of three who currently resides in Pennsylvania. She enjoys gardening and wildlife-watching and dreams of becoming a snowbird.

Books & Plays by Edie Claire

Romantic Fiction

Pacific Horizons
Alaskan Dawn
Leaving Lana'i
Maui Winds
Glacier Blooming
Tofino Storm (2020)

Fated Loves
Long Time Coming
Meant To Be
Borrowed Time

Hawaiian Shadows
Wraith
Empath
Lokahi
The Warning

Leigh Koslow Mysteries

Never Buried
Never Sorry
Never Preach Past Noon
Never Kissed Goodnight
Never Tease a Siamese
Never Con a Corgi

Never Haunt a Historian
Never Thwart a Thespian
Never Steal a Cockatiel
Never Mess With Mistletoe
Never Murder a Birder
Never Nag Your Neighbor

Women's Fiction

The Mud Sisters

Humor

Work, Blondes. Work!

Comedic Stage Plays

Scary Drama I
See You in Bells